Award-winning, bestselling novelist Gianrico Carofiglio
was born in Bari in 1961 and worked for many years as
a prosecutor specializing in organized crime. He was
appointed advisor of the anti-Mafia committee in the
Italian parliament in 2007 and served as a senator from
2008 to 2013. Carofiglio is best known for the Guido
Guerrieri crime series: *Involuntary Witness, A Walk in the
Dark, Reasonable Doubts, Temporary Perfections* and now
A Fine Line, all published by Bitter Lemon Press. His other
novels include *The Silence of the Wave.* Carofiglio's books
have sold more than four million copies in Italy and have
been translated into twenty-seven languages worldwide.

A FINE LINE

Gianrico Carofiglio

Translated by Howard Curtis

BITTER LEMON PRESS
LONDON

BITTER LEMON PRESS
First published in the United Kingdom in 2016 by
Bitter Lemon Press, 47 Wilmington Square, London WC1X 2ET

www.bitterlemonpress.com

First published in Italian as *La regola dell'equilibrio*
by Giulio Einaudi editore, 2014
© Gianrico Carofiglio, 2014

English translation © Howard Curtis, 2016

This edition published by arrangement with
Rosaria Carpinelli Consulenze Editoriali srl.

A CIP record for this book is available from the British Library

ISBN 978–1–908524–61–4
eBook ISBN: 978–1–908524–62–1

Typeset by Tetragon, London
Printed and bound by CPI Group (UK) Ltd, Croydon, CR0 4YY

Supported using public funding by
ARTS COUNCIL
ENGLAND

1

It was around the tenth of April. The air was cool and clean. A fragrant breeze, rare for this city, was blowing, and the sun spattered liquid light over us and the grey façade of the courthouse. Carmelo Tancredi and I were standing near the entrance, chatting.

"Sometimes I think about quitting," I said, leaning against the wall. The plaster was flaking, and a spider's web of small cracks spread worryingly upwards.

"Quitting what?" Tancredi asked, taking his cigar from his mouth.

"The law."

"Are you kidding?"

I shrugged. At that moment, two judges passed. They didn't notice me, and I was pleased I didn't have to greet them.

"Do you know them?" I said, nodding towards the glass door behind which the judges had just disappeared.

"Ciccolella and Longo? I know who they are, but I wouldn't say I know them. I once had to testify in court before Ciccolella, but it was all over pretty quickly."

"A few days ago, I was in a lift with Ciccolella. There were also two trainees and that female lawyer who always dresses as if she's on her way to a Chinese New Year party."

Tancredi laughed. He knew immediately who I was talking about. "Nardulli."

"That's right, Nardulli. She's weird but she's a good person, I find her almost endearing. She defends all kinds of hopeless cases for free."

"True. Whenever we need a public defender and can't find anyone, she always shows willing, even when there's no money in it for her. So what happened?"

"The lift reaches the ground floor and I step aside to let her pass – she was the only woman there. She's just about to get out, tottering on those ridiculous heels, when Ciccolella barges past her, almost knocking her down, then looks at her for a few seconds and cries *Avvocato!* in an angry tone, as if to say: you should have moved aside, you shouldn't even have tried to go before me. I'm a *judge*, in case you didn't know. Then he turns and walks off without saying goodbye to anyone."

"Nice man."

"He did it on purpose, barging into her like that. I felt really bad. I should have intervened, told him that was no way to behave, that he'd been rude. But of course I didn't. Just brooded over it later. In the office, they saw me talking to myself at least three times that day. That's happening increasingly often."

"Your clients know you're crazy anyway. What came out of these broodings of yours? Is 'broodings' even a word?"

"I don't think so."

A police car drew up, and two suspicious-looking guys got out, greeted Tancredi, who replied with a nod, and went inside.

"I was thinking how different it was before," I resumed, "how there wasn't that rudeness, that level of vulgarity when I started, more than twenty years ago. I seemed to remember that relations in the profession were less brutal, less… yes, vulgar's the word. Then I stopped and pinched myself.

I told myself I was going soft, doing what I'd always found pathetic in other people."

"Feeling nostalgic?"

"That's right. Feeling nostalgia for the past as if it were a golden age. Missing your own youth even though when you were in the middle of it you thought everything was terrible. You know the opening of that novel by Paul Nizan: 'I was twenty. I won't allow anyone to say that these are the best years of our lives.'"

"I know the quotation, but I haven't read the book. What did you say the author's name was?"

"Paul Nizan, a French writer."

I shifted a little, sliding along the wall so as to get the sun on my face. I looked for the most comfortable position I could find to support myself and half-closed my eyes.

"Sometimes I think about when I used to imagine what would happen to me in the future. Travel, graduation, marriage, my first hearing at the Supreme Court, a whole lot of things. Those moments when I imagined the future seem very close to me. Whereas the things I imagined that really happened appear very far away. My future is sunk in the past."

"I've heard clearer explanations."

"But you understand, don't you?"

"Only because of my superior intelligence." He also moved his face into the sun and took a couple of puffs on his cigar.

"How would you describe the smell of a cigar?" I asked him.

"Don't tell me it bothers you. I'm constantly reducing my circle of friends through incompatibility: my incompatibility with their intolerance towards cigars."

"It doesn't bother me. Not too much, anyway."

Tancredi lifted his hand to his face and passed it the wrong way over the short beard he'd had for a few months now. "Experts say that the smell – or as they put it, the aroma – of a cigar is a mixture of wet leather, pepper, an old brandy keg and seasoned wood. I've heard this so many times, I've ended up convinced I'm also aware of these smells. Apart from the old brandy keg, of course. I've never seen one or smelt one."

"Pepper, seasoned wood, brandy keg, leather…"

"*Wet* leather."

"Wet leather… That kind of thing. Like the descriptions you get from wine waiters. I always feel like an idiot when I'm having dinner and someone says things like: a fruity feel, a hint of chocolate and liquorice, tannins. I drink wine, but I can't taste these things."

"Haven't you ever smoked cigars?"

"Never. You may remember I smoked cigarettes for many years. Then nothing. Never cigars, never a pipe, thank God."

It felt good leaning against that wall, with that sense you're cleansing your soul that only certain spring days are capable of reawakening. How good it would be, I thought, to go somewhere in the country, lay a blanket on the grass, read, eat sandwiches, close my eyes and listen to the murmurs of nature.

"Do you want to hear a story?"

He made a gesture with his hand as if to say: sure, go ahead.

"A month ago I had some tests done. Routine stuff, my doctor says it's fine to do them every two or three years. A few days after taking the samples the doctor called me – I'd just finished a hearing and was on my way out of here – and told me he had to talk to me. There was something too neutral in his tone. I didn't like it at all. I asked him if anything was wrong and he replied that it'd be better if I came to see him. So I went to his clinic, not in a very calm state of mind."

"What did he tell you?"

"He's a friend, he was very ill at ease. He told me some of the results were *slightly* skewed, but that there are often false alarms in this kind of check-up, so we ought to repeat the tests immediately before starting to get worried. But if the results were confirmed, I'd need an appointment with a haematologist. I asked him if he could please be a bit more specific, and as I said that I realized I'd put my hands on his desk because they'd started to shake badly."

"And what did he say?" Tancredi asked in a thin voice.

"He beat about the bush a bit more, then told me it might be a form of leukaemia. There are many different kinds, he said, and many can be cured nowadays. But it was pointless to say anything until we'd repeated the tests."

Tancredi didn't move a muscle, seemed almost to have stopped breathing.

"We redid the samples. He assured me he would talk to the lab to make sure the results came back within a day. He called me next morning, about eight. He couldn't find the right words, all he could think of was: *Congratulations*. 'I told you there are often false alarms. Actually not so often, I exaggerated a bit, but it does happen. Fortunately, it's what happened this time. Go out tonight and raise a toast to your second birthday.' He also said a few more things, but by now his voice had become distant and I didn't hear them properly. In any case I don't remember. It was one of the most unreal situations I've ever been in."

I heard the sound of the breath being expelled by Tancredi. "So everything's OK?"

"Yes."

"Fucking hell. For a day you thought you had leukaemia?"

"Yes."

"Did you tell anyone?"

"No."

"Why didn't you call me?"

"I thought about it, but I was ashamed."

"Ashamed? To call a friend? You need a psychiatrist, not a haematologist. What does that mean?"

"I felt *inferior*. Suddenly I'd ended up on the side where the sick people are, while the healthy people, those who carry on with their normal lives, who eat, drink, work, travel, make love, make plans, were on the other side, the one I'd just been excluded from. I felt inferior and I was ashamed. I know it may seem strange, but that's the way it was."

Tancredi took a deep breath and screwed up his eyes. He made an angry grimace and shook his head as if dismissing a thought. "It can't have been easy," he said at last.

"I don't know. I can't somehow define my memory of it. It was a day when I was suspended over a void. It was fear, more than anything. As if the fear was throbbing inside me. The actual thought that in a short while, not in some remote, abstract future, you'll cease to exist. The *world* will cease to exist. I remembered what a friend of mine – Emilio – said when he told me about the illness and death of his wife at the age of thirty-four. You think about the walks you didn't take, about the times when you were stingy with your affections. It isn't just the fear of death, it's the fact that you wish you hadn't wasted your time. Then there were moments of perfect calm. As if I'd already got used to it, as if I'd accepted my fate and was able to observe it in a detached way. Something that concerned another person. And there were moments when I thought I mustn't give up, that I should fight, beat the disease, whatever it was. A lot of people have done that. Those were the hardest moments, if you understand what I mean."

"You didn't think about what the doctor had said, that it might have been a mistake in the tests?"

"Not even for a second. I forbade myself from doing that. I think it struck me as a cowardly thought, a way to postpone acknowledging what was happening to me. I'm not the kind of person who wins the lottery, I think I told myself."

"And how did you spend the day?"

"That's the other strange thing. I worked, I went to the gym, I went to bed early, I even fell asleep almost immediately, and I don't remember what I dreamt about. But then I woke up again at four in the morning. I opened my eyes and felt an anxiety I'd never felt before. Like a blanket of metal. I got up, I *had* to get up because I could feel the panic starting. I went out in the dark, I walked for hours, day broke and the streets started to fill with people, and in the end the doctor's call came."

"You must have gone crazy with happiness."

"That's the strangest aspect of it all. For a few seconds, maybe a few minutes, I did actually feel… happy? Yes, I'd say happy. After that, though, it turned into a feeling I'd never have imagined."

I tried to explain it, but it wasn't easy. I'd felt fragile. It had occurred to me that although it hadn't happened this time, it might happen in a few months, a few years. It had turned into a fear different from the one I'd felt the day before. One was a sharp pain, the other a limp fever. Both humiliating, in different ways. When the doctor had phoned to tell me that the first tests were wrong, I'd thought the clocks had been turned back and my life would resume just where it had left off. But it wasn't like that. My life had changed, irreversibly, after those twenty-four hours.

"Since then, over the past few weeks, I've asked myself all kinds of questions, some of them about my work. Whether I want to carry on doing it and for how much longer. Things like that."

Tancredi seemed about to say something, but couldn't find anything appropriate. He relit his cigar and blew yet another dense grey little cloud up into the air. I decided it was time to drop the subject of my medical tests and my existential dilemmas.

"Why are you in court today?"

"I have an appointment with a magistrate from the Prosecutor's Department, one of the few I still like working with. How about you?"

"A hearing in the second division court."

"What kind of trial?"

"A young guy accused of sexual assault."

He looked at me in surprise. The reason was obvious. I don't normally take on that kind of case. I'm not judgemental, but I really don't feel up to defending people who might have committed an offence like that. I wouldn't feel comfortable and I wouldn't be able to guarantee an adequate defence. Don't get me wrong: a little bit of discomfort is indispensable to doing any job that's – how shall I put it? – morally sensitive. It's a good thing. But an excess of discomfort – the kind I'd felt the only time I'd defended a rapist – isn't good. Best to let it go. Tancredi knew my views, that's why he was puzzled.

"The guy's innocent."

"That's what they all say."

"No, really. Come to the hearing, if you don't believe me."

Tancredi didn't reply. He was looking at a point behind my back.

"Your partner's here."

I turned towards the courthouse gates and saw Consuelo hurrying towards us with her leather handbag and her elegantly clumsy stride.

"Good morning, Inspector," Consuelo said to Tancredi, with a smile that stood out against her dark skin.

"Avvocato Favia," Tancredi replied with a slight bow.

Consuelo Favia is Peruvian, born in some remote village in the Andes, but she's also Italian, the adopted daughter of a friend of mine. Years earlier she had come to me to learn the profession and now she was a partner in the practice. One of the few criminal lawyers I'd agree to be defended by.

"Shall we go in, boss?"

"Let's go. Bye, Carmelo."

Tancredi waited until Consuelo had gone into the court-house and couldn't hear him. "Guido?"

"Yes."

"The next time you scare me like that, I'll shoot you."

2

The presiding judge, a dignified, elderly man named Basile, finished adjourning the previous trial and called ours.

Consuelo and I were ready at the bench to the left of the judges, both in our robes. When she'd put on hers, a slight smell of amber had wafted through the air. Having got through the introductory formalities, Basile turned to us.

"The trial of Antonio Bronzino has come to us after being deferred by the previous court. Much of the testimony – I'd even go so far as to say all of it – was heard by that court. I ask both parties, counsel for the defence in particular, if they consent to admit that testimony today."

That's the way it works. The code of criminal procedure says that the verdict must be given by the same judges who took part in the original trial, in other words, those who heard the witnesses. Theoretically, if trials lasted a few days or a few weeks, that would be only right and proper. But as they usually last several months or even years, this rule can be a serious problem. If even just one of the three judges who hear the case is transferred – something that happens quite frequently – there has to be a retrial. Unless, that is, the defendant and his counsel agree to admit the testimony given before the previous court. Often, this doesn't happen. Defence lawyers aren't always cooperative, and having a retrial means gaining time (some would say: *wasting* time, but they would be accused of scant regard for the rights of the individual), especially for guilty defendants who hope that the statute of limitations will come into play. That's not the way I like to work.

I stood up and addressed the judges.

"We consent, Your Honour. Our only motion is to re-examine the injured party, who is apparently present and could therefore be heard immediately. This is not in any way a dilatory motion. In the previous phases of the trial, the defendant was unable to present his defence. The events in question go back several years. Despite Signor Bronzino having gone abroad to work, the summonses were sent to his former residence, and he was unaware of the proceedings until last January. We do not question the fact that those proceedings were carried out correctly. We do not do so because we are not interested in technicalities, nor are we interested in postponements. We want the trial to continue immediately. That is why our only motion is to proceed with the examination of the offended party. The defendant is not present because he is working abroad, as I said. Believing as we do that his presence is not indispensable, we ask for this examination, and it is highly likely that we will rest our case on the outcome of the injured party's testimony."

A few years earlier, our client had met a girl at a party, they started going out together and definitely had sexual relations. There was no doubt about this, nobody denied it. It was on the nature of those relations – whether or not they were consensual – that opinions differed. The girl (Marilisa, she was called, I don't know why the name had stuck with me) had lodged a complaint against him, claiming that he had assaulted her. Bronzino had been arrested on the basis of these statements and held in custody for a few weeks. Then the judge must have realized that something wasn't quite right about the accusation and had released him. A couple of years later, however, there had been a petition for remand. The prosecutor who was dealing with the case, not exactly a lover of hard work, must have thought that filling out a petition for remand was less of a bother than writing a well-argued motion for the case to be closed.

In the meantime, Bronzino, convinced that there would be no further proceedings against him following his release, had moved to Germany. Within a short time, he had been declared a defaulter and was remanded for one of those surreal proceedings that are sometimes seen in our court-houses. The so-called defence had been entrusted to court-appointed lawyers who, from one hearing to the next and one postponement to the next, had put in appearances without ever contributing, for the obvious reason that none of them knew anything about the case.

None of the witnesses had been cross-examined, not even the key witness, the presumed injured party, Marilisa Di Cosmo.

When Bronzino, on his return to Italy, had received a boxful of mail that had accumulated at his old address, informing him of the proceedings, he had come to me.

Things weren't looking too good for him after the previous hearings. There was the injured party's testimony, there was a medical certificate confirming the existence of abrasions compatible with sexual assault, there were statements from the victim's then partner, who had been the first to hear about what had happened when she had returned home in a distressed state. Above all, there had been no real activity on the part of the defence. As things stood, the trial could easily end with a guilty verdict, and the minimum sentence for sexual assault is five years.

*

When I had finished speaking, the presiding judge turned first right, then left, to look at the associate judges. They were two demure-looking women – one with hair tied in a ponytail, the other with hair gathered in a bun kept in place by a chopstick – wearing the expressions of people who would have preferred to be somewhere else. It's the kind of expression that's almost a professional disease for those who've been associate judges for too long. It seems like interesting work, and to an extent it is. For a few months, if you get the right trials. But sitting there three times a week, for years on end, listening to witnesses, defence lawyers, prosecutors and defendants (each category produces its fair amount of nonsense or worse), without saying a word out loud (the only person who opens his mouth is the presiding judge) would be enough to fry anyone's brains. I'd have gone crazy.

Anyway, as I was saying, the judge exchanged rapid glances with his associates to see if they had any observations to make. Both barely moved their heads. That meant no, they had no observations, and yes, they were fine with my motion.

"Prosecutor?"

Assistant Prosecutor Castroni was a very polite person, a nice man in his way, disinclined to get caught up in legal subtleties. He got to his feet and said that he had no observations, no particular motion to make, and no objection to the injured party being examined.

"Very well, then, we have said that the witness is present. Let's hear her," the presiding judge said to the bailiff, who went into the witness room and emerged a few moments later with an attractive young woman. Attractive but with something dull about her bearing and features. A tall, shapely, dull brunette.

She looked around almost furtively, like a scared animal ready to attack in self-defence. The kind of witness – actually,

19

the kind of person – you have to be particularly careful with. Only when she realized that the defendant wasn't in court did she seem to relax a little.

The judge asked her to read the formula of commitment. It used to be called the oath, the sentence witnesses had to recite before making their statement. When I started work as a lawyer, before the new – now old – code for criminal procedure was approved, the oath still existed. I know it by heart: "Conscious of the responsibility that with this oath I assume before God, if a believer, and before men, I swear to tell the truth, the whole truth and nothing but the truth."

There was a perfect balance between drama and farce in the rising cadence of that admonition that lent itself to being mangled in the most surreal ways. My favourite one was when people, nervous at being in court, asked for the formula to be repeated and then swore that they would tell *anything but the truth.* Which of course is what happens in most testimony, irrespective of the witness's good faith.

Then, with the new code that was introduced in 1989, it was considered that taking an oath was somewhat inelegant and ill-suited to a secular State, and the law introduced a formula of commitment, which goes like this: "Conscious of the moral and legal responsibility I assume with my testimony, I commit myself to tell the whole truth and not to conceal anything of which I have knowledge." More correct, certainly, but much less poetic.

This was what our witness recited, reading from a dirty laminated card.

Judge Basile made her give her particulars – the most pointless of obligations, given that these particulars were already on at least six or seven documents in the case file – and at last gave the prosecutor the floor.

"Thank you, Your Honour," Castroni said. "Signora, do you remember already giving evidence in court some months... or rather, about a year ago?"

The young woman nodded.

"You must answer yes, for the record."

"Yes."

"You do remember. Good. Do you remember what you said on that occasion?"

She sniffed before replying. She seemed very ill at ease. "More or less, yes."

"In any case, you told the truth on that occasion?"

"Yes."

"Your Honour, I have no other questions. We have a full record of the previous hearing."

"Wow, he really exerted himself," Consuelo whispered in my ear.

"In that case," the judge said, "defence counsel may proceed with their cross-examination."

Consuelo stood up, adjusted her robe over her shoulders – again giving off that slight scent of amber – and turned to the witness with a smile. Consuelo's smile can be deceptive. She looks good-natured, with a face like a small, friendly rodent in a cartoon. If you look more closely, however, you notice a much less reassuring gleam in her eyes. Consuelo is a good lawyer, someone of almost embarrassing rectitude, but above all she's someone you really don't want to quarrel with.

"Good morning, Signora, I'm Avvocato Favia. Together with Avvocato Guerrieri, I represent Signor Bronzino. I need to ask you a few questions, but I'll try to be brief. Do you feel up to answering?"

The young woman stared at her with a somewhat dazed expression, then looked around in search of help, as if trying to make sense of the situation. You don't expect a girl from the Andes to be a criminal lawyer in Bari, so looks of surprise are the norm. Consuelo is used to it, but it's going to be like that for a while longer.

"Signora, please answer Avvocato Favia," the judge said in an understanding tone.

"Yes, yes, I'm sorry."

Consuelo glanced at her notes. She didn't need to, but we all make pointless gestures when we have to start something, or finish it. "Could you tell us when and on what occasion you met the defendant?"

"We met at a party. I went with a friend of mine."

"When was this party?"

"I don't remember, it was years ago."

"So you can't answer?"

"No, how could I possibly remember?"

"No problem. After meeting the defendant at that party… By the way, whose party was it?"

"I don't know, I told you I went with a friend of mine. She was the one who knew the host."

"So you didn't know the host?"

"No, what's so strange about that?"

"Nothing. I'm sorry. What kind of party was it?"

Castroni stood up. "Objection, Your Honour, the witness is being asked to make a value judgement. That makes the question inadmissible, quite apart from the fact that it's completely irrelevant."

"All right, Avvocato," Basile said, "let's forget about what kind of party it was, unless there's a specific reason to go further into this aspect of the matter. If there is, please tell us."

"Your Honour, knowing the context in which the defendant and the injured party met may help us to understand the beginning of their relationship. But I'll drop the question, it isn't essential. So, Signora, after meeting the defendant at this party, did you have occasion to meet him again?"

"Yes."

"Just once, or several times?"

"I think I already said, he sometimes dropped by the office—"

"You mean your place of work?"

"Yes."

"Did he ever invite you out? For a coffee, for example, an aperitif, dinner?"

"Yes."

"Did you ever accept any of his invitations, apart from the evening with which this trial is concerned?"

"That evening I only agreed to go for a walk."

"Before that evening did you ever accept any invitations, walks or otherwise?"

"Just once, a coffee at a café near the office."

Consuelo paused, turned to look at me, we exchanged knowing looks, and I stood up as she sat down. It was my turn.

"Signora, do you have a boyfriend, a partner?"

"Not at the moment, I'm single."

"But at the time when these events happened, you had a partner?"

"Yes."

"He's the person who went with you when you lodged a complaint the following morning, isn't he?"

"Yes."

"Were you living with this person at the time?"

"Yes."

"What kind of work does your former partner do?"

"He's area sales manager for a confectionery company."

"Was he ever away for a few days?"

"Yes."

"Often?"

"He was always travelling, almost every day. He'd go from one place to another."

"Did he usually come back in the evening?"

"Yes, he'd leave in his car in the morning and get home in the evening."

"And apart from spending all day away, did he sometimes take longer trips which obliged him to spend the night away from home?"

"Yes."

"How frequently?"

She did not reply immediately, but it wasn't clear if the hesitation was due to the fact that she was concentrating on the answer or because, for some reason, the question made her uncomfortable.

"I can't say exactly. A couple of times a month."

"Ah, by the way, when you went to that party with your friend, do you remember if your partner was away?"

"I don't know, it was a long time ago."

"Let me try and help you. Did you ever go out alone when your partner was in the city? Did he mind?"

Marilisa sighed, torn between exasperation and resignation. "I couldn't really say, it's a period of my life I'm trying to forget."

"I'm sorry to be so insistent and to remind you of things you'd prefer to forget, but unfortunately I need an answer. Do you happen to remember if, when you went to that party, your partner was away on business?"

"Maybe yes."

"Maybe?"

"Yes, yes, I remember, he was away."

"I'd like now to get a better idea of the timeline. How

much time passed between that party and the events that concern us in this trial?"

"I can't say for certain."

"Weeks, months?"

"A couple of months."

"So, since the date of the offence with which the defendant is charged is 3 April, your acquaintance presumably goes back to the beginning of February, or maybe the end of January?"

"I think so, yes."

"And between that party and the first time you saw each other again, or spoke to each other on the phone, how much time passed?"

"He called me a couple of days later."

"Where did he call you?"

"How do you mean?"

"On what telephone did he call you?"

"On my mobile."

"So you'd given him your mobile number?"

"Yes."

"Why?"

"He asked me for it."

"Please don't take this question the wrong way, but do you give your mobile number to everyone who asks for it?"

I glanced sideways out of the corner of my eye. The prosecutor shifted in his chair. He might have been thinking of objecting, but then decided to wait and see what would happen. Nor did the judge say anything.

"No, no, I mean, it depends—"

"You had only met Signor Bronzino that evening, is that correct?"

"Yes, but what I mean—"

"I assume you felt a particular liking for him, you trusted him."

She passed her hand over her face. She looked as if she was suffering. I wished I could get this over with as soon as possible.

"Yes, he was… very polite, and besides, he knew my friend."

"Don't worry, Signora, you don't have to justify yourself. I was only asking the question in order to get a clearer idea of the situation. So, Signor Bronzino called you two days after meeting you at the party. I assume there were other calls, other telephone conversations?"

"Yes, he'd phone me and we'd chat."

"And did you sometimes phone him?"

"I can't remember. Maybe I did."

"Maybe you did. When did you meet again?"

"I'm not sure. He told me that he was often in the area where my office was and asked me if I felt like taking a break and coming outside for a coffee. He kept insisting, and one time I accepted."

"Was that the only time you met, apart from the evening of 3 April?"

"I think so."

I let those words hang in the air for a few seconds, with their heavy burden of ambiguity.

"Do you know the Hotel Royal in Milan?"

She looked at me in genuine surprise. "No… I don't think so."

"Did your partner ever go to Milan on business?"

"Yes, he had meetings there."

"Do you know which hotel he stayed in when he went to Milan?"

She half closed her eyes, and let several seconds go by before replying. She was trying to understand. "It may have been that one, yes."

"The Royal?"

"Yes."

"Did he always go there?"

"I think so."

"A couple of times a month, as we said before?"

"More or less. Sometimes he went more often."

"Do you remember if there was a particular day of the week when he went on these business trips to Milan?"

A deep breath. Our eyes met for a few seconds. Then she looked away. "I think it was Monday."

"Thank you. Now I'd like to bring this document to your attention. It's a record of calls made to and from the defendant's mobile phone. To be more specific, the one Signor Bronzino was using at the time of these events. This record shows that there was a call lasting five minutes and twenty-three seconds to a number in Milan late in the evening of 6 March 2006. The number is that of the Royal, the hotel we were just talking about. Do you have any idea why Signor Bronzino should have telephoned that hotel that evening?"

"You should ask him."

"As it happens, I have asked him, but right now I'm interested in your opinion. Can you answer me? If it's any help, I can tell you it was a Monday."

The worst situation for a witness to be in, especially a witness of dubious honesty, is when he or she realizes that something is about to come out, but isn't sure exactly what and can do nothing about it. She pursed her lips in silence.

"Do you know if the defendant knew your partner?"

"No."

"You don't know, or he didn't know him?"

"He didn't know him, as far as I know."

"I ask you the question because it turns out that your partner spent the night of 6 to 7 March 2006 at the Hotel

Royal in Milan. So it's quite likely that he was there when that phone call I told you about occurred. Can you explain that coincidence?"

Castroni tried to object, but didn't sound very convincing. Even he was starting to realize that something was wrong – very wrong – in this affair. "First of all, this is an inadmissible line of questioning. Questions should be about facts, not speculation. Secondly, I'd like to know how counsel for the defence comes to be in possession of this information."

Basile looked at him and turned towards me. He didn't say anything. Castroni's objection made sense, but it was obvious that the witness would have to answer the question anyway.

"Your Honour, the defence has conducted investigations, strictly according to our legal prerogatives. The ways in which we have used the results of these investigations are fully compatible with the defence's powers of discretion. I reserve the right to provide documentation, where necessary, at the end of the cross-examination. May I proceed?"

"You may, Avvocato, but try to make it clear where you're going with this."

"It will all become clear very soon, Your Honour. Signora, I repeat: that phone call from Signor Bronzino's mobile to the Hotel Royal coincides with your partner's stay in Milan, in that very hotel. If you'll forgive a direct question, could it be that you were the person who made that call?"

The pause that followed was a really long one.

"All right, then, let's go on to something else. Was your relationship with your partner happy?"

"What do you mean?"

"Did you agree about things, or did you quarrel? Did you quarrel often, or just occasionally? Did you have problems?"

"The same as any couple."

"Did your partner ever hit you?"

I noticed that she was holding the hem of her skirt between the fingers of her left hand and crumpling it convulsively. "Just the occasional slap."

"Did you ever lodge a complaint following these *occasional slaps*?"

"What's that got to do with anything?"

The judge got in ahead of me and in a sharp tone ordered her to answer.

She seemed to shrink, and I felt sorry for her. "Once I went to the carabinieri, but then I withdrew everything."

"Can you tell us what you told the carabinieri?"

"That there'd been a quarrel."

"Did you say that you'd been hit?"

"Yes, but I withdrew—"

"You withdrew everything, yes. What else did you tell the carabinieri?"

"I just wanted him to stop."

The way she said that made me think of a landslide. No, that's not right, it made me think of the *word* landslide. The fragile structure of her testimony, which had held up because nobody up until then had asked her to account for it, was collapsing beneath her like loose earth or clay.

"To stop what?"

"His fits of jealousy. Sometimes he hit me even when I hadn't done anything."

"Why did you withdraw everything?"

"He said he would change."

"And did he?"

"In a way…"

"After the dropping of the complaint, after you withdrew everything, were there other acts of violence?"

She didn't reply. She was staring into space now, her face very pale, her lips dry and colourless.

"Signora, I'm sorry to insist, but were there other acts of violence?"

"Yes."

"Did you ever need medical attention?"

"Maybe a couple of times."

"Did you go to accident and emergency?"

"Yes."

"Did you tell the doctors there that your injuries were caused by your partner?"

She shook her head.

"Your Honour, can it be entered in the record that the witness shook her head to indicate no?"

Basile gestured to the stenographer, meaning that she could write what I had asked.

"Would it be correct to say that you were afraid of your partner?"

"Objection, Your Honour," Castroni said, leaping to his feet. "The witness is being asked for a personal opinion."

"Objection sustained. Avvocato, let's try and get to the point."

"Signora, you said you met Bronzino outside your office building, where he was waiting for you, and that you accepted a lift home in his car. Can you tell us what time you left the office?"

"The usual time."

"And what time might that be?"

"Five."

"And you found the defendant waiting for you outside your office building?"

"Yes."

"Your Honour, I have to challenge the witness on the statements she made at the time she lodged her complaint."

"Go ahead, Avvocato."

"When you were questioned by the carabinieri the morning after, you stated: 'I left the office at six and met Antonio Bronzino, who had been pursuing me for some time and was obviously waiting for me.' You told the carabinieri six, now you're saying five. Which is the correct time?"

"I don't know, I don't remember. If I said six, it must have been six."

"But when did you usually leave your office?"

"At five."

"At five. In that case, how did the defendant know that on that particular day you would be leaving at six?"

She was about to reply instinctively, but must have realized the trap concealed in the question. "Maybe I got it wrong. I probably did leave at five."

"You probably did leave at five. I still have here the records of Signor Bronzino's mobile phone. That day there was a thirty-three-second call at 5.18. The other number must have been yours, Signora. If you like, I can show you the records."

She moved her hand in a sign of denial, but it looked more like a gesture of self-defence.

"I point this out because if you met soon after five, it's hard to figure out why Bronzino should have called you on his mobile at 5.18."

It wasn't a real question, it was an explanation of what was happening, intended for the judges.

"Was your partner away on business that day, by any chance?"

"I don't remember."

"I put it to you that you had an appointment with Signor Bronzino that day. In other words, that meeting wasn't a chance one at all."

"No, I—"

"I put it to you that your partner was due to be away that day, and that when you got home fairly late that evening, you discovered that he hadn't left."

She didn't say anything. It was time to bring this to an end. I turned to the judge.

"Your Honour, if it can be entered in the record that the witness hasn't answered the last two questions, I've finished."

The judge was just doing as I had asked when the woman spoke again, without warning. Her voice was thin, diaphanous, seeming to come from somewhere else. It was as if her face had dried up in the course of the half-hour she had been in the witness box, as if the skin had stuck to the bones. Occasionally, as if in some terrible time machine, her face looked like an old woman's.

"I'm sorry. Forgive me."

Startled by the sound of her voice, the judge broke off, looked at her and asked her if she wanted to add anything. He, too, without realizing it, lowered his voice. But she didn't say anything else. She was looking somewhere else, outside that courtroom.

3

The judge told Di Cosmo that she could go. He said it in a tone that was meant to be stern, but he couldn't quite manage it. The sense of unease, of defeat that she conveyed had prevailed over his indignation. I turned to watch her while Basile was saying that we would adjourn for fifteen minutes. It's something I usually avoid: watching the actors of the drama (or the comedy) as they leave the stage. I was just in time to see her leave the courtroom, as silent and insubstantial as a ghost.

It was only then that I noticed Annapaola in the public seats. The investigation we had relied on for the cross-examination of the witness was hers. Most private detectives are men: retired former police officers or carabinieri. Usually somewhat elderly gentlemen.

Annapaola Doria doesn't correspond to the stereotype. Firstly, she isn't a man, and secondly, she isn't elderly. She's thirty-seven years old, and has a face like a rebellious schoolgirl, which makes her look younger. Above all, she isn't an ex-cop. She used to be a freelance crime reporter. A very good one, maybe even too good. She managed to gather information where others had to give up, even though it has to be said that she wasn't too bothered about journalistic ethics or the criminal code. I had defended her in a number of trials, some for libel and one actually for receiving stolen goods. The Prosecutor's Department had charged her with obtaining copies of documents relating to a pending criminal case that was still confidential, documents stolen – by persons unknown, as they say – from the clerk of the court's office, the said clerk having left it unattended because of a sudden urgent need for a cappuccino and a croissant.

According to the Prosecutor's Department, receiving three copies of improperly obtained documents was equivalent to buying a stolen TV set or jewellery taken in a robbery, and had therefore to be punished with a prison sentence of between two and eight years. A somewhat singular theory, which the judge did not share. Annapaola was acquitted, and I earned myself a few paragraphs in the papers.

Soon after that trial and that acquittal, Annapaola disappeared. For months, almost a year, there was no sign of her in the courthouse or at police headquarters. When she reappeared she was equipped with a new haircut, an expression that was both harder and more fragile, and a private detective's licence. The first time I needed an investigation to be carried out for a case of mine, I turned to her. The work was rapid and impeccable, even though it wasn't clear where and how (and breaking what rules, or even what locks) she had got hold of her information.

It had been Annapaola who had got me the data on Di Cosmo's partner's stays in Milan; how, I didn't want to know.

When our eyes met, she made me a sign and, as the judges went back into their chambers, she stood up, came towards me and embraced us in turn, first Consuelo, then me.

"Excellent work. If I hadn't felt sorry for the stupid girl, I might even have enjoyed it."

"*You* did excellent work, we just used it," I replied.

"Okay, let's stop right there before things get really treacly. That should be the end of the case, shouldn't it?"

"I think so. We just have to see if they deal with it today or decide on yet another postponement."

"I think the judge will deal with it today," Consuelo said. "He seemed almost embarrassed at the end of the cross-examination. I got the impression he wanted to get it all out of the way as soon as possible."

That was probably true, I thought.

We decided to go for a coffee. I even invited the prosecutor but he said no thanks, he'd rather use that time to look at his other briefs. He seemed on the verge of adding something, maybe a comment on what had just happened, then changed his mind.

Out of the four cafés in the vicinity of the courthouse, we chose the one where the coffee most resembles medicine that's past its expiry date. They manage to make it weak and burnt at the same time, which takes a certain talent. But the barista weighs 260 pounds, and can lift as much again in the gym, so nobody complains.

Consuelo said it was on her, because this was her first and probably also last trial for sexual assault, at least as defence counsel. My colleague doesn't exactly look at cases dispassionately. If she doesn't like the client, if the offence he's charged with strikes her as horrible, and if it isn't clear that the person is innocent, she has no desire to take on his defence. Let's just say that a practice following her criteria for taking on clients might find it hard to survive.

When we were back outside again, Annapaola quickly rolled herself a cigarette and we set off again, walking past the cemetery opposite the courthouse. Some winter evenings, when the hearings go on until it's dark, it's comforting to leave the courthouse and find yourself facing a myriad of grave lights. "In case you'd forgotten," they appear to say, although almost everyone – lawyers, police officers, clerks of the court and judges – has got used to it. The lights, the cypresses and the niches have become part of the landscape.

We passed a small group of carabinieri. Annapaola stopped to hug a couple of them with a warmth reserved for former comrades in arms. As so often before, I noticed the masculine way she moved and related to the outside world.

We went back into court. A few minutes later, the judges emerged from their chambers and the hearing resumed.

"First of all, I ask defence counsel if they wish to examine the defendant."

"No, Your Honour. The statements made by the defendant under questioning and already admitted in evidence appear more than sufficient following the outcome of the cross-examination of the injured party."

"Then if there are no further observations or motions, we declare that the testimony contained in the case file is admissible, including that made before the previous judges. Therefore at this point—"

"Your Honour, I'm sorry, I have a motion," Castroni said.

Basile looked at him for several seconds without saying anything. Not only had he not appreciated the interruption, he could also imagine the reason and didn't like it.

"He's asking for a postponement," I whispered to Consuelo. "If there's an acquittal he wants the other bastard to get it in the neck."

"Go on, prosecutor," the judge at last conceded, although his tone was far from cordial.

"I ask for a postponement in order to have a chance to examine the results of today's hearing, which has... well, which has contained a few surprises. Considering today's developments, it may be appropriate that the conclusions should be drawn by the prosecutor whose case this originally was because—"

"Prosecutor, in the first place don't force me to remind you that your office is impersonal. In the second place, I don't see any reason to grant a postponement. The trial has been going on for too long; the defendant was actually arrested at the time of the events and is entitled to a verdict within a reasonable length of time. You have been present at a crucial stage in the proceedings and are best qualified to draw the right conclusions from them. If you need half an hour to reread the documents, to think about them and then make your decision, I would have no objection to that."

Castroni was about to reply. Then it must have struck him that it wasn't a good idea. Mechanically, he leafed through the file he had in front of him, but without looking at the papers. Equally mechanically, he adjusted his robe over his shoulders and made his closing speech. It didn't take long.

"Your Honour, the evidence against the defendant, which at the time of his arrest, and to tell the truth up until today, has appeared solid, seems less so now. On cross-examination, the injured party has highlighted contradictions and hesitations. It does not seem to the prosecution that it is possible to reach a guilty verdict in the light of these contradictions. The evidence is ambiguous and, in a way, tainted, and therefore we have no option but to ask for an acquittal in accordance with article 530, paragraph 2 of the code of criminal procedure on the grounds of insufficient evidence to support the prosecution case."

The judge nodded and turned to Consuelo and me. "I don't want in any way to limit the prerogatives of the defence, but" – he clearly articulated the words that followed – "I ask you to take the prosecutor's motion into account. The court will appreciate a brief summing up, entrusted if possible to only one of the defenders."

The translation of that phrase was as follows: We will acquit him, don't make us waste any time, and let's all go home as soon as possible. Don't get on my nerves. I exchanged a rapid glance with Consuelo and stood up.

"Thank you, Your Honour, it is always a pleasure to hear your instructions. I will therefore conclude equally on behalf of my colleague, Avvocato Favia. The prosecutor's request for acquittal is the correct one, even though maybe a little timid. In his closing remarks, he did indeed speak of tainted and contradictory evidence, which ought to result in an acquittal according to article 530, paragraph 2: what used to be called acquittal due to insufficient evidence. While it will make no difference in practical terms – the defendant will have to be acquitted and his unfortunate experience of our courts brought to an end – I believe that what happened in today's hearing requires the final ruling to be all the more explicit and well argued. I maintain that the law owes it to the defendant, as a kind of moral compensation."

I had my eye on them. According to my calculations, I had between five and ten minutes to say a few things before Basile lost patience.

"It is not enough to say that the evidence in this trial is contradictory and insufficient, as the prosecutor has just done. No, the evidence is consistent and more than sufficient to prove the defendant's innocence. His innocence emerges in the light of the injured party's embarrassing testimony. It emerged clearly, as it did in the defendant's statements when he was first questioned, that the two of them had a relationship following their encounter at the famous party. They would meet whenever Di Cosmo's partner was away on business. The call from Bronzino's mobile phone to the hotel where the witness's partner was staying demonstrates that. Given that Bronzino had no reason to call that hotel, let alone the man, we may easily infer that the call was made by Di Cosmo, using the defendant's phone, when the two of them were together. It seems a minor detail, but in fact it is the key point in demonstrating, as I said, a pre-established relationship, one that was never admitted by the witness."

I know *a pre-established relationship* is a horrible expression. Many of those we lawyers use are. I try to limit myself, but often it's inevitable. There are judges – or colleagues – with whom you can't avoid speaking in a horrible way. If you speak in correct Italian when addressing the court, they don't recognize you as a member of the profession. You lack credibility. Legal jargon is the foreign language they – we – learn at university in order to become part of the team. It is a language which is all the more appreciated, the more capable it is of excluding those outside the profession from understanding what is happening in courtrooms and what is written in legal documents. A language that's both priestly and ragged, in which mysterious and ridiculous formulas are accompanied by systematic violations of grammar and syntax.

I'm sorry, every now and again I find myself digressing like this.

Judge Basile shifted in his seat and took a somewhat noisy, even ostentatious breath. I still had two or three minutes before he asked me to come to a conclusion.

"Why the witness falsely accused the defendant – because this is indeed, beyond a shadow of a doubt, a false accusation we are dealing with – is obvious. On the day of the events the woman's partner – a violent man, prone to physical abuse that sometimes resulted in injuries, a man of whom the witness was clearly afraid – changed his plans without warning. When Di Cosmo returned home, somewhat later than her usual time, probably in a dishevelled state because of the sexual encounter she had just had with Bronzino, and found her partner waiting for her, she lost her head and invented a story of assault. She stuck to her story, with unfortunate consequences for the defendant, who was completely innocent. I believe therefore that you have to acquit Antonio Bronzino as fully as possible with reference to article 530, paragraph 1. I will leave it to you to consider the possibility of conveying the trial record to the Prosecutor's Department, which may decide to proceed with a charge of slander."

The judge stood up before I had even uttered the last words, and so did the other two judges. It seemed almost as if they were running away.

"We are retiring now. I ask the parties not to stray too far from the courtroom. We shan't be long."

And he retreated to his chambers, followed by his colleagues.

Sure enough, they weren't long. We didn't even have time to take off our robes and go out into the corridor to be jostled by the endless stream of police officers, carabinieri, witnesses, clerks of the court, idlers, lawyers, prison guards and defendants in chains before the bell rang to inform us that the judges were already coming back.

They sat down in a way that suggested – I don't know why, maybe the way they leaned forward, maybe the way they wore their robes – that they didn't plan to stay much longer.

Basile adjusted his bifocals on his nose. "The Court of Bari, having read article 530, paragraph 1 of the code of criminal procedure, acquits Antonio Bronzino of the charge against him on the grounds that there is no substance to the charge. It orders that a record of these proceedings be passed on to the Prosecutor's Department to evaluate the possibility of charging Marilisa Di Cosmo with the offence of slander."

4

Consuelo called Bronzino. She told him it was over, that he had been acquitted, that there would be no follow-up, that it really was over. When he got back to Italy and dropped by the office, we would decide whether or not to bring a case demanding compensation for unfair imprisonment. No, there was no urgency, he could pay by transfer or with a credit card, we would send him an email with all the necessary instructions. The court had already passed on the documents to the prosecutor in order for him to charge Di Cosmo with slander. No, of course he hadn't lodged any complaint, it was good of him not to harbour feelings of revenge, it had been an autonomous decision of the court, slander is an offence it is compulsory to indict. Yes, that means there's no need for a complaint. All right, then, best of luck, speak to you soon, all right, I'll tell Avvocato Guerrieri. Yes, we're pleased too, goodbye.

Consuelo had parked her car in the courthouse car park. She asked Annapaola if she wanted a lift.

"No thanks, I have my motorbike," Annapaola said, pointing to a kind of chrome-plated monster next to the sentry box.

"You ride that thing?" I asked.

"Beautiful, isn't it?"

"Are you in a gang, like the Hells Angels or the Bandidos?"

"Oh, sure. One day I'll pick you up and take you for a ride. It goes like a bat out of hell, but I'm sure you'll be fine."

Then she gave Consuelo a high five and blew me a slightly mocking kiss.

"How about you, boss?" Consuelo asked me while Annapaola disappeared in an unmistakable roar of pistons.

"Thanks, I'll walk. I may stop on the way and have a bite to eat. See you in the office this afternoon."

I didn't stop anywhere. As I walked steadily towards the centre it struck me that it had been far too long since I'd last had lunch at home. I began an inner conversation, the kind where, if there's someone close to me, he asks me after a while if I'm crazy. I start moving my lips, clearly (but silently) articulating a dialogue between Guido 1 and Guido 2. I used to do that when I was a child. Then, to avoid being made fun of (which happened quite frequently), I managed to stop. When I grew up, I started again.

Yes, Guerrieri, it's true, you never have lunch at home. But why should you? You live alone. Much better to sit down where someone knows you and then you can have a bit of a chat. Having lunch on your own is one of the saddest things there is, and it's even a bit sordid.

As usual, you're overstating your case. Sordid, is it? That sense of precariousness you're talking about is only made worse if you try to escape solitude at all costs.

Did you read that profound thought in a cheap magazine? The kind of magazine for men that always publishes the same articles: how to drive her crazy in bed, how to get muscles of steel in three weeks with five minutes' training a day, what food to eat in order not to get ill, and various items about mental health, how to overcome sadness, depression and boils on your nose? Plus recently, a few suggestions on how to prevent an enlarged prostate, a subject which should actually be of some interest to you.

Very witty. You make me laugh like a drain.

Do you even have anything to eat at home? Is there anything in the fridge apart from pathetic ready meals?

I don't have ready meals. I have good, fresh, abundant food, because I know perfectly well that you and people like you are always lecturing me, and I try to pre-empt them. I make myself fantastic salads and seitan burgers. I should also have some strawberries, and anyway, that's enough, I'm going home.

Seitan burgers? Are you turning vegetarian, Guerrieri? Don't tell me that because I couldn't bear it. You've quit smoking, after two glasses of wine you say you've had enough, and gradually you've stopped eating anything that has any taste, like wonderful fried food, burnt hamburgers and fat tasty sausages, mortadella, desserts with cream, pizzas with lard instead of olive oil. You no longer drink spirits, and let's not even mention sex, for heaven's sake, because you're not getting any of that, and now you're even becoming a vegetarian? Do you drink nettle juice?

All right, I almost never eat meat these days. What of it?

You're a vegetarian.

Let's just say I'm thinking seriously about whether or not it's morally acceptable to eat meat.

What? Thinking seriously about what? You've gone mad. Or rather no – you're getting old and you're starting to have obsessions.

Getting old? *You've* gone mad.

How old are you?

Forty-eight. What of it?

When you were a child, what did you think of a man who was nearly fifty?

It's the wrong question. When I was a child a man of fifty was… very grown-up. But now—

When you were a child you thought that at the age of fifty a man was almost old. Your grandfather was seventy, he had friends who were younger, and to you they were all old. Is that true or not?

I arrived home and the conversation fizzled out as quickly as it had started.

For a few moments, as I entered my apartment, I felt legitimate pride. A few days earlier, after many years, I had decided to tidy up a bit.

Actually it hadn't really been a choice. The situation had got out of hand, particularly because of the books. Apart from those on the shelves, there were books everywhere. On the floor, on the tables, on the sofas, in the bathroom, in the kitchen – and let's be honest, not all of them were indispensable.

Even just getting to the punchbag, which hung ever more angrily in the middle of the living room, had become quite difficult. Then, one night, surfing the Internet, I came across the term *disposophobia*.

Disposophobia, also known as pathological accumulation or compulsive hoarding, is a mental disorder characterized by the obsessive need to acquire a large number of objects without using or throwing them away, even if they are useless, dangerous or unhealthy. Compulsive hoarding hampers and significantly damages basic activities like moving about, cooking, cleaning, washing and sleeping. As it happened, cleaning and moving about, at the very least, had become quite complicated in my apartment. The condition is ego-syntonic, according to experts. That is, it is not perceived as disabling. On the contrary, the individual concerned finds a thousand justifications to continue his own compulsive accumulating. Until the point of no return is reached, and the sufferer realizes that the work he'll need to do to tidy up and clear the space is immense and impossible and finds himself torn between the need to keep things and the necessity to get rid of them in order to survive.

I had read enough. I have a certain aptitude for recognizing in myself the symptoms – or at least the early warnings – of the most varied psychiatric conditions. That web page was clearly about me, and I'd have to run for cover before it was too late. To cut a long story short, the following Saturday I got hold of lots of boxes and for several hours filled them with books, to be given to jumble sales or thrown in recycling bins. The idea of throwing books into recycling bins may be upsetting, but what else can you do with volumes called things like *Meditations for the Bathroom, Practical Manual of Self-Hypnosis, 101 Cures for Insomnia, How Proust can change your Life* and many other similar titles?

I had bought those books. When I go into a bookshop, my inhibitors become deactivated, and I can buy all kinds of things. It's only later that I can't remember why and wonder what kind of entity possessed me in the half-hour I spent between the shelves.

It had been rather an exhausting Saturday, but on Sunday morning, when I woke up, I'd felt it had been worth it. The windows seemed larger and the light spread more freely. If the opportunity presented itself, I might even be able to invite someone to dinner.

After enjoying the spectacle of tidiness for a few moments and saying hello to my friend Mr Punchbag, I went to make lunch.

The conversation with my shadow, though, had shaken me a little, and in order to avoid further sarcastic remarks

I decided, just for the day, to do without food that was too healthy. The seitan, the Brussels sprouts and the soya chunks stayed in the fridge and the pantry, waiting for better times. I prepared a dressing of garlic, oil, *very* spicy chilli pepper, black olives, anchovies and fried breadcrumbs, boiled two hundred grams of spaghetti from the Abruzzi, drained it while it was still hard and tossed it in the pan. I also decided to break the *No alcohol at lunch* rule. I opened a bottle of Primitivo and drank a good half of it. At that point, it occurred to me that I could even allow myself a little nap. As I slipped into the delicious no man's land of an afternoon nap, I vowed that it wouldn't become a habit.

Maybe.

5

About ten days had passed since the Bronzino trial and I had just got back to the office after a pointless hearing, which had finished in the afternoon with the umpteenth postponement.

As soon as I entered, Pasquale came to meet me, an almost desolate expression of apology on his face. The expression of someone who would like to have done something to avoid an unpleasantness, but hasn't been able to.

Pasquale Macina has worked his whole life in lawyers' offices. He began at the age of nineteen as a deputy clerk (it isn't true, I invented the rank) in the practice of a leading barrister who was a friend of my grandfather's. He continued with another famous criminal lawyer, also of the old school, a contemporary of my father's. And now, well past sixty, he's with me.

His existence is founded on a few basic, unbreakable rules. Some of these have to do with hierarchies – understood as a metaphor for the necessary order of the universe – and their corresponding rituals. For example, you never call the lawyer you work for by his first name, although it is taken for granted that said lawyer calls you by your first name. Otherwise the relationship, deprived of its form, is impoverished, doesn't work and may lead to negative consequences. Don't think I've invented all this out of my inclination towards conjecture.

Oh, no, it was Pasquale himself, in a memorable conversation a few days after he began working in my office, who explained it to me.

"Pasquale, I have to ask you a favour. I called you by your first name, it seemed quite natural, and I'd like it if you did the same, otherwise I'd feel awkward."

"You mustn't, Avvocato, but I can't call you by your first name."

"Then maybe I shouldn't call you by yours. That'd be more correct."

As I said this, I saw it for what it was. An abstraction, banal and stupid.

"If you don't mind me saying so, I think it would be wrong. Very wrong. Our relationship is honest, sincere and, if you don't mind my saying so, friendly, because it goes along the right tracks. We must see that it stays on those tracks. I'm convinced that we're friends. I think, however, that this friendship follows rules that are a little different from what I might call traditional friendships. They are rules that help to guarantee loyalty and spontaneity between us."

And that was all.

"He's back," Pasquale said.

With a sigh, I dropped my bag on the floor and let my shoulders droop. "That's not possible. What are we going to do with him?"

"I'm sorry. As usual, he rang the doorbell and when I opened, there he was. If you'll allow me—"

"Pasquale, please don't say: if you'll allow me. Just say what you have to say."

"The fact is, Ignazio comes to you because you give him too much rope. When the other people in the building meet him, they pretend not to see him, they don't even answer him and he loses interest. You're too—"

"Pasquale, let's just drop it. Where is he?"

"In the conference room. He switched on the TV. He's watching – what do they call it? – that channel the kids watch—"

"MTV."

"That's the one."

Ignazio is a young man with serious mental health problems. Up until the age of twenty-three, apparently, he was normal. Then, overnight, he went mad. I realize that isn't a perfect description from a psychiatric point of view, but I think it describes what happened to him effectively enough.

He has an invalidity pension and takes various drugs, he lives with his parents in an apartment in the same building as my office, he's harmless (I hope), and above all, he loves animals. The problem is that he's convinced he can talk to them and, at least a couple of times a month (but sometimes, as at this particular time, even more frequently), he comes and tells me what they've told him, because it's usually information about important crimes.

I walked into the conference room. He didn't hear me because he was concentrating very hard on a video – the volume wasn't exactly moderate – and was following the images and the rhythm of the music with unsynchronized movements of his head and shoulders.

"Ignazio!"

He turned, still moving, and gave me the usual gentle, sad smile. "Avvocato Guido, hello."

"Hello, Ignazio, what's up?"

"Something very important. Do you have a cigarette?"

"No, Ignazio, you know I haven't smoked for years."

"Well, I have cigarettes," he said with perfect consistency, searching in a pocket of his jacket and taking out two packets of Marlboro Lights, both open. "Would you like one?"

"No, thanks, Ignazio, I told you I don't smoke."

"It's all right to smoke here, isn't it?"

"Sure, but open the window."

He went to the window, opened it, looked out, waved at someone – probably a dog passing with its master – and went and sat down. He lit his cigarette with a Zippo. "Can I throw the ash on the floor?"

"It's best not to. I'll give you an ashtray."

He took two or three almost ferocious drags at his cigarette, then went back to the window as if he'd suddenly remembered something he had to check. "We have to tap his phone," he said at last, abruptly.

"Whose phone, Ignazio?"

"The owner of the pork butcher's where my mother goes. I'm not eating the mortadella ever again."

"Why, what's the matter with the mortadella?"

Ignazio lowered his voice and leaned towards me, blowing smoke in my face. "He makes it with dog meat."

"How do you know?"

"There's a rumour going around among the neighbourhood dogs. They're very worried. The problem is, I told my parents and they don't believe me."

"No?"

"No, they think the things my friends tell me are bullshit. But they're true. Luckily, you believe me."

There. Pasquale was right.

"But are you sure? How does he manage to get hold of the dogs without their masters realizing?"

He made a gesture of polite self-importance, like a kind

teacher dealing with a stupid pupil. "He takes strays that wander the streets at night."

"But there aren't any stray dogs in this city."

"There are hardly any left because he's taken almost all of them. To make mortadella. The few remaining are hiding. They're afraid. That's why we have to tap his phone, don't you see? Do you have a cigarette?"

"No, Ignazio. I don't smoke."

He lit another cigarette, silently, concentrating hard. Then he turned to me again. "This is the number of the pork butcher's, for the phone tap," he said, taking out a little piece of squared paper, like a page from a school exercise book, and holding it out to me. "I wrote it out secretly from mother's diary. It's the number she calls to have the shopping delivered. I don't want to go there. Do you think it's possible he makes the smoked ham out of dogs too?"

"I don't think so. I think that would be difficult."

"So I can eat the smoked ham?"

"Yes, I'm sure you can. You'll be safe with the ham."

"Oh, I'm pleased, because I really like smoked ham. I like rolls with smoked ham and cheese slices. Do you like them, Avvocato Guido?"

"Actually, it's a long time since I last ate that kind of roll. But yes, I used to like them."

"Then one day I'll bring two and we can eat them together." He let about ten seconds go by and assumed an expression of polite impatience. "So what about the phone tap?"

"We'll do it next week."

He looked at me with disappointment and a hint of suspicion in his eyes. "Can't you do it right away?"

"Unfortunately not, Ignazio. We need to fill in a form."

"What form?"

51

"We need to get a form from the court, write down everything for the phone tap, and give it to the judge."

"So we have to go to the judge? We should go together."

"There's no need, I'll go, don't worry. That's a lawyer's job, isn't it?"

He turned pensive. He was processing the information I'd given him. At last, he nodded resolutely. "If I hear anything else in the meantime, I'll let you know right away."

"Excellent idea. Now, Ignazio, you'll have to go because I have an appointment with another client and I don't want to keep him waiting."

"Of course, of course." And after a brief pause: "Avvocato Guido, can you give me your mobile number? Then, if there's an emergency, I can call you and you can come right away."

"I'd be happy to give it to you, Ignazio. The problem is that I'm changing contracts right now and I think I'll have a new number by tomorrow. There's no point in my giving you the old one, is there?"

"You know something, Avvocato Guido?"

"What, Ignazio?"

"I'm happy when I come to see you, because you understand what I'm saying. Other people are crazy. I tell them what I hear from my animal friends and they look at me with an expression that tells me they don't believe me. You understand, you're more intelligent."

"Thank you, Ignazio, that's nice to hear."

He looked at me for a few moments longer as if to underline the concept, to confirm that he really meant what he had said.

God knows how he was when he was a child. God knows what he dreamt of doing and what his parents dreamt for him. Maybe they imagined he would become a doctor, or a lawyer, or an engineer, and that he would be with them in their old age, instead of which they had found themselves trapped by life, with a fear of dying that was different from the one we all have: the fear of leaving their son, a child in a man's body, alone and helpless.

"Can I give you a little kiss, Avvocato Guido?"

"All right, Ignazio."

He approached and I smelt the stale smell of hundreds of Marlboros, smoked one after the other, with which his clothes and his hair were impregnated. He gave me a delicate kiss on the cheek, like a child kissing its father.

"Now you must excuse me, Avvocato Guido, I have to go. I'll be back soon, though. Please see to that matter."

"Don't worry, Ignazio, I'll deal with it. Let me walk you to the door."

We walked down the corridor together, watched from the other offices.

"We'll see each other soon. Right now, I'm going to work."

"Where are you going, Avvocato Guido?"

"I'm going to my office, to work."

"Do you have a cigarette?"

"No, Ignazio, I don't smoke."

"Then take one of mine," he said, taking out the two packets.

"Don't light it now, or the smoke will linger on the stairs and the other people in the building will get angry. Light it when you're in the street."

"But isn't it forbidden to smoke in the street?"

"No, you can smoke in the street. It's in church that you can't smoke."

A few days earlier, he had been caught for the umpteenth time smoking in church, and for the umpteenth time the parish priest had kicked up a fuss, threatening to call the local health authority, the municipal police, the paratroopers.

"Can you give me money to buy cigarettes?" he said, even though he still had the two half-used packets in his hand.

I took out my wallet, extracted a ten-euro note and gave it to him. "Since you already have cigarettes, keep the money. Or else get yourself an ice cream or fruit juice."

"But when I finish them, can I buy more with these ten euros?"

"Yes, Ignazio, you can." I managed to hold myself back from saying that he ought to smoke less, that smoking is bad for you, and so on. Apart from the fact that it would have been futile, I wondered if it would have been *right*. I once knew a lady, a client, whose two children had been killed in a road accident. She smoked a lot, but not in a nervous way. Methodically, you might say. She would drag fiercely at the smoke, and it was as if each mouthful spread through her body like a medicine that a mad doctor had forced her to take regularly. Once – we were in a break during the trial for culpable homicide of the lorry driver who had killed her children – someone told her that she ought to quit.

She replied, in a calm tone that sent shivers down my spine: "I'm alone, with a grief that won't leave me until I die. I can only bear it thanks to these cigarettes. If I didn't smoke I'd go crazy. And if I go crazy with grief, what do I care about the risk to my heart, or the risk of tumours and all that stuff? I'm killing myself anyway, so it's better to do it this way." And there was nothing else to add.

"All right, goodbye, then," Ignazio said, unaware of the intense activity in my mind.

The afternoon passed normally. Even just a few days later I wouldn't have been able to remember what had happened, but a few minutes before eight a call came in.

"Yes?"

"Avvocato, there's a call for you." There was something odd about Pasquale's voice that I couldn't figure out.

"Who is it?"

A brief pause. "Judge Larocca."

Now I was the one who paused for a moment. "Judge Larocca? The head of the appeal court?"

"Yes."

"Put him through."

6

If a judge calls me at my office – it happens rarely, but it does happen – I start to get anxious. I'm always afraid that something has gone wrong. That I've screwed up in some really big way. So big that it can't be dealt with by a clerk of the court or a secretary.

And the fact that the judge in question, as in the case of Larocca, is kind of a friend doesn't change things one iota. A judge calling you at your office is a flashing red sign saying: *Danger ahead*. I asked myself what I could possibly have done, but couldn't think of anything. We had a few appeals pending, and were waiting for the dates of the hearings. Nothing urgent, nothing important. So I thought.

"Hello?"

"Guido!"

"Pierluigi. How are you?"

A brief pause.

"So-so. I waited for the end of office hours before phoning, because you might have been seeing clients and I didn't want to disturb you."

"That's all right, you can call me when you like."

"Actually I was hoping to see you in court, but it's been a while since you've appeared before me."

"You're right, it must be a couple of months. Come to think of it, I don't have many clients in prison these days."

Another pause, on both sides. Mine meant: Are you going to tell me why you called or do I have to ask you? His, I don't know.

As happens in these cases, we talked over each other:
"Listen—"

"So what do—"

"I'm sorry, it's just that I need to talk to you—"

"Can you tell me over the phone, or would you prefer me to come to your office tomorrow?"

"No, thanks. It's something… How can I put it?… It's better if I come to see you."

"All right. When can you come?"

"As soon as possible."

"As soon as possible could be this evening, if you like."

"That'd be perfect."

"It's eight o'clock now. Maybe it's best if you come when there's nobody around. That way we can talk in peace."

"Thanks, Guido. I really appreciate it. Tell me what time and I'll be there."

"Let's say 9.30. You know the address."

"Of course. If only for the times I've read it on your papers."

Pierluigi Larocca wasn't just anybody. If the expression *top of the class* could be applied to anyone, that person was him.

We had gone to the same high school – although we weren't in the same class – and the same university. He had been a legendary student. Top marks at school, top marks at university, a graduate at twenty-two and at twenty-four already a magistrate.

He had become head of a criminal division of the court while still young, and it was widely thought that when the post became vacant – in a few months, because the old president was about to retire – he would become the youngest president of the Court of Bari. Then – who knows?

The Prosecutor's Department and the police didn't like him. They considered him too much of a stickler for rules. Maybe they were right, but it should be said that his decisions were always impeccably argued and were almost never overturned by the Supreme Court.

We had rubbed shoulders occasionally in our university days, even though we didn't move in the same circles. His was the classic well-to-do Bari of the early Eighties. I don't know what mine was. I hung out with all sorts of people back then, but actually our paths did sometimes cross. The height of our intimacy was an evening when we went for a pizza together with our respective girlfriends. His, as far as I recalled, hardly said a word.

If Larocca wanted to talk to me in my office, he must have some private problem. Either he was the injured party, or he was under investigation. The second hypothesis struck me as extremely unlikely. Or rather, I couldn't imagine that somebody as untouchable as him could be accused of something.

All right, I told myself. I'll go out for a walk now and have a bite to eat. I hadn't had lunch, and I suspected that the conversation with Larocca wouldn't be a short one.

7

By 9.15 I was back in the office.

Going into the office when it's deserted always gives me a touch of anxiety. The anxiety of someone who feels he's in the wrong place, that things are happening somewhere else. The sensation of being left out.

That didn't happen in the old place, nor does it happen if I remain alone when everybody else has gone. Maybe it means something, and someone better than me would be capable of interpreting the phenomenon. So far I haven't succeeded.

At exactly 9.30, the silence of the office was broken by the harsh sound of the entryphone.

"Second floor," I said, opening the door without waiting for a reply.

Larocca walked up the stairs while I waited for him in the doorway. I held out my hand and he took it. After a very brief hesitation, he came closer, moving awkwardly, and hugged me.

He was wearing a well-cut jacket and trousers, a shirt, a neatly knotted tie and classic shoes, and gave off a faint high-quality male scent. I doubt he'd dressed like that as a student, but I couldn't remember him wearing anything different from what he had on now or in court. He had been a somewhat anonymous young man in appearance: average height, average build, average features, the kind you look at and forget immediately afterwards. With the years, he had grown more interesting. The slightly receding hairline, the lines on his forehead and at the sides of his mouth, even the slight bags under his eyes, had conferred personality on his face. This was the first time I'd realized it, outside the context of the courtroom, of our roles, our masks.

"A nice office, it reflects your personality," he said as we proceeded along the corridor towards my room at the far end.

I don't think my office reflects my personality. It was done by an overenthusiastic designer; I simply put up with it and paid. For at least the first two years, I would have liked nothing better than to abandon it and run away. Gradually, I got used to it. Nothing more.

"Please sit down," I said, indicating an armchair in my room, on the opposite side from the one behind the desk.

"It smells nice in here," he said as he sat down.

"That's one of my female colleagues. She's obsessed with natural essences. Yes, it is very nice."

He looked around. He noticed the books, the comics.

"It isn't quite how I expected it. Don't get me wrong, that was meant as a compliment. It doesn't have that – how can I put it? – that sad, dusty look. The offices of old lawyers have something of the sacristy, the bishop's antechamber about them. Those of young lawyers seem like… well, legal offices: furniture all the same, law books, horrible prints. I like it that there are real books here, and even comics. What do you have there, Tex Willer?"

"A few old issues. Sometimes I reread one to relax when I can't work."

"I like that," he said, indicating the framed poster hanging to the right of my desk. It's a black-and-white photograph of two Palestinian children sitting on the ground surrounded by bombed-out buildings. At the bottom, there's a quotation from Brecht: *We sat down on the side of wrong because all the other seats were taken.*

"I've grown fond of it. It's one of the few things I took with me from the place where I lived with my ex-wife. It followed me to my old office and now to this one."

"Your ex-wife. That's right, you're separated. How many years has it been?"

"I'm divorced now. We separated ten years ago."

"Ten years? Incredible."

It wasn't clear what was so incredible about it. Maybe it was just an expression of his embarrassment. He'd come to me to talk about a delicate, urgent matter and somehow couldn't get into the rhythm.

"So, what can I do for you?"

My question startled him. He abandoned the apparently relaxed position he had kept up until that moment. He straightened and leaned forward in the armchair.

"You're right, we've got through the pleasantries. I'm here about something that's been tormenting me for several days. I don't even know where to start."

"Shall we have a drink?"

"No, no, don't worry, calling the bar at this hour—"

"One of the advantages of having such a large office is that there's also a kitchen with a fridge. Will you have a glass of chilled wine, or would you prefer something non-alcoholic?"

"Chilled wine will be fine."

It really was fine. Before starting to tell me what he had to, Larocca knocked back two glasses of Chardonnay as if it were water, ignoring the little tray of pistachios I'd brought in to accompany the bottle.

"Alcohol helps, you can't deny it. Guido, I'm scared that they're bringing criminal charges against me in Lecce."

According to the code of criminal procedure, when magistrates are subject to criminal proceedings, the case is dealt with in a place different from the one in which they work. A rule intended to avoid any conflict of interest. For magistrates from the Bari area, cases fall within the jurisdiction of the court in Lecce.

"Excuse me, Pierluigi, but is that speculation or have you had formal notification?"

"Neither."

"I'm afraid I don't understand."

He snorted in frustration. "I was told by a friend, a colleague of yours."

I had the impulse to ask him who it was, but restrained myself. If he wanted to tell me, he would; if he didn't, my question would just embarrass him.

"What did this colleague of mine tell you?"

He filled his glass again and immediately drained it. "Don't think I always drink like this. It's just that this story is wearing me out. Your... colleague told me that there have been statements made to the anti-Mafia magistrates in Bari by a Mafioso who's turned state's evidence... statements accusing me. This Mafioso supposedly... I'm sorry, I really can't say it. I feel overcome with shame and anger. The man has apparently stated that I accepted money in return for favourable rulings. To get prisoners released, in fact."

I let out a hint of a whistle. There are always unpleasant rumours circulating in the courts about supposed examples of judicial corruption, judges inclined to accept gifts and grant unlawful favours. That happens in Bari too, of course, and there were some names that were bandied about more frequently than others. Some of these rumours had been confirmed and over the years some judges – especially in the civil courts, to tell the truth – had been arrested, sentenced and struck off. But I'd never heard the slightest gossip about Pierluigi Larocca.

"This colleague of mine who told you about this, how does he know? What is his source, if I may ask?"

"This has to be strictly between ourselves, Guido."

I made a slightly self-important expression, to make it clear to him that there was no need to worry, that I was Mr Confidentiality in person. And I also looked somewhat ridiculous, I thought to myself, as I always do when I force myself to act self-important. I don't like self-important. Either from an aesthetic or an ethical point of view. But sometimes I can't help myself.

"He heard it from a woman friend of his who works in the office of the Mafioso's lawyer."

"Do you know who this Mafioso is?"

"A man named Capodacqua."

"Never heard of him. But I don't do organized crime, I don't take that kind of client as a rule, so the fact that I've never heard of him doesn't mean anything. Is he somebody important?"

He shrugged his shoulders, and as he did so a grimace of disgust – of which he probably wasn't aware – drew back his lips and crinkled his nostrils. The expression of someone who has suddenly become aware of a bad smell.

"I don't know much about criminal hierarchies. The police and the Prosecutor's Department say he's a very big fish. I think he's just a dealer who's gone up in the world."

"Did you handle his case?"

"A couple of years ago."

"What was the outcome?"

"Two separate sentences for drugs offences. In both cases the sentences were upheld."

"Fine. That means he didn't get any favourable treatment. So maybe he has it in for you. What could this man have said to the prosecutor? And who's the examining magistrate who's questioning him?"

Larocca passed a hand over his forehead, as if to wipe away sweat, even though there wasn't any. A mechanical gesture, or maybe a metaphorical one. He glanced at the empty glass, thought about it for a few moments, then must have decided that it was better to stop.

"Berardi and Padula are questioning him. So you can already see how objective they are."

Filippo Berardi and Daniela Padula were assistant prosecutors working for the regional anti-Mafia directorate. They had the reputation of being good, competent people and, a year earlier, had been involved in an argument about how easy it was to be released by the court of appeal. In other words, Pierluigi Larocca's division. It was understandable that he didn't care for them.

"What could this Capodacqua have said?"

"My friend didn't see the transcript. As I told you, he just received a few tip-offs from this person, a female trainee he's having a relationship with. I'm not sure if she read the transcript because she was authorized to do so or if she glanced over it when she shouldn't. Anyway, what she told him – and what he then told me – is simple: Capodacqua claims that Judge Larocca took money to have someone released."

"Do you know when these statements were made?"

"It must have been a few months ago."

"Is the fact that this Capodacqua is cooperating well known? Do you know if his statements – not those concerning you, obviously – have been used to apply for custody orders or cited in any trials?"

"I don't know."

"So the idea that a case is already pending against you in Lecce is only your conjecture?"

"Yes, but a very reasonable one. When a judge is accused of an offence, the information is passed on immediately. Not to do so exposes those involved to the risk of disciplinary procedures."

We sat there in silence for a long time. I was thinking about what he had told me, trying to figure out a possible course of action. The only thing that occurred to me was to petition the Prosecutor's Department in Lecce to be informed of the possible existence of the proceedings, although there was no guarantee I'd get an answer I could use.

"How long have you known?" I asked at last.

"A week. And for a week I haven't slept, I've barely even been alive."

"It's an unpleasant situation, but I wouldn't overdramatize it, because—"

He interrupted me almost angrily. As if he'd been expecting me to say something like that in order to come out with what was really eating him up inside. "Guido, I don't trust my colleagues, especially not those in the Prosecutor's Department. The way I've presided over the years hasn't endeared me to them. They like judges who agree with them, more or less. They don't like anyone who follows the rules too strictly. It's always been like that. I've always been afraid they'd find some willing ex-Mafioso to help them teach me a lesson. To make me pay for all the times I've acquitted someone, quite rightly, all the times I've demolished their absurd theories based on flimsy evidence. It's an idea that's obsessed me for years, since before I began presiding over the appeal court."

"But I don't think that—"

"Please let me finish. Let's be clear about this, I'm not saying it's an accusation made up out of thin air. That would be too banal. The likeliest scenario I can imagine – the one that emerges from reading the statements of lots of criminals who've turned state's evidence, and from an analysis of the modus operandi of those in the Prosecutor's Department – is more complicated than that."

It struck me that he had used the term *modus operandi* to talk about the work of the Prosecutor's Department. *Modus operandi* is the expression usually used in police and criminological contexts to indicate the operating style and characteristic features of a criminal or category of criminals. I don't know if he'd done it consciously, but he couldn't have chosen a more effective way of expressing his own contempt.

"One of these criminals decides to cooperate, usually because his is a hopeless case and he's likely to receive a heavy sentence, or because some of his former friends have decided to kill him. The prosecutor and the police who interrogate him ask him what kind of things he's able to tell them, given that, as you know, the possibility of gaining an advantage from cooperating really depends on the nature of the information he can supply, especially on whether it's something they haven't heard too much before. And among the most sought-after information is anything that implicates politicians, public officials, administrators, police officers, carabinieri, and – last but by no means least – criminal court judges. Anyone looking to cooperate knows perfectly well that the degree of consideration he'll get from the investigators, his importance, and therefore the likelihood of his having benefits and the power to cut deals increase if he talks about things like votes for favours, fiddled contracts, and corrupt policemen and judges. But he often doesn't know anything – or at least nothing specific – because these things, assuming they happen, even here, are known only by the bigwigs, the criminal bosses. So although he has nothing concrete to say about these subjects, but is being – how shall I put it? – urged to talk about them, he digs into his memory, and if he digs deep enough, he's bound to come up with something. Even if it's just some wretched piece of gossip he heard in prison. Or maybe the result of influence peddling on the part of some crooked colleague of yours.

"So he says that Judge So-and-So is corrupt because his cellmate or his lawyer told him. The prosecutor nods – it's just what he wanted to hear – and the criminal realizes he's on the right track. When he's questioned again and asked to go further into the subject, which his interrogators – the investigators on whom his future depends – obviously consider important, he tries to remember more, embellishes it, and adds a few speculations of his own, passing them off as actual knowledge. They end up with a flimsy but credible accusation, which they have to investigate in order to find corroborating evidence. Investigating and finding corroborating evidence takes time. I'll be caught up in this business for God knows how long and with my reputation soiled forever. Because even when the case is closed – with either a dismissal or an acquittal – everyone will remember that I was the judge accused of releasing prisoners in return for money.

"Among other things, the position of president of the court falls vacant in the next few months. As you can imagine, I stand a good chance of getting it. Or maybe I should say: *I would have stood a good chance.* With this thing pending, unless we deal with it very soon, my chances are close to zero."

Again that uncontrolled grimace of disgust.

It was my turn to pour myself some more wine, after refilling his glass.

"What would *you* do?" he asked as he drank.

"We could present a motion in accordance with article 335 and see what they reply. Just a try, obviously."

67

According to article 335 of the code of criminal procedure, anyone who supposes he is being investigated can present a motion to the prosecutor asking if his name appears on the register of those under investigation. The prosecutor is obliged to divulge the information unless the investigation is in any way confidential, in which case he can take advantage of this confidentiality for three months.

Larocca shook his head slightly. "I don't know. I think if we present a motion, all we'll do is put them on the alert. They're bound to claim confidentiality, and for at least three months I'll be sat here stewing, wondering what nasty surprise they might have in store for me. It'd drive me mad."

"An alternative would be to take it as read that the process is under way – we don't have to indicate any source – and ask for you to be examined."

I had barely finished speaking before he had already started shaking his head again.

"You're not convinced by that either."

He didn't reply immediately. He pushed back his smooth, thin brown hair, which was falling over his forehead, breathed in greedily, almost violently, as if suddenly hungry for air, then put his hands together. "I heard about that remarkable cross-examination of yours in the second division court, when you demonstrated that the charge was a slander. My colleague Basile says you must have carried out a very thorough investigation. He doesn't see how you could have gathered certain information without help from the police."

"Oh yes, it was a trial for sexual assault. A case that should never have come to court. The investigation was a good one, I agree."

"I don't want to ask you anything that will interfere with professional confidentiality, but I imagine you must have used a private detective." He let a few seconds go by before continuing: "Or else you have some… useful contacts?"

"I know a very good private detective. She's the only one I trust. And I think she has… useful contacts, as you put it. Including among the police."

"Is she an ex-policewoman?"

"No. She's not your average detective. She used to be a journalist. You may remember her, she was always hanging around the courthouse years ago, as a crime reporter: Annapaola Doria."

"Doria, of course I remember her. Pretty face, good figure. Now that you mention it, it's true, I haven't seen her around for a while. Why on earth would a journalist become a private detective?"

"I tried asking her once, and I soon realized it was best to drop the subject."

"But you say she's good?"

"Very good. She gets results others don't even dream about."

"What would you say if I asked you to carry out a pre-emptive investigation, using this woman, to find out more about what's going on before we take any formal steps with the Prosecutor's Department in Lecce?"

"What are you thinking?"

"I don't have any specific ideas. Anything we manage to find out – about the Mafioso and about the case they're building – will help us to decide what to do next. I know several people in the police. In theory, I could ask any of them, but I don't think they can be trusted any more about these things. It's a tricky business. You talk to someone you consider a friend, and the first thing he might do is write a duty report and take it to the Prosecutor's Department. Better to strangle it at birth, don't you think?"

Strangle it at birth. The expression bothered me. I had to make an effort to suppress my disquiet and say, all right, I'd talk to Annapaola and ask her if she was in a position to carry out that kind of investigation. I wasn't sure it was possible, I wasn't sure what she'd reply, but I'd try.

"To be on the safe side, I'd like to formalize this, if you have no objection."

"Of course not."

"Then I'll immediately prepare a proxy document giving me authority to carry out investigations – I'll make it general, without going into details – and you can sign it now. That way you won't need to come back here. I'll call Annapaola tomorrow."

"Don't discuss it with her on the phone."

"Don't worry."

Ten minutes later, I was walking Larocca to the door. On the threshold he hesitated for a moment.

"Guido…"

"Go on."

"I want to be treated like any other client. You'll incur expenses with your detective. Can I pay you an advance? I insist on it. If you can tell me how much—"

"You *will* be treated like my other clients. But right now, it's after eleven and I think it'll be a bit difficult for me to take the money and write you a receipt. For the moment, it's time to go home."

8

The next morning was full of things to do at the courthouse, the kind I hate. Engaging an expert for a pretrial hearing; examination of an individual in the police cells; hearings related to building violations. As far as possible, when there are tasks of this kind I delegate Consuelo and Maria Teresa, my other colleague, or, for simpler things, one of the trainees. That morning, however, there were too many things to do. We all went to the courthouse together at nine and got back to the office around lunchtime.

"Who drank a whole bottle of wine?" Maria Teresa asked, a few moments after going into the kitchen to make herself a salad.

"A client. A new one. We drank the bottle between us, talking about his case. I'll tell you about it later. I didn't take any girls to the sleeping quarters, I swear."

Maria Teresa rolled her eyes and shrugged her shoulders.

"I can't find Annapaola Doria's phone number," I said, dismissing the subject of my nocturnal drinking bouts in the office with my clients. "Can you get it for me, please?"

"Do you want me to call her for you?"

"No thanks. I'll do it."

Annapaola answered at the second ring. "Guido Guerrieri!"

"Am I disturbing you? Is this a bad time?"

"On the contrary. At moments like this, it's great to get a phone call."

"What you mean by *moments like this*?"

"I've been stuck in a van for the past two hours, glued to a pair of binoculars and a camera with a telephoto lens. My only company is a flask of water and mineral salts. I thought it'd be better than grappa in the circumstances."

"So maybe you can't talk?"

"Yes, I can. I'm a hundred metres from the target. I can talk and watch. Especially as I have to be here for quite a while. Dammit."

"The target?"

"I'm waiting for a guy to come out of a place where he shouldn't be. One of those cases that puts food on my table, even though they aren't really my passion."

"Marital infidelity."

"Technically, no. Not until there's a law on gay marriage."

It took me a couple of seconds to get my head round this. "They even ask you to investigate infidelity in homosexual couples?"

"Much more than you might imagine."

"Why? It can't be used in court."

"Even hetero couples often don't know what to do with these investigations, legally speaking. You know as well as I do they can only be used to reduce the amount of alimony in a divorce settlement. They want proof their suspicions are correct, they want photos, they want things they already know to be confirmed. They want to feed their resentment. It's just another form of masochism. Then, of course, they throw the photos in their partner's face or throw them out of the house or walk out themselves, it all depends. An expensive and rather crazy kind of satisfaction. But it's fortunate for me, because at least fifty per cent of my income comes from crap like this."

There were a few moments' silence. I was thinking about what she had said, while she was catching her breath.

"Sorry to go on like that, but I was about to go out of my head. The guy still hasn't come out and I'd like to be somewhere else. A long way away. But I assume you wanted to tell me something, you didn't call to give me moral support."

"I need to talk to you about a possible assignment. It's a rather delicate matter. When can we meet?"

"Are you in the office in the afternoon?"

"I've been in the office in the afternoon for over twenty years."

"Excellent. Then you won't mind waiting for me. I don't know what time I'll be free, it depends on this bastard. As soon as I'm done, I'll go home, take a shower, and come to see you. If you're busy with clients, I'll wait. That's what I'm best at, after all."

"Waiting?"

"Waiting. Bye, Avvocato, I'll see you later."

The job must have lasted quite a while because it was after seven by the time Annapaola got to the office. She wore faded jeans and a black leather jacket, and was carrying a menacing-looking wraparound black helmet.

"How did the surveillance go?"

"I took at least a hundred photos, then a really long shower. Sometimes I wonder why it's so hard for me to find an honest job."

"But you enjoy it, don't you?"

"I did at first, but I get bored easily. What did you want to talk to me about?"

I told her about the case. She sat motionless in the armchair, listening attentively without so much as a nod, until I had finished.

"Let me see if I've got this right. You'd like me to make some enquiries, ask a few questions, talk to—"

"I don't want to know who you talk to, assuming you're able to talk to someone, and also assuming you accept the assignment."

"Okay. You want me to ask someone you don't want to know the name of if there are proceedings pending at the Prosecutor's Department in Lecce against Judge Pierluigi Larocca for the offence of corruption, if they originated in the statements of an ex-Mafioso named Capodacqua who's cooperating with the law, and... what else? It's okay to smoke in here, isn't it?"

"Sure. It reminds me of the good old days when I used to smoke. This office has never had the privilege of being immersed in the bluish smoke that hovers in the light of evening. I quit some time ago, when I was still in the old place."

"What poetry. *The bluish smoke that hovers in the light of evening.* Who are you, Szymborska? If you like, I can roll one for you, too."

"Best not. Do you like Szymborska?"

"Very much."

"Me too. I'll get you an ashtray and open the window."

She rolled her cigarette, lit it, smoked half and let it go out.

"If you don't want to do it, I'll understand. I already told Larocca that I couldn't guarantee you'd accept. I know I'm asking you for something a bit out of the ordinary, but on the other hand I understand the man's state of mind. For someone who does that kind of job, it's quite a blow to find out you're implicated in something as nasty as that."

"You like the sound of your own voice, don't you? Did I say I don't want to do it? I was just... emphasizing the unusual

74

nature of the assignment. That doesn't mean I'm not going to accept. It'll cost you, though."

"Larocca insists on making a down payment."

"Congratulations," she said, relighting her cigarette. "You've told me what he told you, but you haven't told me what you think."

"I don't think anything. I don't have enough to go on yet."

"He isn't a pleasant man."

"Not really, you're right about that. But I'd be quite surprised if I discovered that he took a bribe to get someone released."

"Why?"

"Maybe I'm biased in his favour, but I find it hard to believe that someone so competent and with such an illustrious career behind him would run the risk of squandering it all for a bit of extra cash, like any old crook. I'm not saying I consider him morally incapable of doing so. I have no idea. For me, it's a matter of… personal strategy, intelligence, the ability to weigh up the pros and cons of situations. He's an intelligent man, and an intelligent man wouldn't do something as stupid as that. That's how I see it, anyway."

"They say he might become the next president of the court."

"Precisely. Who'd risk an opportunity like that for something so petty?"

"Okay, let's try. It'll do me good to get away for a few days from betrayed husbands seeking revenge. I'll ask a few questions around and see what comes up. As soon as I find out anything – or as soon as I realize I won't be able to find anything – I'll give you a call. And thanks: it was nice to smoke a cigarette in peace in a place that's not a balcony or the door of a restaurant."

9

Every now and again people ask me, with the guarded expression reserved for eccentrics, why I carry on boxing. The implication is: now that you're the age you are, maybe it's time you learnt to play golf and stopped engaging in fisticuffs with guys young enough to be your sons. Depending on the moment, my mood and the person asking me the question, I reply: that it's as good a way as any other to keep fit; that I practise boxing because it's a literary sport (possibly throwing in a quote from Hemingway or, if I want to seem self-important, George Bernard Shaw); that I like having conversations with the punchbag I keep in my living room; that I appreciate the picturesque ambience of the gym, the characters you run into there, even the smells, which are often not very pleasant.

There's an element of truth in all these answers, but the real reason – which I almost never give – has to do with the magic power of ritual.

I continue to box because the always identical liturgy of training takes me back to a mythical period in my life, when I was a boy and the world was a place that glittered with possibilities. In that world, in that mythical territory, twice a week I would go to the gym, empty my bag, change, skip with the rope, do press-ups and pull-ups, shadow-box, then bandage my hands, put on my gloves and work on the punchbag, try out techniques with an opponent, and at the end of that always identical sequence I would take a shower and let the pains and tiredness slip away along with the shampoo and cheap shower gel, while my head was empty and free and light and everything was perfect. So much for Monsieur Nizan and his disciples.

Nowadays, twice a week, I go to the gym, empty my bag, change, skip with the rope, do press-ups and pull-ups, shadow-box, then bandage my hands, put on my gloves and work on the punchbag, try out techniques with an opponent, and at the end of this always identical sequence I take a shower and let the pains and tiredness (and the fear, which I didn't know about in those days, because as a boy you're immortal) slip away along with the shampoo and the shower gel.

For an hour and a half, twice a week, I'm the boy I was many years ago. An explanation you don't really want to give when you're talking to someone in a bar.

I was doing pull-ups, counting the repetitions with stifled groans, when I heard the phone ringing in my bag. I considered ignoring it, but when I saw it was Annapaola I changed my mind. I moved to the door of the changing rooms, away from the sign saying *The use of mobile phones is forbidden. Offenders will be punished*, which in a boxing gym sounds quite menacing.

"Hi."

A few seconds' silence, then: "Were you jogging, or do you just get excited when you hear my voice?"

"I'm a bit out of breath… I'm at the gym."

"I have to talk to you, I have some news," she said, leaving the sentence hanging.

"What kind of news?"

"I'd rather not talk about it over the phone."

"Okay. I just need to take a shower, and then I'll join you."

77

"Better if I come there. It's complicated, getting to my place. Where is the gym?"

I told her the address: a godforsaken spot in the heart of the Libertà district.

"That's not a place for mummy's boys. What gym is it?"

"Boxing. Why should it have been a place for mummy's boys?"

"I'd have said you were the kind of guy to go to a fitness club in the city centre, with all that ridiculous apparatus and bored women who go there to get picked up."

"This is the perfect place to get picked up. If you like men with squashed noses and bad grammar."

She gave a brief, harsh laugh. "See you in half an hour."

Exactly half an hour later, Annapaola was outside the gym with her black leather jacket, black helmet, black shoulder bag and carbon-coloured motorbike. She wasn't exactly inconspicuous.

"Take this," she said, holding out another helmet, also black.

I wasn't dying to go by bike. I don't like motorbikes in general, I don't like riding on them as a passenger, and above all (no offence) I don't like riding as a passenger with a woman at the controls. It's not a sexist prejudice. Rather, it's a kind of post-traumatic phobia. Once, many years ago, I let myself be persuaded to go out with a girl who looked like Gene Wilder, smoked big joints and rode her brother's Enduro 600 without having any aptitude. She was convinced that doing stupid, reckless things while under the influence of cannabis and laughing smugly while I begged her to stop was an effective seduction technique. Inevitably, we ended up plunging down an embankment. Luckily, neither of us was hurt, but the bike was ruined. The adventure ended with the arrival of an ambulance, a breakdown truck and her brother, the owner of the bike – or what remained of it. He took me aside and, with an inquisitorial expression, started asking me repeatedly who was driving when the accident happened, while ignoring my answers. At the fourth repetition of the question, I told him in a neutral tone that if he asked me again I'd smash his face in. There followed a few seconds in which he must have been wondering about the meaning to ascribe to the expression *I'll smash your face in*. Joke? Metaphor? Genuine threat? I don't know what interpretation struck him as the most appropriate. I only know that, after throwing me a final, not very cordial glance, he turned and walked away.

I never saw him again, just as I never saw any member of that family again.

The episode didn't increase my liking for motorbikes, especially not motorbikes ridden by girls who looked like Gene Wilder.

It should be said that Annapaola didn't look anything like Gene Wilder, but all the same I had a moment's hesitation when she told me to put on the helmet and jump on. Now, though, I didn't have much choice: I should have thought of it earlier and told her that we could meet at my office. So, with little enthusiasm but trying to appear as casual as possible, I obeyed.

Annapaola rode very differently from Eleonora – the girl I'd tumbled down the embankment with.

Calm, careful and fast. Relaxing, almost. The bike glided between the cars, producing a muted roar like the friendly cry of a domestic pet. A big cat purring. For about ten seconds I even closed my eyes, breathing in almost voluptuously the smell of her leather jacket.

"Where are we going?" I asked, barely raising my voice.

"You haven't had dinner, have you?"

"No."

"If you like, we could go somewhere quiet where we can talk and have a bite to eat. I'm starving. But if you don't think that's very professional, we could go to your office and talk on an empty stomach."

I felt like laughing. In itself the line was nothing special. It was the *way* she said it. That's always the case. With jokes and with almost everything else.

"Let's go and eat. As long as the bar association doesn't hear about it."

She rode calmly for a few minutes, leaving behind her the Libertà district, sailing through the Murat district and its square, regular streets, running between the lighted windows of the shops selling clothes and shoes and electronics, skimming past the groups of young people starting to gather in front of the nightclubs. I could have gone on a journey with that bike and that rider. I could even have dozed off. How great to cross the country and the cities, ride along the coast, without being imprisoned by the windows of a car.

"Are you still there? Or have you fallen off and will I have to turn round and pick you up?"

"I almost never go by motorbike. I was enjoying the ride."

A couple of minutes later, she stopped outside a wine shop. "We've never eaten together. I hope you're not a teetotaller?"

"As a child, I was."

"Where we're going, they don't have wine. We have to take our own, if you don't want to drink just tea. Wait for me."

She went into the shop and came out with a wrapped bottle. She gave it to me and we set off again. After another three or four minutes we arrived at our destination, in front of an old door in Via Celentano – one of the streets of the city most populated by Africans. I decided not to ask any questions and just wait. Annapaola pressed the entryphone a couple of times. Nobody answered, but soon afterwards a boy with an olive complexion and Middle Eastern features appeared and propped the bike in the entrance.

"Let's go up," she said. By this point, not asking questions had become a matter of principle, so I followed them in silence up the dimly lit stairs as far as the second floor. Over one of the doors that faced the landing, there was something written in Arabic. The boy opened the door and let us in. I found myself in a restaurant with low lights, dark wooden tables and chairs and a frieze of small indigo bricks around the walls. There were a few customers having dinner, the air smelt of spices, and an Arab tune was playing.

A man of about fifty who looked like the boy came towards us.

"Hello, Khalid," Annapaola said.

"*Ahlan*, Anna." He turned to me with a very slight bow. "At your service," he said, making a ceremonious gesture with his hand.

"Thanks, Khalid. I brought wine, can you open it for us?"

"Of course. Will you order or shall I see to it?"

"Is there anything you don't eat?" Annapaola asked me. I shook my head and she told Khalid to go ahead.

"What is this place?" I asked her when we were alone.

"A private club, sort of."

"And you're a member?"

"Sort of."

"I see. Sort of. Is the food good?"

"The only other place I've eaten such good Middle Eastern cuisine was in Beirut. The only drawback is the thing about wine."

She was right. The dinner was amazing. So amazing, in fact, that I forgot the reason we had met.

When the last glass was drained, the last piece of baklava swept away and the table cleared, it struck me that the moment had come to talk about work.

"Fantastic food. Maybe you have something to tell me."

"Do you want the narghile?"

"Better not, or I might feel like having a cigarette."

"When did you quit?"

"Almost ten years ago. But right here and now, I'd smoke half a packet."

She looked at me for a few seconds, as if checking that my words didn't hide a double meaning.

"Your client is in trouble," she said. "Serious trouble."

"So there are proceedings in Lecce?"

"The Prosecutor's Department did its investigation, along with the customs police, and even filed a petition for a custody order."

"Are you joking?"

"To be precise, the Prosecutor's Department asked for your client to be put under house arrest on a charge of judicial corruption. Luckily for him, the judge who received the petition rejected it for lack of evidence."

"I assume it's pointless to ask if you're sure of your information."

"I assume it is."

"And I assume it's pointless to ask you how you got hold of it."

"Someone owed me a favour. That's how it works. Exchange of favours, exchange of information. Or rather, not to be hypocritical: *traffic* of information."

"And after the petition was rejected, the Prosecutor's Department didn't contest the decision?"

"It did. That's why I'm able to tell you about it."

"This isn't my evening. I don't understand."

"The Prosecutor's Department contested it and the documents were sent to the appeal court, which, apparently, hasn't yet fixed a date for the hearing. It'll take several weeks, but you would have found out soon enough anyway, when you received notification of the appeal and the date of the hearing. The person who helped me owes me several favours, but wouldn't have told me the whole story if there hadn't been this new development."

"A harmless infraction of the rules, in other words."

"Although I wouldn't feel very sure of that as a line of defence in any possible trial for breach of confidentiality."

"Nor would I. Did he pass on any papers? The prosecutor's petition, the judge's ruling…"

Annapaola looked me straight in the eyes as if I had made a really inappropriate request. This lasted a few seconds. In the end she leaned down to the big bag she had placed next to her chair, opened it, took out a red folder and passed it to me. Without changing her expression.

"Consider them copies released on an emergency basis. Which influences my fee, obviously."

I took the folder. It was cheap and anonymous, without writing or logos. Before opening it, I measured the thickness of it between my fingers. An old habit, a neurotic little game: I try to guess by touch the number of sheets of paper in a file. I usually get quite close.

"About thirty."

"I'm sorry?"

"Nothing. I was saying the number of pages out loud."

I glanced at the papers. The petition for the custody order was much longer than the judge's ruling. I resisted the temptation to start reading there and then.

"I can keep them, right?"

"I told you they'll cost you extra. So of course you can

keep them. If by any chance the customs police come to your office to notify you of the date of the hearing, put them neatly through the shredder. You do have one in your office, don't you?"

"Couldn't I have a memory stick with the files instead?"

"Memory sticks are dangerous. Files leave more traces than a dog in mud; anyone who's any good can track down the computers they come from, even when you think you've deleted everything. Good old printed papers are more manageable. After they've been through the shredder, there's no way anyone can put them back together, except in films."

"I'll see you home," she said when we were out in the street.

"There's no need, thanks. I can get there on foot in five minutes."

"All right. So we'll talk on the phone after you read these."

We were about to say goodbye when we heard someone yelling. Annapaola raised her head, as if to sniff the air. "It's coming from Via De Giosa."

"I'm going to see what's happening."

I turned the corner of Via Celentano and Via De Giosa. Some fifty yards away, over towards the Petruzzelli, a small, disorganized crowd had gathered. Some were shouting insults, others running about, and I thought I heard someone weeping. As I increased speed, I noticed that Annapaola had joined me. In her left hand she was clutching a baseball bat.

"Where did that come from?" I asked, walking quickly.

"Mind if I tell you later? It looks like someone's getting beaten up."

She was right. Some boys of about fifteen were taking turns attacking a plump boy who seemed a little older than them. Maybe that was why the image was particularly humiliating,

84

even obscene. He was leaning against the wall, shielding his head with his hands and weeping, saying "Please, please" between his sobs. The others were laughing, punching him on the head, slapping his ears. One of them, who probably practised some martial art or other, hit him with a flying kick to the face. Another was filming it on his mobile phone.

"What the hell are you doing?" I said, approaching the group. I grabbed the first one within reach by the jacket and pulled him away. I took it for granted that I'd give them a few slaps and disperse them. The last thing I expected was for them to turn against me.

"Fuck off, shitface," was the not very ambiguous phrase snarled by the biggest of them, as he landed me a punch that was as nasty as it was futile. I was so unprepared I didn't even try to dodge it, but a moment later I reacted: I dropped the gym bag and responded with a left hook to the face. He collapsed to the ground like an empty sack.

Then the others arrived and all I remember of what happened next is a kind of video game: they attacked me like stupid evil aliens, I hit them and they fell one by one. I also took a few blows, but the only one I felt was a kick to the face, with the tip of the shoe, from the one who obviously did karate or something like that. I responded with a straight right and he, too, ended up on the ground. In the thick of the fight, I saw Annapaola almost casually hitting one of the boys in the pit of the stomach with the point of her baseball bat and then sending him flying with a blow to his leg.

It lasted little more than ten seconds. In the end, there were four of them on the ground and as many on their feet, although a little unsteady on their legs. A couple of them were bleeding. The victim of the beating had vanished. The one who had been filming the scene earlier now stood motionless, his arms dangling.

"Come here," I said to him.

He stared at me in terror.

"Come here right now, or I'll come over there."

If he'd run away I wouldn't have been able to catch up with him, but he was too scared. He approached.

"Don't hurt me, I beg you. I didn't do anything." That was what he said. The voice of a son of the bourgeoisie. Like the others. Now that they were in focus, I saw how they were dressed – expensive clothes from shops in the city centre. Comfortable and basically rather boring lives. You need a distraction from time to time. What was that poem by Pasolini about the events in Valle Giulia? "You have the faces of daddy's boys... You have the same nasty eyes."

I noticed that my hands were shaking.

"Give me the phone."

He didn't even try to object. He stretched out his arm, trying to keep the greatest possible distance between us. I took the phone, held it between my fingers and looked at it as if it were a strange object I had never seen before.

"There are people at the windows," Annapaola said. She meant that it was best to get out of there in a hurry, given the chaos we'd caused. I calmly put the phone down on the ground and crushed it with my heel. Three, four, five times, until I was sure it had become unusable.

I recovered my bag with its load of damp sports clothes and illicitly obtained court papers. We turned onto Via Celentano and walked back to where the motorbike stood waiting for us. Annapaola shoved the baseball bat into her bag.

"Let's go. Get on."

"I'll walk. I told you, I live nearby."

"Don't talk crap. A patrol car is bound to be here soon. We had an audience back there, do you really think nobody called the police or the carabinieri? Let's get out of here, now. We'll drive around a bit and I'll take you back home when the coast is clear. Maybe you don't realize what your face and hands look like."

"What's on my face and hands?" I said, touching my face.

"Blood. Let's go."

Before long, we found ourselves on the seafront, heading south.

"Why do you carry a baseball bat with you?"

"For times like these."

"You're crazy. Who taught you to use it like that?"

"I used to play softball."

"I thought that in softball you only hit a ball, not boys."

"You weren't exactly handing out sweets."

We got to Torre a Mare. She stopped in a dark, silent, deserted street.

"Let's take a look at your face," she said, getting off the bike.

"It's just a scratch."

"That's hardly a new line. You must have read too many Tex Willer comics as a boy."

"Sometimes. What do you have against Tex?"

"A great gay icon, he and his boyfriend Kit Carson. His son Kit Willer and the Indian Tiger Jack are another lovely couple."

"I won't allow you to make these insinuations about Tex and the others."

"Are you homophobic?"

"Of course not. But Tex isn't gay."

"All right. Neither are Batman and Robin, neither is Elton John." She switched on the little light on her mobile phone and held it to my face.

I had a small swelling on the temple, where I had taken the kick. She cleaned me with a wet wipe.

87

"It's a small cut, but it's bleeding a bit. Was it the Bruce Lee guy?"

"Yes."

"There's no need for stitches. When you get home put a plaster on it and in a few days you'll be fine. Do your hands hurt?"

"A little. Punching without gloves is a problem for the hands, more than for the face."

"Those boys might not agree."

"Yes, it's possible they don't share such tactical considerations. Anyway," I said, holding out my hands with the palms turned downwards, "do you think I'll be able to play the piano in a week?"

"Of course. Tomorrow, even."

"I'm really pleased, because I couldn't play the piano before."

It took her a moment or two to realize it was a wisecrack. She looked at me as if I were a lunatic. *Probably* not a dangerous one, but you can never be too careful.

"I think you're the crazy one."

"It's an old joke by Jerome K. Jerome. I've been waiting ages for a chance to use it. I'm only sorry it's that gang of idiots I have to thank for the opportunity."

"Let's hope none of the idiots was too badly hurt, or we might be in trouble."

"If they say what happened nobody will believe them. 'Who beat you up like that?' asks the inspector. 'A middle-aged man with clear anger management problems and a girl in a black leather jacket who looks like a member of the Baseball Furies.'"

"Who are the Baseball Furies?" Annapaola asked.

"Don't tell me you've never seen *The Warriors*."

"Right, the uniformed ones with painted faces and baseball bats. The battle in Central Park. Great scene."

"Next time show up with a painted face."

"Talking of films, Clint Eastwood in *Gran Torino*—"

"…Has one of the greatest lines in history. When he approaches the car with the thugs—"

"That's the one I was thinking of, but I don't remember it exactly."

"'Ever noticed how you come across somebody once in a while you shouldn't have fucked with?' Then he spits on the ground and says, 'That's me.' And mimes firing a gun."

"It's obvious you were ready before you came out."

"Of course, those little sons of bitches were extras."

"All right. Now it's time to sleep."

We dropped by one of the duty pharmacies. Annapaola went in and bought a box of plasters.

"If you like, I can put it on you now, but I don't think you'll have any problem doing it yourself when you get home."

"None at all. Actually, it makes me feel nostalgic. When I was about twenty, I sometimes used to go home with my face bashed in."

Ten minutes later, we were outside my front door. I got off the bike and removed the helmet. She removed hers, too, and shook her hair out. It was the first feminine gesture she had made all evening.

We looked at each other for a few moments.

"How old are you, Avvocato?" she asked.

"Why?"

"You don't look it, but you must be nearly fifty, as far as I remember."

"What do you mean, you remember?"

"I must have read your date of birth somewhere. I like to keep myself informed."

"I'm forty-eight."

"You moved well. You weren't even breathless afterwards."

"Oh, believe me, I was."

I wondered if I should invite her up. In the end I went to her and gave her a kiss on the cheek.

"Goodnight. I'll call you tomorrow after I've read these papers."

She looked at me with an expression that was hard to describe. It was if there was something she couldn't quite grasp. I felt the same.

"Goodnight," she said finally, in the slightly irritable tone of someone who would like to add something but can't find the words.

I listened to that muted roar, confident and reassuring, moving away into the distance.

10

I took a shower. A fight – like some trials – leaves you feeling dirty. To get back to normality, it's essential to spend about ten minutes under the warm water without thinking about anything.

After drying myself, I checked my face and hands. I had a few light grazes on the knuckles; the cut on the temple, on the other hand, wasn't exactly invisible, and wouldn't close so easily without a little help. I applied a couple of the plasters, put on shorts and a T-shirt and made myself a bourbon with crushed ice. I was sure the adrenaline coursing through my body wouldn't let me sleep for a while, so I might as well satisfy my curiosity and read what was written in the papers from Lecce.

Before throwing myself down on the sofa, which is my favourite workplace at home, I gave Mr Punchbag a slight push, making him sway just a little.

"No punching tonight, my friend. I'm sorry, but my hands are sore. First I went to the gym, then I actually came to blows, if you want to put it like that."

"…"

"You're right, I'm a bit too old for these things, but really there was no way to avoid it."

Mr Punchbag let the chains he was hanging from squeak a little, as a mark of discreet but clear disapproval. His idea is that fists should be reserved for punchbags; punching people in the face strikes him as somewhat inelegant. *Everything in its place* is his philosophy. Sometimes I listen to him, sometimes I don't. I would have liked to talk to him about Annapaola – another strange character – but just then the idea made me feel slightly embarrassed for some reason. If right now you're thinking I'm a little bit off my head, I suppose I'd have to agree with you.

I took a big swig of bourbon with ice (it's a dangerous drink; the crushed ice makes it deceptively light), opened the file and counted the papers. There were thirty-two; the fact that I'd guessed almost right put me in a childishly good mood.

The prosecutor's rejected petition was twenty-five single-spaced pages; the judge's ruling rejecting it just seven. I decided to read the latter.

The heading, as usual, contained the names of those under investigation – Pierluigi Larocca, Rocco Ladisa and Caterina Amendolagine – and the charges.

Pierluigi Larocca was being investigated

for the offence, as under articles 319 and 319c of the criminal code, of having, in his capacity as head of the appeals division of the Court of Bari, received the sum of 50,000 (fifty thousand) euros as payment for the release – after an appeal hearing held in the said division – of Rocco Ladisa, under investigation for the offences of usury and extortion and held under a custodial sentence; an offence committed in order to favour a party – the said Ladisa – in Bari on or about 3 July 2008.

Rocco Ladisa and Caterina Amendolagine were under investigation for the offence, as under articles 110, 319, 319c and 321 of the criminal code, of having, in collaboration with Corrado Salvagno, now deceased (and availing themselves of the material assistance of Nicola Marelli, bearer of the envelope containing the sum, without being aware of the contents of the said envelope or of the criminal collaboration), paid Pierluigi Larocca the sum of 50,000 (fifty thousand) euros as remuneration for the reversal of the custodial sentence and the subsequent release of the said Ladisa. Offence committed in Bari, on or about 3 July 2008.

The paper then went on:

On 6 May 2009, Salvatore Capodacqua, held in custody for a number of serious offences including association with a Mafia-style organization, multiple aggravated homicide, drug trafficking, illegal possession of explosives and heavy weapons, extortion and usury, expressed to the prosecutor at the Court of Bari his intention to cooperate with the law, in the first place admitting his own responsibility for most of the offences of which he was accused and also claiming responsibility for numerous others of which he had not even been suspected.

Apart from admitting his own responsibility, Capodacqua, in his many interviews before the prosecutor in Bari, reported a large number of events and circumstances of direct and indirect relevance to other individuals. In particular, as far as the present proceedings are concerned, the said Capodacqua reported supposed illegal conduct on the part of Judge Pierluigi Larocca, head of the appeals division of the Court of Bari.

It may be useful at this point to refer to Capodacqua's statements on this subject, taken from the transcript of an interview of 15 October 2009 with the prosecutor of Bari:

ANSWER: I also know about lots of illegal things done by public officials: in particular police officers, directors of local organizations, officials of the court and even judges [...] One of these episodes concerns Judge Larocca of the Court of Bari...

ANSWER: It was an episode involving my friend and associate Rocco Ladisa, about whom I have already spoken repeatedly. Ladisa was under investigation for an episode of usury and subsequent extortion for which he had been arrested even though the victim had not cooperated with the police. Ladisa had been released by the court of appeal presided over by Larocca, who had received a payment of fifty thousand euros for that ruling.

ANSWER: I am aware that each time I report something I have to indicate the source of my information. If, that is, these are episodes of which I have direct knowledge (maybe through having been personally involved) or about which I have been told by third parties. In this latter case I have to indicate the person who passed on the information, along with the time and place. Having noted this, I specify that I have knowledge of this fact because it was told to me by the person directly involved, Ladisa. He had boasted on many occasions of being able to count on the favours of police officers and carabinieri. On this particular occasion he boasted about the fact that he had even managed to get to an important judge like Larocca.

ANSWER: The episode was told to me by Ladisa some months after his release, in other words in the autumn of 2008. If I remember correctly, we were having dinner at a restaurant called Il Pescatore. Ladisa and I often had dinner together, in that and other restaurants, and often talked about confidential matters. Nobody else was present. Ladisa would not talk about certain things in the presence of people he did not trust absolutely.

I broke off reading, thinking that Ladisa's ability to identify those people he could *trust absolutely* didn't seem faultless, given that a few months after these confidences Signor Capodacqua had decided to spill the beans to the prosecutors. I thought of asking Mr Punchbag for his opinion, but saw that he had dozed off. So I took another sip of whisky and carried on.

ANSWER: The contact with Judge Larocca was Avvocato Corrado Salvagno, who died in a road accident at the end of last year and who was apparently a friend of Larocca and other important judges, both civil and criminal. It was rumoured in our circles that Salvagno was able, for the appropriate fee, to fix trials of every kind.

ANSWER: I repeat that it was a rumour in our circles. It was spoken about, and I am unable to say from whom and on what occasion I heard it for the first time. But apart from the episode concerning Judge Larocca, of which Ladisa spoke to me, I am not aware of other specific instances of corruption regarding the late Avvocato Salvagno. Actually, it was the news of the death of Avvocato Salvagno that led Ladisa to tell me about this episode. To introduce the subject he said to me something like: "Did you hear about Salvagno's accident? A pity, partly because he really could do anything. You know how he got me out the last time I was arrested?" And he told me the story.

ANSWER: As far as I know, in the episode we are talking about, the other two judges were not involved. In any case, Ladisa said that "Larocca gave the orders" in that court. He meant that if there was any conflict, his opinion easily prevailed over that of the others.

ANSWER: Salvagno had told him that his situation was somewhat compromised, in the sense that the evidence was strong and there was a distinct possibility that he would remain in prison for a long time. The same lawyer, who was his defence counsel, told him that there was the possibility of obtaining a favourable ruling by paying a large sum of money, because Judge Larocca was his friend and, if the request came from someone he trusted (like Salvagno), he was willing to oblige.

ANSWER: Salvagno had told him these things in prison, during their client–lawyer interviews.

ANSWER: I think that when they talked about such delicate subjects they were very careful because of the risk that they were being bugged. For example, it is possible they communicated by writing, with little notes that the lawyer then tore up and took away with him. I make it clear that this is my conjecture, because Ladisa did not go into details when he told me the facts.

ANSWER: Ladisa told me he had agreed and had paid, through his wife Caterina Amendolagine, the combined sum of one hundred thousand euros in cash to Avvocato Salvagno, who had then made sure that half of it got to the judge a few days before the appeal hearing. The other half was his own fee.

ANSWER: I do not know how Ladisa's wife was able to get hold of such a large sum in cash. He did not tell me and I did not ask him. I can tell you, though, that Ladisa had considerable amounts of cash available, partly linked to the activity of usury in which he was involved, so when he told me that a sum of that size had been collected and paid I was not at all surprised.

ANSWER: From everything that Ladisa said it was obvious that the things for which he had been arrested, and then released by Larocca, were things he had actually committed. It was not anything explicit like "I did this and that", but it was clear that he was not innocent of the offences.

ANSWER: Ladisa told me that the money had been delivered to the judge by an employee in Avvocato Salvagno's practice who I think is named Nicola – I do not know his surname. I think the money was in an envelope together with other papers, or in a package. On this point Ladisa was not specific because he was reporting what he in his turn had been told by Salvagno. In fact, when the payment was made, Ladisa was still in prison.

ANSWER: From what Ladisa told me, this Nicola was unaware of the contents of the envelope. He was a clerk in Avvocato Salvagno's office and was simply doing what he was told to do.

The quotations from the interview transcript continued for a few more lines with other non-essential details about what Capodacqua knew and how he had learnt it. But that was the gist of it. Ladisa told him he had paid – through his wife, his lawyer and an apparently unwitting office clerk – five thousand euros to Pierluigi Larocca to obtain his release from a sentence for the serious crimes of usury and extortion.

If it were true, it would be a pretty repulsive story.

"Is there anything more disgusting than a judge who sells himself out? What do you think, Mr Punchbag?"

Mr Punchbag doesn't like bastards, so the question was a rhetorical one. I drained my glass, resisted the temptation to refill it, and went on reading.

After the fragments of Capodacqua's first interview, there were references to a second transcript, this time of a statement before the Prosecutor's Department in Lecce, subsequent to the case being transferred there. There was nothing new: he had basically confirmed what he had said before to the magistrates of the anti-Mafia directorate in Bari.

Before moving on to an analysis of the evidence, the judge in Lecce made a digression on the criteria prescribed by the Supreme Court for evaluating statements made by those who have turned state's evidence.

It may be useful at this point to recall the obvious guidance given by the law in regard to evaluating statements by individuals under article 210 and interpreting articles 192 and 195 of the code of criminal procedure. It is obvious that in the first place it is necessary to examine the reliability intrinsic to the statements of the said individual in accordance with the provisions of article 192, paragraph 3. The judge must firstly address the problem of the credibility of the declarant in relation, among other things, to his personality, his socio-economic and family conditions, his past, his relations with those he is accusing and how recently he has decided to confess and to accuse fellow perpetrators and accomplices; secondly, he must verify the intrinsic consistency of the statements of the declarant, in the light of criteria including, among others, precision, coherence, constancy and spontaneity. Finally, he must examine the so-called external evidence. The judge's examination must be carried out following the indicated logical order, because he cannot proceed with a uniform evaluation of the accusation and the other elements of evidence that confirm his reliability if he has not first clarified the possible doubts that gather around the accusation itself, independently of the elements of proof external to it.

It should finally be specified that where the statements of the individual concerned are ascribable to the paradigm indicated in article 195 (indirect testimony) the onus to find corroborating evidence is of an even more pressing nature. Those statements that report, even if in a framework of personal reliability and intrinsic credibility, things learnt from others (including those under investigation), pose a twofold demand for corroborating evidence and therefore impose an examination of particular rigour.

The statements of an indirect witness require corroborating evidence; the statements of someone who has turned state's evidence require corroborating evidence. The statements containing the indirect testimony of someone who has turned state's evidence (which therefore do not report facts directly perceived but only *heard about*) require twofold corroborating evidence, even in the custody phase.

Whoever had written that ruling, a woman, was a competent magistrate – although a little verbose. I thought, as I often do, that the same concepts, for which hundreds of words had been used, could have been summed up in a few sentences. More or less like this: you first of all have to work out if the person making the accusation is intrinsically reliable (that is, if he isn't an obvious liar or if his statements aren't patently contradictory and implausible), then you have to see if there is corroborating evidence to confirm these statements. The need for corroborating evidence is even stronger if the statements are hearsay and not based on direct personal knowledge. The end.

Jurists, with rare exceptions, are unconsciously and tenaciously averse to clarity and brevity.

Having defined her methods, the judge addressed the question of Capodacqua's intrinsic reliability. His story – she wrote in her ruling – was consistent, devoid of contradictions, with accents of sincerity (I wondered for a few moments how it was possible to identify the "accents of sincerity" in statements you haven't heard for yourself and that you read only in the bureaucratic summary of a transcript) and no reasons emerged as to why Capodacqua should have lied and made false accusations.

Having therefore clarified that Capodacqua appeared *intrinsically* reliable, the ruling went on to examine the so-called objective, or external, corroborating evidence.

This examination hadn't produced very inspiring results: reading between the lines, it was clear that the judge hadn't much liked the way in which the Prosecutor's Department had conducted the investigations. The phone taps carried out on Larocca's landlines and mobiles had not shown anything substantial. According to the records, there had only been two contacts between Larocca and Salvagno, but it was an element – so the ruling said – devoid of unambiguous significance. Firstly, the contacts had taken place at a period of time different from that of the presumed corruption; secondly, the two of them, according to what had been reported by Capodacqua, were friends and therefore there was nothing strange in the fact that they sometimes (sporadically, in any case) communicated by telephone.

The investigations into Larocca's bank accounts and assets had not highlighted any unusual cash flow. Larocca took his salary, had shares in a quantity that was entirely compatible with his income, and owned the apartment where he lived. Nothing abnormal there.

The only element classifiable as corroborating evidence in a technical sense was the statement of Nicola Marelli, Avvocato Salvagno's office clerk, the person who, according to Capodacqua's statements, had handed over (without knowing the contents) the envelope containing the fifty thousand euros. The ruling quoted extracts from the transcript of Marelli's brief statement to the prosecutor in Lecce.

ANSWER: I have worked for more than ten years in the office of Avvocato Corrado Salvagno, who unfortunately died last year as the result of a road accident.

ANSWER: It is a group practice and I have continued to work there, with Avvocato Salvagno's partners, since his death.

ANSWER: As far as I know, Avvocato Salvagno and Judge Larocca had been good friends for a long time.

ANSWER: I did not spend time socially with my employer, so I could not say with any certainty how often, and under what circumstances, he saw Judge Larocca. I remember that the judge was sometimes a guest on Avvocato Salvagno's boat, occasionally for trips lasting a few days. I think they sometimes met for dinner but, I repeat, I am not in a position to supply details on these meetings.

ANSWER: Every now and then, over the years, I delivered packages from Avvocato Salvagno to Judge Larocca. They were mostly Christmas presents, and I delivered them to the judge's home.

ANSWER: I deny having ever delivered envelopes or documents of any kind to Judge Larocca. Whenever I had to file papers of relevance to the appeal court on behalf of Avvocato Salvagno, I would go to the clerk of the court's office and definitely not directly to the judge.

ANSWER: I cannot say for certain that I delivered packages – mostly bottles of wine – to Judge Larocca only on the occasion of the Christmas holidays. It is possible it happened on other occasions. In fact, now that you draw my attention to the circumstance and urge me to remember more clearly, I am able to say that it definitely happened. One of Avvocato Salvagno's clients is a producer of excellent wines. Sometimes bottles of wine came into the office and Avvocato Salvagno told me to take some to Judge Larocca, who is apparently a lover of good wine.

ANSWER: Avvocato Salvagno would give me ready-wrapped packages and tell me to take them to the judge's apartment. Sometimes I left them with the porter, sometimes I delivered them to the judge personally.

ANSWER: I do not know when the last time I made a delivery to Judge Larocca was.

ANSWER: I am aware that you are urging me to make an effort to remember more clearly, in particular if I made any of these deliveries between the month of June and the month of July 2008, that is, a few months before the death of Avvocato Salvagno. I cannot rule out the possibility that I made a delivery before the summer holidays, but I cannot be more specific than that.

ANSWER: I think I made that delivery to the judge personally, in other words without leaving the package with the porter.

ANSWER: Handing over the package, I said it was from Avvocato Salvagno. The judge thanked me. He seemed to know that the package was going to be delivered.

ANSWER: I did not deliver any envelope.

ANSWER: I cannot rule out the possibility that the package contained an envelope, but I do not know because I was not present when the package was wrapped.

ANSWER: Now that I remember more clearly, I can confirm that from the way the judge received me I had the impression he was waiting for me.

Nicola Marelli's statements – wrote the judge – constituted a small corroboration of Capodacqua's statements, but were "insufficient in themselves to prove to any acceptable degree the truth or otherwise of the accusation of corruption".

Continuing her ruling, the judge now clarified her thinking by summarizing its essential points. Capodacqua was reliable when he reported Ladisa's confidences. It was likely that Ladisa had given Avvocato Salvagno the sum of one hundred thousand euros in the belief that half of that sum would be used to bribe the judge. And it certainly couldn't be ruled out that the fifty thousand euros really had been paid to Larocca as payment for Ladisa's release. But nor could another hypothesis be ruled out, which allowed for an alternative explanation of the evidence and prevented the granting of the requested custody order: Salvagno might have been influence peddling.

No element to support the accusation – in fact, rather the opposite – emerged from an examination of the ruling, later confirmed by the Supreme Court, with which the appeal court under Larocca had overturned Ladisa's sentence and ordered his release.

Such a ruling did not present any evident anomalies, appeared well argued, although perhaps a little too formalistic, and in any case, as already stated, had been confirmed by the Supreme Court.

Even an examination of this ruling did not produce any elements to corroborate the accusation of judicial corruption and therefore, *as things stood,* the petition had to be rejected.

*

When I'd finished reading, I stopped to think.

It was a correct ruling, and all the more admirable when you realized that the judge wasn't at all convinced of Larocca's innocence. On the contrary. Reading between the lines, I had the impression she was saying: If I had to – or was allowed to – base my decision purely on my own intuition, on my inner conviction, I would gladly grant the petition for a custody order. Since, however, I am required to observe strict rules on the evaluation of evidence, I can't do that. Not today, at least – *as things stood*: there was a menacing undertone in those words at the end of the ruling.

All right, I've exaggerated a bit, but that was pretty much the impression I got from reading those papers. And, paradoxically, that impression made me even more nervous than I would have been if the ruling had ordered my client's arrest.

There are times when hints of suspicion feel much more unpleasant than things that have been openly declared, whether real or presumed. At this point, all I could do was call Larocca and ask to meet.

Or rather, to be more precise, at this point all I could do was throw myself into bed, seeing that it was now late and my eyes were clouded by the exhaustion of a rather intense day and the bourbon that had concluded it. I would phone Larocca the following morning.

As I tossed and turned between the sheets, a troublesome thought occurred to me. If I met that group of boys in three or four years' time, they would slaughter me.

Time was on their side.

The last image I had before I fell asleep was Annapaola, with her baseball bat, moving with nonchalant elegance.

It's funny when a man feels safe because he's physically protected by a woman.

11

I woke up quite late. It was Saturday: I had to call Larocca and I really didn't feel like it. I looked for every possible excuse to put it off. Shower, shave, breakfast, reading the news online, meticulous checking of a few pointless emails. I thought of having a chat with Mr Punchbag, but he's not really a morning person. So I decided to look at the local news, just in case they mentioned a night-time brawl in Via De Giosa in which a few kids had got hurt and that a police investigation was under way to identify those responsible. I didn't find anything, and felt somewhat relieved. The last thing I needed was to find myself being investigated for aggravated assault and grievous bodily harm.

In the end, having run out of excuses, I phoned. It only rang twice, but the voice that answered wasn't Pierluigi Larocca's.

"Hello?"

"Good morning, Avvocato Guerrieri."

"I was looking for Judge Larocca. Who am I talking to?"

"This is Manfredi. The judge left me his phone because he's in the lecture theatre for the seminar." Then he added, in a tone of apology or justification: "He asked me to answer if there was any call for him."

He was a clerk of the bar association, and he spoke as if I should have known what seminar he was talking about.

"I'm sorry, Manfredi, what seminar is that?"

"The seminar for the postgraduate students. Wait, let me read you the title: 'Ethics and roles in criminal trial procedure.' Judge Larocca's lecture will be starting soon."

I decided to go. I would tell Larocca what I'd found out when he finished his lecture or if there was a break in proceedings. It seemed to me a less disagreeable way to communicate such unpleasant news. Of course, I told myself, it would have been even more unpleasant if the examining magistrate hadn't rejected the custody petition, but I didn't suppose it would be amusing, for a man whose job was concerned with other people's freedom, to find out that someone was trying to deprive him of his.

I put on a pair of jeans, a blue shirt and a blue casual jacket. I chose rubber-soled shoes that were maybe a little garish, and didn't bother with a tie. I hesitated for a moment, then told myself: This isn't a hearing, it's Saturday, and anyway, who cares?

As usual, it took me exactly a quarter of an hour to cover the distance between my home and the appeal court, on the sixth floor of which the bar association has its offices. Sometimes the obsessive predictability of my movements, their times and rhythms, feels oppressive. It's as if my life is like the sum of the routes taken by the ball in an old pinball machine. You had the feeling at first, if you were not expert at the game, that there were a lot of possibilities, accidents, surprises. Then as you continued playing – maybe it was a pinball machine in the bar near your home, or at the seaside, or in the pool hall near school – you realized that the routes repeated themselves. You got to know them all, and after a while you didn't want to play on that pinball machine any more and went to find another. Finding a new and different pinball machine would be the right cure, I told myself, dismissing the subject from my mind as I got into the lift that would take me up to the bar association.

The lecture theatre was quite crowded and all the seats were occupied, except those in the front rows, to which I'm incontrovertibly allergic and so didn't even consider.

At the speakers' table were the head of the bar association, Larocca and a cadaverous-looking man I didn't recognize. Glancing at the posters for the event, on both sides of the door, I learnt that he was a professor of judicial administration I had never heard of before. He would have been perfect at the reception desk of an undertaker's.

Larocca must have started just a few minutes earlier, because he was still at the preliminary stage of thank-yous and pleasantries.

I looked around. Most of the seats were occupied by trainees and young lawyers. There were also a few old workhorses who were there to be noticed by Judge Larocca and to congratulate him immediately afterwards or in the succeeding days for his wonderful lecture. Whatever he said.

There weren't many magistrates present, and those who were had the embarrassed air of people who have ended up somewhere by mistake and now don't know how to leave without being noticed. A colleague of mine who was part of the bar association and whose name I could never remember – Tommaso or Lorenzo? – appeared at my side, a fine fellow who had inherited an excellent practice but was genetically incapable of understanding the law. "Hello, Guido, what on earth are you doing here? We don't usually see you at these events."

"Hello. I had to go to the secretariat for some information, and I saw that this meeting was on. It sounded interesting, so I thought I'd stay." I didn't think it was appropriate to inform him of my professional relations with Judge Larocca, let alone the nature of the latter's legal problems.

"Whenever you need anything from the association or the secretariat, just call me and I'll see to it. Not that I'm not glad to see you. Quite the contrary. You get my drift, of course?"

"Of course, thank you, you're very kind," I said, hoping he would stop there.

"Guido, you know the respect and friendship we feel for each other. If I could do you a favour, I'd be more than happy. But what happened to your face?"

A street fight: I smashed a few heads, but took a couple of blows too. Now I'd really appreciate it if you could piss off. If you don't, and keep talking, I'll headbutt you. Keeping in mind the respect and friendship we feel for each other, of course.

I didn't say that. I nodded and replied that it was nothing, I'd fallen off my bike and grazed myself. Then I smiled, trying to convey, in a single expression, respect and friendship and an urgent request to go away and leave me in peace. It must have worked because Tommaso-Lorenzo gave me a slap on the back and told me he'd leave me to follow the lecture. Result.

In the meantime, Larocca had started his presentation.

"For lawyers as for magistrates, identifying – and respecting – the rules of ethics requires before anything else an effort of intellectual honesty.

"When we observe the world of criminal justice without allowing ourselves to be misled by rhetorical and moralistic prejudices, we discover some disturbing truths. We have to take these truths into account if we want to interpret our respective roles in an ethically correct and unhypocritical way."

I noticed he had some papers in front of him, but he barely looked at them. He simply turned one over at regular intervals and glanced quickly at the one underneath.

"The first disturbing truth is that very often – certainly in the vast majority of cases – defendants, regardless of the constitutional presumption of innocence, are wholly or partly guilty of the crimes with which they are charged. Of course, some are innocent, but they're a minority."

He made a studied pause and looked around at his audience, who were hanging on his every word. The argument was deliberately provocative, although basically true. Larocca was a good orator.

"Both magistrates and defence attorneys are aware of this truth, even though, for different reasons, they often deny it or don't admit it. One of these reasons is a defective or hypocritical understanding of the presumption of innocence as defined in article 27 of the Constitution. A criminal lawyer who makes his living from that work and who maintains that most of his clients are innocent is either a liar or a fool. And if you'll allow me a little personal digression, there are few things that annoy me more than certain lawyers who babble on about their clients' innocence as if they feel uncomfortable with their role, or as if they think that all judges are stupid. Not that I'm saying that the group to which I belong is immune from the virus of stupidity…"

Another pause, underlined by an expression of false innocence – almost a grimace – to allow his audience, composed mostly of lawyers, to enjoy the joke. Some laughed, some exchanged a few words with their neighbours: they felt united in the healthy complicity of the intelligent against the stupid. Those who feel this solidarity most strongly are the most stupid, I thought. The joke, in any case, was classic

Larocca. It spoke of his contempt for the incompetence and trickery of some of his colleagues.

The murmur died down and he resumed.

"The work of the criminal lawyer consists, mostly, of representing guilty defendants – guilty, often, of serious and repugnant crimes – and of trying, by all legitimate means, to get them acquitted. I repeat: *representing guilty defendants and trying, by all legitimate means, to get them acquitted.*

"If that is the case – and it is – it's necessary to understand how the work of a lawyer can be compatible with ethics. And not just the work of a lawyer, but the work of a judge too, for even the work of a judge – and this is something we often neglect – can be sensitive from an ethical point of view. We should never forget that judges have other people's freedom in their hands and, consequently, often their lives, too. It's an aspect that should fill us with dismay and yet we take it for granted.

"Our problem, therefore, is twofold: how to admit the ethical legitimacy of defending someone guilty of terrible crimes, and how to admit the ethical legitimacy of one person depriving another person of his personal freedom.

"Where do we locate the ethical legitimacy in these two problematic spheres? Where do we locate the single idea of justice that we can all share without being influenced by the diversity of our moral standpoints?

"We locate it in the rules of procedure. The rules of procedure and our respect for them are the only way to see that *justice* is done. Basically, there can be no real justice outside a respect for the rules of procedure.

"The judge and the defence attorney mustn't let their personal beliefs and their moral frame of reference interfere with their work and the respective choices they make. The only shared and shareable common ground is that of the rules of procedure, which judges must make sure are observed without worrying about the consequences, and which lawyers must respect without worrying about the consequences.

"You don't like what I'm saying? You'd prefer a more romantic idea of justice? So would I, but unfortunately such an idea is often a rhetorical device, and it's often precisely those who talk about it the most who are the least interested in obtaining it. Often those involved in the proceedings aren't interested in getting justice. They're thinking about other things, because they're human beings.

"Defence lawyers don't want justice. In other words, they don't want the guilty to be sentenced or amends to be made to the victims. They want to win cases. And I add: they're right to do so, because that is their role in the mechanism, in the overall picture. If defence lawyers didn't want to win cases, defendants would be deprived of real protection, and in particular innocent defendants – however few of them there are – would be at greater risk of being unjustly sentenced. When a defence lawyer says he wants justice to be done, he's almost always lying, consciously or unconsciously.

"You know the old joke about the lawyer who's just won a difficult case, phones his client and tells him that justice has triumphed. Without hesitation, the client replies: Never mind, we'll appeal immediately…"

Again a few laughs, a few murmured exchanges. I noticed that I, too, was smiling. It was an old joke, but the kind that endures because there's an element of truth in it.

"The defendants don't want justice, they want to be acquitted. The defendants' counsel don't want justice, they want their clients to be acquitted.

"And now I'll say something that's a bit hard to take. Even prosecutors don't want justice. But – except in a few rare cases of clear bad faith – they don't know it. They think they're pursuing justice, but they often confuse the idea of justice with a sentence passed on a defendant they consider guilty. And since for many of them, a sentence passed on those they consider guilty *is* justice, they're ready to accept, to ignore, or even to cover up the breaking of the rules of procedure, which if followed might lead to the acquittal of a defendant they consider guilty, especially if it's of a serious crime."

It struck me that if I were a prosecutor, one of the good ones I knew and who behaved impeccably, I'd have been annoyed to hear a statement like that.

"You might object: at least judges are interested in seeing that justice is done. They haven't – they shouldn't have – any interest in one result rather than another. Unfortunately, things aren't so simple.

"Do you have any idea how many rulings by examining magistrates that I have to deal with as head of the court of appeal are a copy – without a single word changed, without a shred of genuine argument, without a shred of critical control – of the prosecutor's petition?

"Does a judge who copies a prosecutor's petition word for word, even leaving in the occasional grammatical error, want justice? Maybe he's only trying to do as little work as possible. Or maybe he feels he's on *the same side* as the prosecutor and the police. Maybe he's convinced that his job is to get rid of criminals, or presumed criminals, rather than guarantee that the rules are respected.

"Does the judge who realizes he's made the wrong decision, but argues it in the most nit-picking way possible because he doesn't want his rulings to be thrown out on appeal or overturned in the Supreme Court, want justice or is he thinking of his career? Is his own narcissism the dominant factor?

"I could give many other examples, but I think you get the idea. The members of each of the groups working in the criminal courts are convinced, often in good faith, that they're pursuing justice, but it's an optical illusion."

He leafed through the pages he had in front of him. Caught up in the momentum of what he was saying, he had raced ahead of his own notes and was now finding his place. Or else it was only another theatrical ploy to make the most of the pauses and keep the audience's attention.

"I'm sure many of you have felt a sense of unease in listening to the things I've said so far. That's what I wanted. I *wanted* these unpleasant truths to make you uneasy.

"My intention was to prompt you to think outside the conventional patterns, to think about the elements of hypocrisy and even brutality lurking in our criminal justice system. To draw your attention to these elements, I've used the weapon of paradox and exaggeration. Of course not all prosecutors, not all judges are unaware of their duties; and of course many defence lawyers know perfectly well that their task isn't basically to see that justice is done, but to carry out a role which guarantees that the rules are respected.

"The reality isn't only the anguished and surreal one we see in the distorting mirror of paradox. But nor is the legal system an idyllic place where we always succeed in harmoniously combining the rules of the law with the demands of justice. Such an idyllic place doesn't exist.

"Anyone who experiences the everyday reality of the criminal courts knows perfectly well the kind of influence that incompetence, hypocrisy, often mistakes, and sometimes even dishonesty may have on the final outcome of the legal system. He knows perfectly well how often the principle of equality before the law is damaged by a lack of culture and a poor sense of rules and roles, because

113

of bias, illegitimate personal aspirations or even simple intellectual laziness.

"To make sure that justice is done, we need to free ourselves of false myths about justice. And in order to free ourselves of these false myths, we need to destroy them, because they're tenacious. If we merely set them aside, they come back and again overwhelm our minds, preventing them from functioning in the right way. The right way is the way guided not by emotion, but by reason.

"To be aware of what I've said shouldn't lead to a resigned recognition or cynical acceptance of the rules of a game that's inevitably unjust and brutal. We all of us, judges and lawyers alike, have a duty to reject cynicism and resignation.

"This rejection would be meaningless and futile if it were not solidly argued, if it were merely a general, however noble, aspiration to justice and an equally general willingness to respect the rules.

"Of course, it's certain that the guarantees embedded in the process are also limits to a free – indiscriminate? – search for the truth. If, for example, we could order phone taps merely on the basis of suspicion, of conjecture by the investigators, it would be easier to capture criminal conversations and discover the perpetrators of serious crimes.

"If it were possible to question suspects without a lawyer present, it would be easier to obtain confessions.

"Does that mean that rules and guarantees are incompatible with an effective search for the truth? I don't think so."

At that precise moment, for no reason, or rather, for no reason I was able to pin down (maybe because I was surrounded by young people who were embarking on their legal careers), I recalled a few scenes from my first months as a trainee prosecutor. Trivial things – queueing up at a clerk of the court's office, filing a petition, asking for a postponement in a hearing at the magistrate's court – that I would never have thought could still make me feel emotional. And yet, unexpectedly, those memories broke my heart. They filled me with an almost unbearable sadness and nostalgia. It was a strange nostalgia, because the painful memory of my youth was mixed with a different sensation, something like a feeling of having wasted my time, of not having done what I should have done, of having – out of fear, cowardice or laziness – been content with second best.

I remembered a sentence I had read a few weeks earlier: *It's never too late to be who you might have been.*

By the time I tuned back into Larocca's lecture, he was nearing his conclusion.

"Does nobody really want justice? And, in a broader perspective, can we dispense and, above all, obtain justice? These are questions to which it is not possible to supply an answer in the brief space of an event like this. Among other things a shared answer would imply a consensus – one that doesn't in fact exist – about the meaning of the concept of justice, which at one time or another has been compared with legality, impartiality, equality, whether formal or substantial, and so on.

"What is certain, however, is that, between the radical scepticism of those who consider the very aspiration to justice as utopian and hypocritical and the more or less concealed fantasies that are basically just new versions of 'an eye for an eye', there exists a space of rules, guarantees and rights. Rights of defendants and suspects, of course, but also of the victims of crimes. It is in this space, the space of jurists, our space, that it is possible and lawful – with difficulty, but protected from abuse and prevarication – to try to reconstruct the truth, establish responsibility and, last but not least, dispense punishment. With an awareness of our limitations and an acceptance of the idea that in many cases a guilty person will be acquitted and that this is the price to pay for a system in which it will be difficult (although not impossible) for an innocent person to be found guilty.

"Each one of us is free to call the results of this effort whatever he chooses. Even justice, of course.

"Thank you for listening to me."

For a moment, silence hung in the air, almost dizzyingly. Then loud applause broke out. After a few seconds, I, too, started clapping.

12

While the applause was still ongoing, I moved towards the exit. I was at the door when our eyes met. Larocca changed expression, losing the smug self-confidence he had exhibited until that moment. My presence reminded him of an unpleasant thought, something he had dismissed for the space of that morning and which now reappeared in all its disturbing force. He nodded in my direction and made a barely sketched gesture with his hand, indicating that he wanted me to wait for him. For at least five minutes, there was a flurry of smiles, congratulations, thank-yous and handshakes. With a touch of contempt, I observed the collective servility of that little crowd. Then I, too, was struck by an unpleasant thought. I was there. Larocca was a client of mine, but if he hadn't been an important judge would I have gone to see him to talk about questions regarding his case? Or would I have considered it completely natural to summon him to my office for that kind of communication? I felt uncomfortable and tried to think about something else. I went back to watching the action that was taking place behind the speakers' table. From the grimace of regret the head of the bar association was giving, I grasped that Larocca had just said that he had to go. The two men shook hands for a long time in an overly emphatic way. Larocca also said goodbye to the undertaker, whose expression had remained unchanged the whole time.

When I saw that he was starting to move away from the table, while still shaking hands and saying goodbye, I left the lecture theatre to wait for him outside. I didn't want everyone to notice that I was the reason for his haste.

"Hello, Guido," he said. His face was torn between surface cordiality and an underlying apprehension.

"Hello, Pierluigi. Can we go somewhere and talk?"

"Do you have good news or bad news?"

"Half and half. Partly good, partly a little upsetting."

He was unable to repress an expression of impatience, mixed with a slight dismay.

"We could go to my office, but we'd have to move to the other courthouse. Or else your office, even though it's a bit further. Or even to a nearby bar or café, whatever you prefer. In any case, you can start to tell me while we're walking."

We headed for the centre and looked for a café that had slightly isolated tables. Going to the courthouse together on a Saturday would have attracted attention. Not that there was anything unlawful in what we were doing, but the more secret we could keep this matter – and therefore our relationship, which wasn't judge–lawyer but client–lawyer – the better it was.

"I heard your lecture."

"What did you think?"

"Very good. A few years ago I read a book by Alan Dershowitz that said lots of similar things about the hypocrisy of legal systems."

"I haven't read it. What's it called?" There was a hint of tension in his voice when he asked this, as if he meant: they were my ideas, I didn't get them from anyone else.

"I don't think it's ever been translated into Italian. It's called *The Best Defense*. It's a collection of cases. Very interesting, even instructive, I'd say."

If I think about it now, there was a touch of wickedness in my talking so calmly and in such a detached manner, taking my time in getting to the point when he was so obviously on tenterhooks.

"I've found out something."

"I was right, wasn't I? There are proceedings pending?"

"Yes."

"Where does the information come from?"

"I'm sorry, Pierluigi, but I can't—"

"No, no, forgive me. I just wanted to know if the source is reliable."

He was speaking quickly, much faster than usual, clearly embarrassed at my denying him something. He couldn't object to it, but it clearly bothered him. People used to having others say yes, to always being right – and there are several judges who fall into that category – don't easily accept refusals.

"Yes, very reliable. I've also seen copies of some documents."

"Do you have them? What kind of documents are they?"

I'm not sure why I decided to lie. Maybe a vague sense of caution, maybe irritation at the overbearing and slightly hysterical tone of his questions. I told him that I'd read the documents and then given them back.

As we walked along Via Calefati we met a colleague of mine, Carbone, who specializes in defending burglars and fences, and is also a notorious frequenter of the East European prostitutes on the southern seafront. I say *notorious* because he made no mystery of his predilection – the main reason being that they were such excellent value for money – and also because he had once been caught in one of the periodic police raids. The officers hadn't been discreet and, the morning after, the fact that Carbone had been taken to police headquarters in the company of whores, pimps and crooks of every kind had been the main subject of conversation at the courthouse. I would have died of shame, but he paraded around the place like a star, pleased with the sidelong glances that were thrown at him.

He greeted Larocca obsequiously and threw me a questioning glance that I ignored.

"Let's go into the first decent place we find," Larocca said. "It unnerves me, talking like this while we're walking."

A couple of blocks further on, there was an old café, the Cristal, which had been there for as long as I could remember. When I used to go there as a little boy, there were five flavours of ice cream – hazelnut, coffee, chocolate, strawberry and pistachio – and there was lemon and coffee granita, with whipped cream, of course. It had tables at the back where nobody ever sat apart from a couple of very old ladies (the barman had once said that they'd both been born in 1900) whose presence could be sensed from a distance because of the very strong smell of mothballs mixed with eau de cologne and the stink of cigarettes. They would have coffee granita with double whipped cream, and they would smoke and peddle malicious gossip about everyone. They both died well into their nineties, cigarette addicts to the end, having avoided the indignity of the smoking ban being introduced in public places.

If those two were there, it was impossible to get to the table area without gas masks and bulletproof vests. If they weren't there, the barman – a very thin man, with a face devoid of expression, but capable of rare, unexpected and scathing one-liners – let us park ourselves there all afternoon, even though we consumed almost nothing. There were three of us, three friends, fifteen years old, and spending time at a café table, immersed in interminable discussions – the subjects ranged from sport to girls, from politics to books – made us feel like men.

It struck me that I hadn't been in that place for at least ten years and that I hadn't sat at those tables – assuming they were still there – for more than thirty.

"Let's go in here."

At the counter there was a young man with a gaunt face, maybe the grandson of the barman who'd let us camp out there all those years ago. The tables were still in their places, the same as before, three-legged Formica tables of different colours – what remained of the different colours. And just as before, there was nobody there. Apart, maybe, from the ghosts of the two old ladies.

Larocca looked around somewhat uncomfortably.

"Nobody will disturb us here," I reassured him.

Over a coffee and a Prosecco I gave him a summary of the situation. He let me speak without interrupting or asking any questions. His facial expression wavered between incredulity, dismay and anger.

When I finished – I'd tried to be as concise and neutral as possible – he rubbed his forehead with his hand. "I can't believe it. I can't believe it. I was working, going out, sleeping, and those bastards were investigating me. They were bugging my phones, checking my phone records, my bank accounts, my assets. It's unheard of. *Unheard of.*"

I was about to reply that actually they were only doing their job and that it would be best not to take it too personally. Then I told myself that Larocca wasn't in a state of mind to consider the matter objectively.

"They asked to arrest me. They *wanted* to arrest me, and if the file had ended up in the hands of a judge less scrupulous than that woman, they'd have succeeded. It's astonishing they haven't searched my home or office, quite astonishing."

121

"Maybe they would have done it when they arrested you. I don't want to give you any further reasons to worry, but it could still happen, maybe a few days before you're notified of the appeal hearing. Or maybe at the same time."

He shook his head, dejected, angry and powerless. Then he looked at me and noticed the plasters on my temple. "What happened to you?"

"Oh, nothing, a little scratch at the gym."

"In our university days you used to box."

"I still do, a little."

"Good for you, you're in great shape. I should do something too, I'm too sedentary, just sit writing rulings."

The waiter came and asked us if we wanted anything else, and I told him no before Pierluigi could order another Prosecco.

"What do we do, Guido?"

"We go to the appeal hearing when we know the date, and we argue the case. I wouldn't be too pessimistic about it. The judge's rejection was well argued, and in my opinion doesn't leave much room for discussion. We'll see what the prosecutor writes, but if I'd been him I wouldn't even have contested it."

"What would you have done?"

"I'd have tried to make further inquiries, and if the outcome was positive, I'd have presented a new petition to the examining magistrate. But with the situation as it is, the appeal will almost certainly be rejected and the Prosecutor's Department will have had two unfavourable decisions in a row. Not exactly the best conditions for going ahead with such a delicate case."

"*Almost* certainly."

"I'm sorry?"

"You said the appeal will *almost* certainly be rejected. So you think it may also be accepted?"

When someone in the profession – a judge, a police-man or a lawyer – ends up entangled in the legal process, he loses, as if by magic, the ability to look at things lucidly. Like a doctor who falls seriously ill. His intelligence and his technical competence are completely obscured by anxiety and a paranoid vision of events and people. If this case had been about someone else and that other person had asked him for his opinion on the possible outcome of the appeal, Larocca would have smiled somewhat contemptuously and said that there was no way the court would overturn the examining magistrate's ruling. But now he was asking me with a worried look on his face to tell him what I meant by the expression *almost* certainly – a "get-out clause", as they say.

"No, I really don't think so. And even in the very unlikely event that this happens, the decision, as you know much better than me, is suspended until the Supreme Court can give its verdict. But in all honesty I wouldn't worry about it. The more general question concerns the strategy we adopt, always bearing in mind that we don't want the news to leak out."

"You're right, I hadn't thought of that. If they don't succeed in arresting me, they'll try to bad-mouth me in the press. I can already imagine the headlines: *Former Mafioso accuses the head of the appeal court of corruption, Umpteenth scandal at the Palace of Justice*, or—"

"I'm sorry, Pierluigi, but this isn't the right way. It's very unpleasant, I won't deny that, but the most effective way of confronting the matter is to avoid emotionalism. Let's try to be cool and practical, if we possibly can."

He sighed, clenched his jaws – it was likely he didn't appreciate my paternalistic exhortations to keep calm, and come to think of it I wouldn't have appreciated them in his

123

place either – then lowered his gaze and let about ten seconds go by. "All right, let's try to be practical. What do we do?"

"The first decision to make is this: do we wait for the notification of the appeal hearing or until they institute something like a search, or do we reconsider the possibility of presenting a petition based on article 335, with a request for you to be examined? The scenario has changed a bit since we first talked about it, and there may not be the disadvantages that we considered back then."

"What would you choose?"

I took a few seconds to think, even though there was really no choice. The only thing that made any sense at that moment was to wait for the Prosecutor's Department to make its next move.

"I'd wait. I realize it's a little more nerve-wracking to remain in suspense, waiting for other people to make a move, but right now it'll only be a matter of a few days before they notify us of the date of the appeal hearing. Then we'll know formally about the proceedings, and we'll be able to consult the papers, make copies, ask to be questioned, all without any particular urgency. Then we'll go to court and challenge the appeal, which in all probability will be rejected—"

"And what if it gets into the newspapers?"

"If it gets into the newspapers, we could emphasize that the original petition for a custody order was rejected for lack of evidence. But we'll decide that if and when the time comes."

He nodded. He seemed calmer. "So we wait?"

"We wait, yes. But while we're about it, I'd like to ask you a few questions, just to get a better idea of the overall picture, to understand why it all happened in the first place, why on earth Capodacqua made those statements."

"I don't follow you."

"Capodacqua made those statements. That's a given, and we can't argue about it. He may have made it all up. He may have said those things thinking they were true. Because Ladisa told him a pack of lies, to boast or for some other reason I can't quite figure out. Or because Salvagno was influence peddling. To work out a line of defence, we need to try and figure out which of these hypotheses is the right one. The judge thinks it was influence peddling, and in my opinion that's the likeliest hypothesis."

He seemed uncertain, and said nothing. He loosened his tie, unbuttoned his shirt, passed his hand across his forehead again and pinched one of his cheeks. I realized that these rather obsessive gestures were making me feel uncomfortable and I resumed speaking.

"Maybe you could tell me something about your relationship with Salvagno. I only knew him a little. Was he really your friend? Did you see each other often?"

"*Friend* is an overstatement. We played tennis sometimes, and sometimes I was a guest on his boat."

"Did you meet regularly?"

"A couple of times a month, no more."

"Lunches, dinners together?"

"Every now and again, and always with other people."

"Obviously he appeared before you in court."

"Of course. He dealt a lot with organized crime, he often had clients who were in prison."

"Please don't be annoyed by my next question. Did you ever think of abstaining in cases where he was counsel for the defence?"

"No. There were no grounds to do so, which you know as well as I do. I saw Corrado Salvagno occasionally, but no more than I did other lawyers. If I had to abstain in all cases defended by someone I've played tennis or been to dinner with, I might as well quit this job. Same for many colleagues. Anyway, Corrado Salvagno was an excellent lawyer and an honest person. He never asked me for anything. He appeared before me and always argued his cases well. When he was right we agreed with him. When he was wrong we rejected his appeals. Just like with anyone else. Just like with you, for example."

Actually, things weren't quite the way he said. It wasn't at all clear, for example, that there had never been any grounds for abstention. According to the code, a judge is obliged to abstain in a number of different circumstances: in particular, *if there are serious conflicts of interest*. One of these serious conflicts of interest is when the judge is a friend of a lawyer and sees him regularly outside the courtroom. Larocca had just told me that he didn't see Salvagno more than occasionally, but I had the impression that things weren't so cut and dried. It was a subject we would do well to go into in more depth before the Prosecutor's Department brought it up.

"Listen, Pierluigi, I'd like one thing to be clear. I'm your lawyer until you decide to brief someone else. To do my job, which is in your interest, I need to ask you questions and to acquire information. So please try not to react so irritably. It doesn't make the situation any easier."

Maybe I wanted to add something more, or maybe I'd finished. At that moment the barman with the gaunt face appeared. Larocca ordered another Prosecco. Putting on my health fanatic guise again, I settled for an orange juice. We sat in silence until our drinks arrived. I tried to remember what there had been on the walls, now bare, when I used to come here as a boy. Posters? Stiff boards propped on the floor? A mirror with advertisements for Campari, Martini or Peroni?

He drank half a glass in one gulp. I sipped at my juice. Somewhere, a defective machine was buzzing.

"I'm sorry, Guido, you're right. You're only doing your job. It's just that this business is eating me up inside. I can't believe it's happening to me. It's a nightmare."

He rubbed his forehead again with his hand and finished the Prosecco in another gulp. If he ordered another, I'd tell him it was better not to.

"What else do you want to know?" he said.

"Something about Salvagno. What kind of man was he? Did he talk a lot, or not very much? Was he someone who might have boasted about his friendships, including his friendship with you?"

"He was an honest person. I find it really hard to believe he could have—"

"Do you think Capodacqua made up the things that are in that transcript? Or worse still: that someone suggested to him that he make false statements against you? In other words, that it was a case of slander, which the police and even the prosecutor may have been a party to? Do you think it's feasible to construct our line of defence on that hypothesis? Personally, I don't. We have to figure out why he made those statements. I repeat the question: insofar as you knew him, was Salvagno the kind of person who might have boasted, perhaps saying more than he should have done, about your friendship?"

Larocca sighed. "It's true that sometimes he talked too much. He had a tendency to… as you say, to boast: about his boat, his villa, his women, his professional successes. And now that I come to think about it, yes, he had a tendency to talk a little too much about the people he knew. Prefects, members of parliament, judges, actors." He paused for some time, as if trying to retrieve a piece of information that was re-emerging from a shadowy area of his memory. "But to go from that to imagining that he—"

"Do you know if he had financial problems?"

"He was always complaining about his expenses. That he needed a lot of money to maintain the boat, the houses, the ex-wife, the girlfriends. But I always thought he was just saying that. It was another way of boasting, part of his character. I never knew if he really did have problems with money."

"Because if he was struggling financially, the hypothesis that he peddled influence in order to get his clients to pay him more, on the pretext that he had to pay you or other judges, might make sense. It wouldn't be the first time. We'll have to run some checks on his finances."

"All right. What I find incredible is the idea that Corrado could have implicated me in something like that. But you're right, we have to figure out what happened and why this Capodacqua said those things."

"What about his fatal accident? I remember reading about it in the newspapers, but I don't know any of the details."

"A German lorry driver dozed off at the wheel, and skidded into the other lane. That's all. Pure chance."

"Was he travelling alone?"

"Yes, he was on his way back from Rome. He'd gone there for a hearing at the Supreme Court."

"Was the lorry driver hurt?"

"Not seriously, as far as I remember."

"Were there any suspicions about what happened?"

"What do you mean?"

"Did anybody suggest any kind of criminal intent? In other words: were things the way they seemed?"

He looked at me in surprise. "Do you seriously think someone might have…" He couldn't finish the sentence. The idea must have struck him as much too far-fetched.

"I have no reason to suppose so. But trying to find out what happened to Salvagno, who may have talked a bit too much – maybe even to the wrong people – could be useful to us. I think it's something else it might be worth investigating."

I told myself that I was ready to go into politics, since I'd just come up with a perfect *non*-answer. Larocca seemed to be on the verge of replying. Then he dropped it, as if he'd said to himself, in some kind of inner dialogue, that it really was too absurd to contemplate.

"Another couple of questions, and then we can go. The question of the wine: is it true that Salvagno sent you bottles of wine?"

For a moment, an almost imperceptible grimace of impatience appeared on his face, but he suppressed it. "Sometimes. He had a client who produced a respectable Primitivo. He sometimes gave me a few bottles."

I couldn't have looked too convinced.

"We're talking about ten-euro bottles," Larocca said, unable to avoid a defensive tone.

How on earth had Capodacqua known about that? Or in other words, how had Ladisa known about it, in order to be able to tell Capodacqua? Whether or not there was any mystery behind his death, Salvagno had clearly been someone who talked too much. It was likely that his death really had been an accident and that there was no reason to let my imagination run away with me.

But.

But I would ask Annapaola to include the accident on the list of things to be checked out. If only to get it off my mind.

Soon afterwards, we left the café and stopped on the street to say goodbye.

"Careful with your phones, Pierluigi."

"Do you think they might be tapping them again? Or that they never stopped?"

"The first is more likely. In all probability they stopped tapping your phones when they petitioned for the custody order. They might start again closer to the notification of the appeal, to record any possible reactions to the news that proceedings do indeed exist. Assuming that the examining magistrate agrees to it, which is by no means certain. Given that we don't know for sure, don't say anything on the phone that might lend itself to being misinterpreted. In other words, say as little as possible. As soon as you get any kind of notification, call me and tell me what happened and ask to meet without making any comments and without any reference to these conversations of ours. Sorry to be pedantic, but is that quite clear?"

"Yes, quite clear."

13

We didn't have long to wait. The following Tuesday, at seven in the morning, I was woken by a telephone call from Larocca. His voice was cracked and even a little breathless, as if he'd just been running or making some other physical effort.

"There are men from the customs police in my home, with a search warrant from the Prosecutor's Department in Lecce. I told them I want my lawyer to be present. Do you think you could come?"

"Give me a quarter of an hour and I'll be there."

To hurry things up I took my bicycle, and about a quarter of an hour later I was at Larocca's home, at the end of Via Dalmazia, in the Madonnella area, not far from the RAI offices. An ambiguous part of the city, between early twentieth-century apartment buildings with spectacular views over the blue and green of the Adriatic and the streets of Rione Japigia, which had been – and maybe still were, despite the many arrests, trials and sentences – the uncontested kingdom of powerful criminal gangs. Ruthless bosses with nicknames, lookouts posted at the borders of the neighbourhood to give the alarm when the police arrived, rivers of drugs of every kind sold wholesale to buyers from all over the region, or exchanged for other illegal goods – arms, stolen cars, sometimes even human beings. A lot of money had changed hands in that area. In quantities it's hard to imagine, if you have a normal job. When many of those people had ended up in prison, very little of the money had been found. It had been channelled into activities that were beyond suspicion, or had disappeared into the pockets of greedy advisers abroad, transported God knows how, intended for God knows whom.

I seemed to remember that even as a boy Larocca had lived around there. What did his father do? I wasn't sure I'd ever known. I wondered if the anonymous Seventies condominium I was entering now was the same one he'd grown up in.

There were no names next to the entryphone. I rang number four, as I had been told to do, and went up to the second floor. There wasn't any nameplate on the door either, but he was in the doorway waiting for me. His hair, usually well combed, was falling over his forehead and curled a little pathetically at the sides of his head. He hadn't shaved – when would he have had a chance to do so? – and, as happens in such cases to men who don't have much of a beard, he looked like a mixture of the scruffy and the forlorn.

"Thanks for coming, Guido. This business is driving me mad. It's a good thing I don't have to be in court today."

I couldn't find any appropriate words of comfort, so I limited myself to a slight smile and a gentle pat on the shoulder.

"Where are they?"

"There, in the living room."

As I walked into the apartment I felt a slight but immediate sense of anxiety. There was an artificial smell, of detergent, of synthetic lemon. Everything was perfectly tidy. In the entrance there was a series of framed lithographs. All of the same size, with the same frames, perfectly equidistant one from the other. The living room was divided in two. On one side, a sofa, two armchairs, a large TV set and a stereo; on the other, a bookcase, with a couple of encyclopaedias and rows of books arranged strictly by order of height, an Eighties walnut table and a large abstract painting hanging exactly in the middle of the wall. It gave the impression that it had been done to commission, specifically to decorate that particular stretch of wall.

There were three officers from the customs police: a lieutenant-colonel and two marshals in jackets and ties, with well-cut clothes that showed no bulges where they carried their guns. They were modern policemen, looking more like managers or bank officials. They greeted me politely, almost cordially, as if trying to apologize for causing so much bother.

One of the marshals was sitting at the table in the living room, in front of a laptop computer to which he had connected a small printer. The complete text of the record appeared on the screen. The lieutenant-colonel, a tall, slightly overweight man in his forties with a noticeably receding hairline and intelligent eyes, asked me if I wanted to read the search warrant. As I skimmed through it – there was nothing in the stated grounds that I didn't already know – he noticed my plasters, which were still there and quite visible.

"What happened to you, Avvocato? A dissatisfied client?"

"Unfortunately I got into a fight with some hooligans in the street."

He gave a little smile. That morning he had an unpleasant chore to dispatch, but at least he'd ended up with a pleasant lawyer. "I think we can start," he said, dismissing the subject of my plasters.

I replied that it was fine by me. Larocca did the same, but he seemed like someone who has taken an overdose of prescription drugs. His voice was shaky, his eyes were glassy, even his posture had something bedraggled about it. That can happen, when someone comes into your home and claims the right to rummage among your things.

I asked myself for a moment how I would behave in the same situation. I couldn't find an answer – usually the case when I ask myself that kind of question – and I moved on.

The three officers proceeded calmly and methodically, inspecting every room from top to bottom. A textbook job. Whenever they had to open drawers or cupboards or look behind pictures, they asked permission. Whenever they plunged their hands into piles of clothes and underwear or when they searched the safe in the bedroom, they apologized. They were so nice about everything that I started to get nervous and felt the impulse to tell them to just get on with their work without being so obsequious.

After finishing in each room, we would come back to the living room, where the lieutenant-colonel would dictate the respective part of the record. From time to time he would break off and ask us if we had any objections or clarifications to make. Larocca would shake his head, and I would say no, thanks, there was nothing I wanted to add. Partly because, as was to be expected, the search wasn't producing any results. They rarely do. Either when the object of a search is something specific, or when the warrant refers in general terms to "objects, documents or anything pertaining to the offence being investigated", as in this case. There are many reasons for this, including the objective difficulty of actually finding anything in an inhabited house or apartment, where there are enormous quantities of objects and clothes and cubbyholes and hiding places. Carrying out a truly effective search, one that really checks out what there is and what there isn't in a given place, takes much more time than police officers can devote to it. Sometimes, in searches as in life, you pass by something crucial and don't notice it. Because you don't know what to look for, or maybe because what you're looking for is so obvious, you don't see it. In searches, as in life, it isn't a matter of technique, it's a matter of eyes and time.

I watched the lieutenant-colonel and the other two officers proceed conscientiously – emptying and then refilling the cupboards, beating on the walls in search of possible secret cavities, opening the books and leafing through them in search of hidden papers – and it struck me that, good and professional as they were, the only way they would find anything (assuming there was anything to find) would be through a stroke of luck. So I lost interest in their operations and started looking around to get a better understanding of the apartment and its occupant.

I knew that Larocca had been separated for several years and that he had no children. I couldn't remember his wife's face at all.

I opened the windows and looked out onto Via Dalmazia. The RAI sign was just opposite. I came back inside and examined the books – mainly stuff about current affairs and American bestsellers. Larocca joined me while I was browsing among the shelves.

"What do you think, Guido?"

"Professionals, very correct, partly or wholly unconvinced of the point of this search."

"Why do you think those bastards in the Prosecutor's Department in Lecce decided to order it?"

"So that nobody can tell them in future that they should have done it and forgot. Plus, they don't know we were already aware that proceedings were under way. So even though this search is late, it isn't completely meaningless from an investigative point of view."

He nodded absently. He would have liked a different answer, but didn't know what.

"Where are they now?" I asked.

"In the bathroom."

"Let's join them. We don't want them to feel lonely."

The bathroom was spacious and aseptic. I noticed a white dressing gown hanging on a coat hanger, with the words *Plaza Athénée* on it. A very expensive hotel in Paris. I had stayed there once, many years ago, when I was still married to Sara, because we'd decided to do something crazy. And when we saw the bill we knew we'd achieved our objective.

I wondered if Larocca had bought that dressing gown, or if he had stuffed it into his suitcase as an unauthorized souvenir of his stay. I took a closer look at the contents of the drawers that the officers were opening, checking and closing again, and realized that the dressing gown wasn't the only thing that had come from a grand hotel. There were towels from the Mandarin and the Ritz, bottles of shampoo and bath gel from Claridge's.

Judge Larocca clearly liked luxury and had a slight – slight? – obsession with objects from big hotels. I remembered an uncle of my father's. Uncle Michele. A really respectable person, a good doctor, someone who would never have jumped his place in a queue – just one example of how strictly he obeyed the rules. He was a Dr Jekyll, and like every Dr Jekyll there were times when he turned into Mr Hyde. Those times were when he stayed in a hotel, either on business or on holiday. Then an uncontrollable predatory impulse would well up in him. Anything that could be taken away without hiring a removal van, he would take. Towels, dressing gowns, ashtrays, bars of soap, shampoo, bath gel, notebooks, pencils, small cartons of jam, snacks, tubs of Nutella and even an entire set of plates, glasses and cups. Whenever my parents talked about it, they referred to it as if it was an illness – a kind of kleptomania, my mother said once, looking at my father with a suspicious expression, as if speculating on the possible genetic nature of the condition.

Well, I thought, Larocca must have a similar problem to Uncle Michele's.

The officers didn't pay any attention to it. Why should they? I wondered if I would have noticed if I'd been in their shoes.

The last room to be searched was Pierluigi's study. They didn't find anything there either, even though they leafed through law books and codes, opened drawers and lifted the rug on which the desk stood, exactly in the middle. Larocca didn't keep case files at home – or at least there weren't any that morning. I wondered how he managed to write his rulings: it struck me as unlikely that he only worked in his office. I told myself that in all probability he used the digital versions of the documents.

The officers made copies of the hard disk from the computer and of a few memory sticks, then said that as far as the apartment was concerned they had finished.

The record was printed and read out loud, with particular emphasis on the statement that no damage had been caused in the course of the operation, and we all signed it in triplicate.

"I'm sorry, Your Honour," the lieutenant-colonel said, "but we have to go to your office now. It's included in the prosecutor's warrant."

Larocca seemed to have regained his self-control. "Very well, colonel. All I ask is that you… keep this as discreet as possible. We don't want it to become public knowledge."

"Don't worry. If you can make sure that nobody comes in, we'll get through it in half an hour. As discreetly as we can."

We decided that I wouldn't be present at the search of the office. My presence there, along with three strangers, might have generated suspicion and speculation. I would drop by in an hour, as if by chance.

I went to the clerk of the court's office to check the registers of proceedings or the release of copies, had a burnt coffee, and chatted in a corridor with a female colleague who had been a noted beauty in her youth and who all at once, without warning, declared that she had no objection to extramarital relations. I replied that if I were married I would share her opinion, but she didn't seem to appreciate the joke.

One way or another, the hour passed, and I went to Larocca's office.

They hadn't found anything there either.

"They also gave me these," Larocca said, handing me a few sheets of paper.

They were a petition for an extension of the period for the preliminary investigation and a petition for a pretrial hearing. In other words, a request to bring the examination of witnesses, which would usually be done during the public trial, forward to the investigative phase.

The prosecutor wanted to proceed with the examination of Capodacqua and Marelli. In the case of the former, who had turned state's evidence, no specific grounds were required.

In Marelli's case, the reason cited was that he was not in good health. There was a strong possibility he wouldn't make it through to the trial, and so needed to be examined as soon as possible. My first reaction was that there wasn't much point in objecting.

"Was there anything else?"

"No. I think that's quite enough to be getting on with."

"No date for the appeal of the custody order?"

He shook his head.

"They're taking their time," I said. "Or else the prosecutor has given up on the idea."

"Why should he?"

"I don't know. A change of strategy, perhaps. Maybe they think they can acquire more evidence, so there's no point carrying on with an appeal they probably won't win."

"Do you think they're tapping my phones?"

"It's quite likely. They do an apparently pointless search just to rock the boat, hoping that the suspect then says something untoward on the phone or calls the wrong person. Or the right person, depending on your point of view."

"Could they have put bugs here or at home?"

"If the charge is just what's written here, they can't do that. You haven't been caught in the act."

"I know, dammit, I know. But that's the problem. I can't predict their moves, I don't know how to react. Who would ever have thought I'd be in a situation like this? Shit, dammit, shit. Those bastard sons of bitches, I always knew they'd try to fuck me over one way or another."

It had been many years since I'd last had occasion to meet Larocca outside our respective professional roles, so it was quite natural that I wasn't used to hearing him swear like that. From what I remembered from our university days, though, he had never been inclined to use bad language. It made quite an impression on me now, seeing him lose control.

"Okay, let's think," I said. "We have a petition for a pretrial hearing, which means they must have filed the supporting documents. I'll go to Lecce tomorrow, look at the case file and ask for a copy. Then we'll decide what to do."

"All right."

"If you don't mind, I'll take these for now. I'll scan them in my office, then give them back to you."

"As far as I'm concerned, you can keep them. I feel disgusted just looking at them."

14

That evening I went out with my friend Nadia. She'd called me a few days earlier. "I have two tickets for a concert at the Petruzzelli. I'll buy you dinner after it."

As the lights dimmed, I recalled that whenever my father had taken me to concerts as a child that had always been my favourite moment: the moment when the auditorium slipped into semi-darkness and the music began.

The pianist, who had an exotic name, played Chopin and Liszt and ended with a piece by a contemporary composer.

For dinner, we went to a restaurant near the theatre. It's called Perbacco and I like it a lot because, among other things, it stays open late, even when there are only a few customers.

"So what did you think of the concert, did you like it?" Nadia asked me after the owner had uncorked an Aglianico from Basilicata.

"Chopin and Liszt were… well, they were Chopin and Liszt. I understand them, I like them, and the playing seemed good, as far as I could tell. The sonata by that Armenian was a bit more problematic."

"He isn't Armenian, he's Lithuanian."

"The fact remains that for the whole of that half hour I had homicidal impulses."

"You aren't a real intellectual."

"You can bet on it."

Nadia took a sip of her wine and smiled slightly shame-facedly. "I found it unbearable, too. At university I took an entire course on contemporary music, and thought I'd started to understand. So there are two possibilities: either I'm stupid, or this Lithuanian fellow is completely beyond comprehension."

"Or else the problem is with a certain kind of contemporary music in general. Maybe only those who compose it and study it are capable of understanding it. In fifty years' time, will anybody still be listening to it, apart from specialists? For example, who today still reads the *nouveau roman* writers, like Robbe-Grillet?"

"Robbe-Grillet wrote the screenplay of *Last Year at Marienbad*."

"My point exactly. Apart from those who've studied cinema, like you, who today still watches *Last Year at Marienbad*? Even supposing anybody watched it fifty years ago when it came out."

"It won the Golden Lion at Venice. Have you seen it?"

"Yes. But I've done all kinds of things I'd rather not boast about."

"It's beautifully photographed."

"You're right, it's beautifully photographed, but the story is unbearable. It's a theoretical and self-important exercise. But I'd prefer to drop the subject of avant-garde art. It always makes me a little nervous, I'm probably too common for it."

As so often, the restaurant wasn't crowded. Partly because of the dim lighting, there was the usual pleasant sensation of intimacy, a little like having dinner at the house of friends.

Our dishes arrived and our glasses were refilled.

"So, what's been happening in your life in the months since I last saw you?" Nadia asked after tasting the smoked scamorza in an orange and spicy oil preserve.

For a few moments, I had the impulse to tell her the story of the mistaken tests, but I decided to avoid it; it would merely have thrown a pall of gloom over the evening.

"Nothing worth reporting. Every now and again, I consider the possibility of quitting this job. But it's only a whim."

"I think it'd be a terrible idea. You like being a lawyer, except that for some strange reason you're ashamed to admit it, even to yourself."

I made a gesture with both hands to stop her and go on to something else. It always makes me nervous when people say sensible things about me.

"I invited you to dinner because I'm leaving next week and I wanted to say goodbye," Nadia said.

"Oh, you're leaving. Actually, you've been doing nothing but leaving for some time now."

For years, Nadia had had a place – a mixture of bar, restaurant and nightclub – called Chelsea Hotel No. 2. I'd really liked going there, late, and staying and chatting with her after closing time, when there was nobody left except her Corsican dog Pino. He was her bodyguard and her family.

One evening, right there in the Chelsea, the dog had died of a heart attack and she had lost all desire to work there any more. She had sold it – I had stopped going there – and started travelling, in search of some new idea that would change her life. She's something of an expert in changing her life, because for many years in her youth she was a high-class prostitute. Although nobody meeting her and talking to her would ever think so, or even thought so at the time.

"This time I'll be away a little longer."

"Where are you going?"

"Sydney, Australia. I'll be there for three months."

"And what are you going to do in Sydney for three months?"

"A friend of mine who lives there has to be away on business. I'll be staying at her place. All I have to do in return is water the plants. A pretty good deal, I think."

"All right, but I repeat my question: what are you going to do in Sydney for three months?"

"Improve my English – I know, most people go to London for that, but when do I ever do what most people do? – and look around to see if it's worth considering a more permanent move there. It's an idea I've often fantasized about, going to live in Australia."

"I feel really bad about it," I said.

She stared at me. "Are you joking?"

"No. I'll feel much more alone when you're not here. *Knowing* you're not here."

She hadn't expected me to say something like that, and nor had I, to be honest. She took my hand across the table and squeezed it. "You're one of the very few people I'll be sorry to leave."

Her words hung in the air between us for a long time. When she spoke again, she had a tone of forced cheerfulness.

"Maybe I won't like Australia. Apparently there are more deadly creatures there than anywhere else in the world."

We didn't say any more about her leaving. We let the time pass pleasantly, eating and drinking and talking cautiously about books and films. We were both careful to avoid sad subjects. By the time I saw her home it was after one, and we said goodbye as if it had been an ordinary evening.

I've never been very good at putting my thoughts in order, but that night they were particularly tangled. Regrets, twinges of fear, faces, voices, flashes of old desires, images of long-forgotten places crowded into my head in time to my footsteps in the empty street, mixing with the façades of the buildings, the signs on the walls, the billboards.

Without intending to, I took a bit of a long way round and passed the building where I had lived as a boy with my parents. It was as if I was seeing it again after an absence of many years, that dark wooden front door, with the cracks in the paint, the oxidized handle, the rust on the hinges. A shudder went through me as I realized how many times, how many thousands of times, I had come close to my past without paying any attention to it, without hearing the frantic murmur of time. My thoughts started moving at an unusual speed, succeeding one another in my feverish head without any apparent connection.

I was forty-eight and my life was more than half over, unless – which seemed unlikely – I turned out to be like one of those people on the island of Okinawa, apparently the place with the highest number of centenarians in the world. It would have been much more than half over if that diagnosis had been correct. It could have been *almost* over. My parents' home. My father and my mother. How strange, I almost never think about them. No, that's not quite true. I almost never *thought* about them, until that business with the tests. They both passed away when I wasn't yet thirty. When my mother died, the house was cool and full of wind. It seemed like a kind of hymn to life, that wind. Dad joined her a few months later, silently, like a leaf falling from a tree. They often talked about how they were going to enjoy their retirement. They would travel, write, learn Chinese. They would live for a year in Paris, in the home of a friend who was a diplomat. Instead of which neither of them reached retirement age. They didn't have time. That's the mistake we all make, thinking we have time. Now strangers live in that apartment. I don't want to know who they are. Strangers also live in the apartment I shared with Sara, my ex-wife. All my places have been expropriated by strangers, one by one.

Is that a banal thought? I don't know. I feel as if I'm in the middle of some kind of centrifugal movement. Things and people rush away from me while I remain still. Even Nadia's nightclub. Even my old, small office. Only Maria Teresa and I were there, when she was still my secretary and not a colleague. Maria Teresa is a good person, spontaneously and effortlessly honest, I think she was just born that way. She and Consuelo looked at me in amazement when I told them that Judge Larocca was suspected of judicial corruption and had turned to me for his defence. I didn't go into details; for some reason I was too embarrassed. I met Sara a few days ago, with her husband. Her second husband, I was the first. Greeting her and embracing her and feeling the strangeness of that body, that perfume, that voice, I felt a kind of dismay. How could you have loved a woman so much, suffered so much because of her, *laughed* so much with her, and now feel so distant from her? And her husband seems like such a cretin. I know it's hard to be objective in certain situations, but he really does seem like a cretin. Had I been wrong about her, all those years ago? Had it all been a mistake? I thought I was in love with her. I thought I loved her. For a long time, I thought I loved her for her intelligence. I thought she'd chosen me for the same reason. But maybe that wasn't the case. You can hardly say she prefers intelligent people, considering the one she's married to now. We shouldn't start thinking like this. We risk coming to dangerous conclusions. We shouldn't go back over our own thoughts and our own actions, it isn't a nice thing to do. Even though Hannah Arendt thought differently. She said that moral action is born out of inner dialogue, and that it's the absence of that dialogue, the inability to enter into it, that turns banal people into agents of evil. Though I'm not so sure what this has to do with Sara, who I don't recognize any more. Or with my parents, who I feel I never really knew. I haven't thought of them for a long time. Only a few vague, fleeting memories from time to time, quite by chance. Just images without voices, without sounds; no conversations, discussions, arguments. God knows why. Just mute presences, distant and sweet. I've recently started dreaming about them. That happened in the past, too, but those were silent dreams. Now, though, I sometimes hear their voices, they talk to me, and I talk to them. They're normal conversations, like the ones in my childhood and adolescence, the ones I'd forgotten. Sometimes I wake up from these dreams weeping softly.

It isn't unpleasant. They aren't sad tears.

15

I gave instructions to Consuelo and Maria Teresa to deputize for me in court, then went to the garage, took out my pointlessly expensive and rarely used car, and set off for Lecce.

Consuelo had asked me if I needed company for the ride. I'd said no, thanks, there were lots of things to do at the courthouse in Bari and it was best if we divided the tasks. Actually, Maria Teresa could have dealt with that morning's chores on her own, but I preferred to be alone for those three hours there and back. I like driving without anybody beside me, especially if I don't have to keep to a schedule. It may be because it doesn't often happen, but it makes me feel free, like those first times when I took my father's car and drove outside the city, at the age of twenty. When I was surprised that I could do what adults did. When I was surprised that I had *become* an adult.

At elementary school I had the recurring thought that I would never get to middle school. That I would die first. I didn't have a specific fantasy about *how* that would happen, just that it wouldn't be anything traumatic or frightening, or even upsetting. It was just a thought tinged with a slight regret for what I could have been and would never be.

I got to middle school and the belief crept in that I wouldn't reach the age for high school. Then I entered high school and forgot all about that strange romantic fantasy. I remembered it five years later, when I graduated. I thought, with surprise and gratitude: I didn't die and now I'm an adult. I can even drive a car and go around the world. I'll never die.

It was a fine spring day. Trees, big friendly clouds, the wind, the sky a very light blue, blinding near the sun, and an intense, darker blue on the side opposite the horizon. The whitewashed houses, the brown of the earth, the green of the vegetable gardens, the spotted red of the poppies, the yellow and white dots of the little daisies.

The perfect day to remember those times in April when we had our first bathe in the sea. Had Larocca ever come with us? I didn't think so, but I wasn't sure, there were lots of different groups, people would arrive, others would leave, and he may have been there, but I couldn't remember.

Most times we went to a place between Cozze and Polignano, on this very road I was driving down. Pietra Egea, it was called. Maybe it's still called that, I don't know. I don't know if we gave it that name or if that was what it was called on the map.

At that time, the dual carriageway and the parallel roads didn't exist. We'd leave our cars on a dusty dirt track and cross the countryside, climbing over drystone walls and pointless gates until we reached some large, flat white rocks, where we'd lie sunbathing or dive off them into the clear water.

Almost unconsciously, I left the dual carriageway, turned onto the exit for Cozze and drove down the parallel road in search of that dirt track from thirty years earlier. It didn't take me long to find it, but now there was a gate and a fence that stopped me from going any further. I parked the car, looked around to make sure there wasn't anyone there and, in my grey suit and regimental tie, climbed over the gate, hoping no angry peasant would suddenly appear accompanied by a fierce dog. Apart from the seagulls, though, there wasn't a soul in sight. A slight sirocco brought me the smells of the scrub, which could be seen at the far end of the fields. The same smells as before. Juniper, wild bay, caper, rosemary and God knows how many others whose names I don't even know.

I stopped for a moment to fill my lungs with that warm, scented wind. I loosened my tie, resumed walking, and within a few minutes reached the white rocks, which sloped down to the sea like slides for cyclopses.

Often, when you go back to a place from your childhood or your remote youth, it seems smaller, and all at once your memories lose that mythical dimension where you've kept them for years.

Pietra Egea, though, was just the way I remembered it. Not just the rocks, but the countryside, the scrub. I felt as if it was only a week since I'd last been there. It was a sensation that was both reassuring and painful.

There was nobody in sight, not even on the sea. Not even a fishing boat in the distance. The water was green and so transparent, I felt like taking my clothes off and diving in without thinking or hesitating. If you hesitated, when it was still April, the fear of the cold would stop you. It's always the fear of the cold that stops you. In general, I mean. Was that meant to be a profound thought? You can do better than that, Guerrieri. Or maybe not. Maybe the best you can come up with are these rather didactic metaphors. All right, as long as it remains between the two of us, nobody else needs to know.

I didn't bathe. Too complicated.

I took off my jacket, lay down on the rocks, closed my eyes, felt the warm wind between my layers of clothes and accustomed my ears to the nearby rustling and the very slight lapping of the water.

I remained like that for a minute, without thinking. Then they came back. The thoughts, I mean. The usual ones. Where I would have been at that moment if the first tests hadn't been wrong, if I really had had *that illness* – it was hard for me to say the name even in my head: *leukaemia*. It wasn't a question. I would have been in some more or less aseptic, more or less white room, as weak as an old man, feeling nauseous, with needles stuck in my veins. Maybe I would already have lost my hair. Maybe I would have been on the verge of dying.

Almost always, thinking these things – but was it really *thinking*? I asked myself and immediately gave up looking for an answer – left me with a painful sense of fragility, of incurable precariousness. That morning, lying on the flat, friendly rocks, as gentle as they'd always been, immersed in the swarming of so many invisible and invincible lives, I felt instead an overwhelming sense of wonder. I was capable of walking, driving a car, skipping rope, hitting the punchbag, doing press-ups, climbing over a gate. Just like a boy.

In those same years when I thought I would die before getting to middle school, I also imagined that when I grew up I'd be a scientist. Is that a contradiction? I'd say it is. But tell that to the child who was afraid of everything and made up stories he didn't have the courage to tell anyone. He didn't know F. Scott Fitzgerald, but the adult he would become would one day read a phrase he'd never forget: "The test of a first-rate intelligence is the ability to hold two opposed ideas in the mind at the same time, and still retain the ability to function." There, that's it.

So I would be a scientist, in a light-filled laboratory like the one in an American university that I'd seen in a documentary. The campus was drowned in greenery and peopled by serious but friendly young researchers, happy to be doing what they were doing. Ready for great discoveries. I would be like them: a happy adult.

In remembering my unrealized childhood dreams, I felt an absurd joy – the same I'd felt back then – such as I hadn't experienced for a very long time. As if those fantasies, and others, could still become reality.

A curious phenomenon, I told myself as I walked back along the dirt road between the low drystone walls, the prickly pear and the olives. It must be a result of the shocks imprinted on your psyche by the business of those tests, I concluded, getting back in my car and setting off again in a southerly direction.

In Lecce, I bought the newspapers because I wanted to check if news of the search had leaked out. There was nothing. That surprised me, and I didn't know how to interpret it. Had they chosen to keep it secret, or was it a tactical move that I couldn't figure out?

Still puzzling over this dilemma, I entered the courthouse. It's a concrete block, quite ugly, though it certainly can't compare – in ugliness, I mean – with the courthouse in Bari.

I went to the clerk of the court's office that deals with the work of the examining magistrates, identified myself, handed over the paper signed by Larocca appointing me as his attorney, and asked to consult the case file for the pretrial hearing.

As I expected, there wasn't much: three transcripts of Capodacqua's statements, heavily redacted; two transcripts of Marelli's statements, the second of which had been taken in hospital; a report by the customs police, with a medical certificate attached, stating that Marelli was seriously ill.

I took a few notes, so that I could pass on to Annapaola the data she would need for her enquiries, and requested a complete copy of the documents filed, to be collected in a few days' time by my counterpart in Lecce.

I thought of going to the Prosecutor's Department to talk to one of the magistrates who were handling the case, then told myself there was no real reason to do so: there was no further information they could give me, even supposing they were in the office and could see me without warning and without an appointment. So, about half an hour later, earlier than anticipated, I was outside again.

I called Larocca, and gave him an account of what I'd learnt, deliberately keeping it brief. I didn't have any desire to hear another series of complaints and curses about the Prosecutor's Department.

Just as I was about to leave the city, I remembered the instructions I'd received from Consuelo and Maria Teresa. I was supposed to buy a tray of *pasticciotti* – the excellent local sweets made of crisp short pastry filled with cream – to be handed over to them, without fail, when I got back. If I didn't bring *pasticciotti*, I wouldn't be allowed back into the office. So I did an about-turn, drove to the area near the beautiful Piazza Sant'Oronzo, glanced at the Roman amphitheatre, found the usual pastry shop, where they had just been taken out of the oven, and carried out my instructions.

The delicious, almost hallucinogenic aroma of the sweets accompanied me all the way back.

16

I was in my office with one of the trainees, the latest to arrive and the grandson of an old schoolteacher of mine who had asked me to take him on. Unfortunately, considering the nature of the request, I hadn't been able to object, even though the young man had the expression of a psychotic pigeon and the pernicious habit of wearing the same shirt for two or three days, with all the olfactory consequences you would expect.

We were discussing the first document I had entrusted him with drawing up: an action for fraud, with a request for the seizure of a number of bills of exchange. The young man had thrown himself into the task with great enthusiasm, but also with a somewhat idiosyncratic, even Dadaist interpretation of grammar and syntax. The vocabulary wasn't any better. It was full of expressions like *aforesaid, above-mentioned, herein enclosed, your lordships* and things like that.

Federico had graduated with first-class honours and hadn't yet decided whether to be a defence lawyer or a magistrate. My plan, when I heard about this dilemma, immediately became clear: to urge him, using all means possible, to opt for the second of these. Not a very good prospect for the magistrature (even supposing he passed the exam), but excellent for me and my practice.

"Why do you use these expressions, Federico?"

"What expressions, Avvocato?"

I leafed through the action and pointed almost at random at a line towards the end of the document. "This, for example: 'May your lordship be congratulated on granting the seizure as a matter of urgency…'"

He threw me his best pigeon look and remained silent.

"All you have to say is: *we ask for this seizure as a matter of urgency.* If you meet a flesh-and-blood prosecutor, do you say to him: 'Good morning, your lordship'?"

He didn't know what to reply. In his first six months as a trainee, in another practice, they had inculcated certain teachings in him as if they were gospel truth. One of these was that in legal documents, and in particular those addressed to a magistrate, this was the way you wrote. Now he was being told that maybe things weren't like that. In all probability, he was thinking that he had ended up with the wrong lawyer, and on that point I couldn't gainsay him. At that moment, the internal telephone rang.

"What is it, Pasquale?"

"Signorina Annapaola has arrived. She's in Consuelo's office. They say to take your time, and when you've finished join them or they'll come to you."

I had no desire to take my time with the psychotic pigeon. Annapaola's arrival was timely. A real lifesaver.

"All right, tell them I'll be there in two minutes." I hung up and gave the draft of the action back to Federico. "Please look at it again. Try to use shorter sentences, twenty, twenty-five words maximum. If you think of a longer one, break it up. Drop the *your lordships*. Write as you'd speak – not in a bar, obviously. Write as you'd speak if you were trying to explain the situation out loud to a judge. I'll see you later, or tomorrow."

He walked to the door, looking dazed and dejected.

"Oh, Federico?"

"Yes, Avvocato."

"My impression, from this first period of acquaintance with you, is that your disposition is more geared towards the work of magistrate than that of defence lawyer."

Disposition more geared... What are you talking about, Guerrieri? Have you gone mad?

"Maybe you should think seriously about your future prospects. Partly because there's one sure way to fail in everything, and that's by doing many things simultaneously, and badly. If you decide to continue in this profession, I'll be happy to have you" – *dirty liar,* I thought – "but if, as I think would be better suited to your gifts, you decide to take the magistrature exams, well, I think you should devote yourself body and soul to that, and not waste time on other activities."

The pigeon assumed a grateful expression and I smiled at him paternally, feeling like a worm.

The door of Consuelo's office was ajar. I could hear non-stop chatter and muted laughter. The two women seemed very much in sync, as if they were exchanging amusing female confidences. I knocked gently at the door. Consuelo said: "Come in", sounding like someone trying to regain composure without really wanting to.

"Am I disturbing you? I could come back in half an hour, when you girls have finished."

"Hello, Avvocato," Annapaola said cheerfully, but with a touch of irony.

"Would you like us to come to your office, Guido?"

"Here is fine."

Annapaola pointed at me. "Did you know your boss is some kind of Rocky Marciano?"

Consuelo threw her a questioning glance, then turned to me.

"She's talking about boxing," I intervened, to avoid – in case that had been the intention – the story of our nocturnal feats.

"Oh, of course," Consuelo said. "Middle-aged men have their obsessions. Best to be indulgent."

I noticed a new poster on the wall facing the desk. Consuelo goes around the streets – in Bari and elsewhere – looking for unusual graffiti, which she photographs and collects. She even held an exhibition once and sold everything. Every three or four months, she has one of the photographs blown up to poster size, frames it and hangs it on the wall of her office, replacing the previous one.

That afternoon there was a new one. A wall overhanging a marble staircase, maybe the entrance to a school or another public building. At the top, someone had scrawled in black: *Do you learn from your mistakes or what?* And about eight inches below, in bright blue, the answer: *What.*

"When did this arrive?"

"I brought it in yesterday. Nice, isn't it?"

"Fantastic. I could have written it."

"I already said that before you arrived," Annapaola said.

"All right. I give up. Shall we work?"

"I'll make the coffee," Consuelo said.

After having the coffee, we sat down at the desk and I told Annapaola what we needed to prepare Larocca's defence for the pretrial hearing.

"In a nutshell: everything we can find out about Marelli, Capodacqua, Ladisa and Salvagno. I don't think Capodacqua made it all up on his own initiative or because he was induced in some way by the prosecutors. Our line of defence can't be: It's all lies, it's just a nasty slander. When Capodacqua says that Ladisa boasts a lot, it's likely that he's telling the truth. He may be embellishing it a little, without even realizing it, because he knows it's the kind of thing the Prosecutor's Department likes to hear. Larocca is one of the judges the prosecutors and the police hate the most."

"So how would you like to formulate the defence?"

"We have to evaluate two hypotheses and work on those. The first is that Ladisa was talking rubbish just to boast. The second is that Salvagno was influence peddling to increase his fees, and I think that's the likelier of the two. It wouldn't be the first time: there are a good number of supposed leading lawyers in this city who've got rich by claiming they could oil the wheels and getting paid triple."

"I know who you're referring to," Annapaola said.

Consuelo seemed to be on the verge of asking who these leading lawyers were, but she held back. Another time, maybe.

"Anyway," I resumed, "in order to explore these hypotheses, thinking of the possibility that the case might go to trial, we need to know everything about the four individuals concerned. In particular, we need information about Salvagno's financial situation, and something more about the accident in which he died. Assuming there is any more. But not for now. Right now, to speed things up, I'd like you to prepare me a dossier on Marelli – who's the least important of them from our point of view, because I think he told the truth – and one each on Capodacqua and Ladisa."

"Do you want dossiers you could show to anyone, or complete ones?" Annapaola asked. She meant: dossiers containing only information that could be acquired without breaking the law, or – well, *complete* dossiers.

"Nobody's supposed to see them. I need them to figure out the best way to cross-examine Capodacqua. Providing it suits us to cross-examine him. It might be better not to ask him any questions at all and wait to see how the case develops. Having said that, I have no interest in knowing who your sources are."

Annapaola nodded.

"So we don't inquire into Salvagno's financial situation until later?" Consuelo asked.

"No, because that'll take time. Right now, the urgent thing is to prepare for the hearing."

"But the date hasn't been fixed yet, has it?" Annapaola asked.

"We haven't received anything, but I think we'll get the ruling giving the go-ahead for the hearing in a few days and then we'll know the date."

"So when do you need these dossiers for?"

"No rush. Yesterday."

"Sounds reasonable."

17

Five days later, two things happened. Notification arrived of the ruling granting a pretrial hearing – it was one week away: as I'd foreseen, they hadn't wasted any time – and the existence of the investigation was revealed by a news agency. That meant it would be picked up by various websites, the TV news and finally, the following morning, the daily papers.

There was no way of knowing the source of the press agency item, but evidence pointed to the likelihood that the information had been leaked by somebody involved in the investigation. The clearest proof was that there was no mention of a previous petition for a custody order or its rejection on the grounds of insufficient evidence. As usual, the item was brief and neutral, but the gist of it was clear enough: the head of the appeals division of the Court of Bari was being investigated in Lecce for the crime of judicial corruption. The charge, based on statements by an ex-Mafioso who had turned state's evidence, was that he had taken fifty thousand euros in return for ruling a prisoner's release. Judge Larocca's counsel for the defence was the "well-known Bari lawyer Guido Guerrieri". That mention gave me a few moments of cloying smugness, which fortunately faded quickly.

I was in the office seeing clients when Larocca's call came in.

"Did you read it?"

"I was about to call you."

"Those bastards in the Prosecutor's Department. It was them, I'm sure of it. What do we do, Guido?"

"Could you get here…" – I glanced at my diary, where two appointments were still marked – "… in an hour?"

He said yes. By the time I said goodbye he had already hung up.

An hour later he was sitting in the armchair in my office. The ringing of the entryphone had been so punctual as to make me think that Larocca had come early, maybe immediately after our phone conversation, and had waited outside.

He conveyed a sense of neglect that I hadn't noticed the previous times. He was wearing a rather old-fashioned suit, a purple tie and a blue striped shirt with a white collar.

There aren't many things I boast about, but one of them is never having owned a shirt like that.

"Did you see how they gave it?" He meant: the news.

"I assume they're convinced nobody knows about the custody petition or its rejection."

"Do you think we should try talking to a few journalists and bringing that out into the open? That way people would know the examining magistrate already fucked them over."

Why did it bother me so much when Larocca swore? The words he employed may have been inelegant, but they were in common use. And yet, every time he came out with one, I had the same sensation I would have felt if he had used it during a hearing. Maybe because there was a kind of ostentation, a vulgar bit of role playing, an awkwardness in the pose he was striking. It was an affectation, and it didn't ring true.

"I've thought about that, and I don't think it's a good idea. We'd only be spreading the news even more. People would know that the prosecutor has contested the decision and that there's going to be a pretrial hearing, and the press would go wild. On the day of the hearing, they'd be all over us. I really don't think it's the sensible thing to do. Best to keep it all as quiet as possible."

"And what if they leak the news of the hearing?"

"Then, of course, we'll have to reveal that the custody petition was rejected. But let's wait and see."

Angrily, he passed his hand over his face, screwed up his eyes and clenched his jaw. These gestures, too, had something unnatural about them.

His expression, though, was genuine enough: that of a man terrified at the possibility that what he has constructed in life might fall to pieces, a judge dismayed by the sense of powerlessness that comes from finding yourself implicated in a criminal case. Few people are more upset at being under investigation than magistrates.

"Listen to me, Pierluigi. I know this is all very unpleasant for you, but I'm convinced we'll sort it out. First, I want to complete our inquiries in readiness for the hearing, then—"

"I want to come to Lecce, too. I want to be present at the hearing."

Technically, the defendant's presence isn't necessary at a pretrial hearing. The only people who really have to be there are the judge, the prosecutor, counsel for the defence and the person who is to be examined.

My general feeling is that we lawyers work much better, and more soberly – at least those who understand the meaning of the word – if our clients aren't present in court and we don't have to demonstrate how much we deserve our fee. There are trials in which it's obvious that the defendant will be acquitted. The prosecutor knows it (if he's a real professional he'll ask for acquittal himself), the judge knows it and defence counsel knows it. In such cases, there is no need for long pleas. In fact, there's often no real need for a plea at

161

all. If his client isn't in court, the defence lawyer speaks for a few minutes, just as the judges linger in their chambers for only a few minutes. If, on the other hand, he is in court, we have to justify to him the money we have asked, or will ask, for our work. If you speak for five minutes, it's very likely that he'll question the amount once he's acquitted. That makes it necessary to speak at length and with indignation about what the defendant has unjustly had to suffer so far, along with all kinds of learned legal references and calls for justice. In the end, the result is the same, but the client is happier to pay. Or, if nothing else, puts up less resistance.

"I'm not sure it'd be a good idea. What use would your presence serve? It'd only arouse the journalists' curiosity."

He took three or four short, violent, angry breaths through his nose. "Arseholes, damned arseholes. A judge only has to behave like a judge and not like a servant of the Prosecutor's Department who rubber-stamps everything, and it drives them crazy. You're a lawyer, so you understand me. If a prosecutor screws up – and you know they screw up a lot – I consider it my duty to punish that, not to smooth it over. I've rejected intercepts that were badly done, I've released individuals who in all probability were criminals of the worst kind when the investigations had been improperly and thoughtlessly conducted, with serious legal errors. It's obvious they're out to get me."

"Pierluigi, I understand how perturbed you are..." – *Perturbed?* What is this vocabulary out of a nineteenth-century novel? I asked myself – "... but we have to keep a clear head. It's evident that quite a few people don't like you, and it's evident that the news that there are proceedings against you will please these people – including some magistrates in the Prosecutor's Department. But to go from that to imagining that Capodacqua was prompted to accuse you is

162

quite another matter. I really don't think that should be our line of defence. Not even as a back-up. It's a frontal attack that won't yield any useful results, apart from the fact that it's based on what I think is a false premise: that there's a conspiracy against you. We have to shift our ground. We have to look for alternative explanations, otherwise we'll be on a collision course. It's in our interest to lower the temperature and find a plausible version of events that'll allow you to come out of this business clean, as you should, without the prosecutors feeling that they're likely to lose face. We have to demolish the charge while giving them a get-out. That's always the best way."

The telephone rang. I replied, and said that until further orders – I actually said *further orders*: my vocabulary really was getting out of hand – they weren't to put any calls through to me. As I hung up, I noticed that Larocca's feet were moving – moving of their own volition, he wasn't moving them – in the sequence tip-heel, tip-heel, almost as if they were miming a slightly grotesque walk.

"I'm really pissed off, Guido, I don't just want to *come out* of this business, I don't just want to be exonerated as soon as possible. My name has been bespattered by this garbage, and I want those who are responsible to pay."

It often happens to me when I'm not convinced by something that someone is saying or when I see a false note in it: I allow myself to get distracted. And I have rather a personal way of doing that: I linger over *how* the person is talking rather than *what* he's saying.

If you're going to nitpick, I thought, you can't be bespattered by garbage, only by soft things like mud or – not to put too fine a point on it – shit. Saying that you've been bespattered by garbage is to construct a defective metaphor. To mean something, a metaphor has to have an inner

163

coherence. I can say that a certain investigation is garbage, and I can say that I've been bespattered by mud, meaning that my honour has been tarnished by something, but to talk about being bespattered by garbage means mixing metaphors and creating a small linguistic monster.

All right, I'm sorry. I know it isn't the mark of a balanced mind, but while Larocca was repeating things I had no desire to hear, this was more or less what I was thinking. For at least a couple of minutes, he spoke without knowing that the person he was talking to was somewhere else. At last I returned, and his voice faded back in.

"Guido, we have to prove that the accusations are *false*, not just that they're insufficient for me to be committed to trial. I want whoever set all this up to be tried for slander. I want it to be quite clear at the end of it all that they can't make such serious accusations with impunity."

The problem with clients who are magistrates is that they think they know what has to be done and demand to frame their own defence. But the profession of magistrate and that of defence lawyer are very different. You may be a very good magistrate – Larocca certainly was – and not understand what the work of a lawyer really consists of, day to day and in detail. There are so many small invisible decisions that you have to make; there's your duty towards your client; there are balances to maintain: with judges, with prosecutors, with the police, with the employees of the clerk of the court's office; there are your relations with your colleagues. Magistrates – most of them, at least – have no idea that you think a lot about the judge: who he is, his psychology, what his priorities are: priorities which are sometimes noble but more often very human, if not petty.

When judges are investigated, they realize at last that finding yourself caught up in criminal proceedings can be very unpleasant, and that courtrooms are places it's best to keep away from.

"One thing at a time, Pierluigi. Our first objective is to put an end to these proceedings without too much damage. Which means, before anything else, handling this pretrial hearing as best we can. I understand your reasons, I understand that you have a sacrosanct desire to protect your name and career, but we have to avoid letting our emotions interfere. Let's make sure of the result first. Later, maybe, we can weigh up the possibility of bringing charges for slander. I can tell you right now, though, that I'm not very convinced by the idea."

"Why not?"

"Because if you then end up with no decision being made – which is the likeliest hypothesis, given that criminal intent in this case is going to be hard to prove – there will always be someone who says: Look, Judge Larocca may have been acquitted, but his accuser was also acquitted, so there must be something true in the accusation. You know the script."

He seemed in search of an argument with which to reply, and luckily for me didn't find one. At this point, given that we had nothing more useful to do, my main desire was for him to leave me alone. Clients can be troublesome. Clients who are magistrates can be *very* troublesome.

So I decided to trust in my body language and stood up, trying to convey the idea of a friendly goodbye. It took him a few seconds, but finally he understood and also stood up.

I placed a hand on his shoulder as I guided him towards the door. "Within a couple of days, I'll have personal dossiers on Capodacqua and Marelli and I'll be able to prepare my cross-examination. If I need anything, I'll call you. The hearing is in a week. We have plenty of time."

18

Annapaola came into my office with her usual big bag, the one from which she had taken the baseball bat, plus a plastic bag from a supermarket, full of white and brown paper packages.

"Sorry to burst in here with the food, but I didn't want to leave this stuff attached to my bike."

"What's so precious in there?"

"Cardoncelli mushrooms, soft cheese filled with butter, and truffles from Murgia."

"I didn't even know there were truffles in Murgia."

"The area around Castel del Monte is full of them, but almost nobody knows that."

"And why are you going around with truffles, cardoncelli mushrooms and soft cheese filled with butter?"

"Gifts from a friend who's also a client, to repay a kindness. I solved a problem for him. Tonight I'll have to eat them."

"There are worse misfortunes. Cardoncelli are my favourite mushrooms, I like them more than porcini."

"Of course, there's no comparison. They're firmer and tastier."

She realized she was still holding the shopping bag. She put it down on the floor and also divested herself of the big bag across her shoulder. "As long as you don't get the wrong idea, I'll invite you."

"How do you mean?"

"I'll invite you to dinner at my house and we'll eat some of this stuff. But no sex."

"You don't beat about the bush, do you?"

"No, not really."

I said all right, I accepted the invitation and the proviso, even though it wasn't so good for my self-esteem. I asked her where she lived – I realized at that moment that it was something I'd never known – but when I heard the address I couldn't hide my slight surprise.

"In the San Paolo district?"

"Yes. Is that a problem?"

"No, it's just that I wasn't expecting—"

"You weren't expecting me to live in the Cep."

The San Paolo district, better known as the Cep or, to its inhabitants, simply "the Neighbourhood", has for many years been synonymous with urban decay, marginalization, organized and disorganized crime in Bari. Things have changed a little lately, but Annapaola was right. I hadn't expected her to be living there.

"If you come by car, call me when you arrive and I'll open the garage. Otherwise, come by taxi."

"I'll come by taxi."

"That's best. I'll expect you at nine."

"Shall I bring wine or a dessert?"

"Don't bring anything. I have wine, and I'll make dessert. Now let's get to work."

She took some folders from her bag and put them on my desk, one beside the other.

"I've made three dossiers, one for Marelli, one for Capodacqua and the last for Ladisa. There isn't much in the first one. A perfectly normal legal clerk, no criminal record, no secrets. I didn't find anything interesting. He really is ill: he's in hospital, and I don't think he'll be able to appear at the hearing."

"In that case, the judge will adjourn and we'll hear his testimony in the hospital. What can you tell me about the other two?"

Annapaola assumed a didactic tone. "Rocco Ladisa, known as Il Flippato. There's a story behind that nickname. Specializes in moneylending, an activity in which he launders money from drugs and extortion. Crazy about bodybuilding, somewhat inclined to megalomania and fits of temper. Among other things, he's suspected of having killed a young man in the Casamassima area. The cause of the quarrel that led to the murder is said to have been a question of who should give way to whom when leaving the car park of a nightclub. The case was shelved for lack of evidence. Not a very nice person at all. Everything I found out about him is in here. The sentences underlined are confidential information whose reliability I don't think I can guarantee. Then there's our Salvatore Capodacqua, known as Molletta, after the flick knife he's carried with him ever since he was a boy. Starts his career at the age of fourteen with car theft, bag snatching and robberies. Before long he steps up a notch and gets into the big time – drugs and extortion – while still a teenager. Joins the Mob and becomes one of the trusted men of Trentadue Cosimo, known as the Viceroy, undisputed boss of the Libertà district. Involved in a number of violent acts, and probably has at least three murders and a number of kneecappings on his conscience. Decides to turn state's evidence last year, after being arrested for various serious charges and spending a not very pleasant vacation in maximum security. He's considered fairly reliable as ex-Mafiosi go; among other things, he's relatively well spoken. In the dossier you'll also find a bit of information about some minor aspects of his criminal record. Things that may have escaped the notice of the Prosecutor's Department and may help you in your cross-examination."

"Did you find out anything about Salvagno's fatal accident?"

"A genuine accident. I talked to the inspector from the traffic police who was called to the scene. When I asked him if there was any likelihood the episode could have been criminally motivated, he almost laughed in my face. I haven't made any enquiries yet about Salvagno's financial situation because you told me it wasn't so urgent. Any questions?"

"I'll have a glance at the dossiers and tell you if everything is clear."

"Needless to say, these documents aren't for exhibit. I must run now, I have guests for dinner."

"See you at nine, then?"

"At nine." After she'd put one bag over her shoulder and picked up the other bag with the food, she added: "I heard a good one today about lawyers. You'll like it. A lawyer and an engineer are on a beach in the Maldives, sipping a cocktail. The lawyer says, 'I'm here because my house burnt down and with it all I possessed. The insurance company paid up and I've changed my life.' The engineer replies, 'What a coincidence. I'm here because my house and all I had were destroyed by a flood. The insurance company paid up and I've also changed my life.' The lawyer looks puzzled. 'There's something I don't understand,' he says. 'What?' asks the engineer. 'How the hell,' says the lawyer, 'did you manage to start a flood?'"

"How nice to belong to a group that's the object of universal respect and admiration," I said with a laugh.

"Bye for now, Avvocato, see you later for the cardoncelli party."

*

When he heard the address, the taxi driver turned and looked at me. "Are you sure?"

"Yes, of course."

"It's in the middle of San Paolo."

"I know," I replied, in the tone of someone who prefers to drop the subject.

He hesitated for another moment or two, then shrugged and started the engine. About twenty minutes later, he dropped me outside a fairly new apartment building, in the part of the district that was closest to the airport. Outside the front door stood a boy.

"Are you Avvocato Guerrieri?" he asked.

"Yes, why?"

He opened the door, motioned me to go in, walked me to the lift, said, "Top floor," then left without another word.

On the landing, before I could ring the bell, the door opened by itself, as if there were an invisible butler to greet me. From inside I could hear Tom Waits singing "Ol' '55". The volume was turned down and Annapaola's voice sounded over the music.

"Come in. The door closes by itself." Which did in fact happen, once I was inside. The place I found myself in was an open space of at least eight hundred square feet, with a large window – in front of which stood a table with a rough wooden top and metal legs – from where you could see the airport and a thousand lights in the distance. Everywhere, shelves filled with books. No overhead lighting. The illumination came from spotlights placed on the floor and the walls. A blue tapestry covered almost the whole of the right-hand wall; beneath it, an old-looking leather sofa on which an animal lay dozing, an animal that looked like a cat but was as big as a cocker spaniel.

Annapaola emerged from a door on the side opposite

that of the tapestry, the sofa and the cat. She was wearing her usual jeans and a black sleeveless top that revealed more than I'd have liked, considering the proviso I'd agreed to a few hours earlier.

"I like punctual people," she said, wiping her hands on a dishcloth and coming closer to give me a kiss.

"Are there ghosts?"

She looked at me for a few moments before realizing that I was referring to the opening and closing of the door. "Oh, yes. I have a slight obsession with home automation. Everything here can be controlled remotely. And if anyone comes in when I'm not here, I get a video of it live on my mobile phone."

"And that?" I said, pointing to the cat.

"Do you like him? He's a Maine Coon, an American breed. A rather large cat."

"Rather large is an understatement. He's beautiful, but I wouldn't like to be alone with him. What's his name? Mephistopheles?"

"When he was given to me, I thought for a long time about what name to give him. In the end, I decided to call him Cat."

"That must have taken a bit of effort."

She laughed. "It's a kind of quotation. *Breakfast at Tiffany's*, don't you remember?"

"Right, I'm losing points, it's official. I can smell truffles."

"Let me tell you the menu: fresh pasta with cardoncelli mushrooms and truffles; soft cheese with truffles; fig tart with cream ice cream."

"Excellent. And what does the kitten eat? Do you leave live sheep around the apartment and let him get on with it?"

"Actually, Cat's like a dog. He even eats pasta and pizza. And drinks beer."

"You're joking, of course."

"Cat!"

The animal raised itself, got down off the sofa, and trotted over to its mistress.

"That's the first time in my life I've seen a feline" – I found it hard to call him a cat – "obey an order."

"Come with me," she said, addressing the lynx-like creature, which promptly followed her. We went into the kitchen, where Annapaola took a can of Peroni from a large bow-fronted orange refrigerator and poured a little into a bowl on the floor.

"Here's your beer, Cat."

The animal lapped it all up with gusto. Annapaola drank what was left in the can.

"Do you want one?" she asked me.

I replied that I'd rather move straight on to the wine and, as she turned to uncork a bottle of red Castel del Monte, I noticed the tattoo – an image of Betty Boop – she had on one shoulder, which continued under the line of her top. I looked away and tried to concentrate on the kitchen. The furniture was white and orange, like the refrigerator; there was an old table with a marble top; hanging on one wall were chilli peppers, dried tomatoes and strings of garlic; next to them was a poster: Frank Lloyd Wright's house over the waterfall.

"Nice poster."

"I took that photograph."

"Were you there? It's a place I've always wanted to go."

"I was taken there by a girlfriend who taught the history of architecture." She broke off and looked at me. "Why are you looking at me like that? Oh, because of the girlfriend. Yes, it's true, I also like women. Maybe *especially* women, but let's say I haven't really clarified my ideas on the subject.

Which sometimes creates problems. You like them, too, don't you?"

"I seem to remember that I do. I'm just a little out of practice."

"Seeing that place was one of the most emotional things that's ever happened to me. Wright was a genius. Well, enough of that. Let's eat."

We had dinner by the window, which offered a spectacular view of the planes landing and taking off.

"You must have wondered why I live here."

"Well, yes."

"I couldn't have afforded an apartment like this in other parts of the city. Plus, I like the idea of being ten minutes from the airport and from the possibility, even if it's only theoretical, of flying in two hours to Paris, Berlin or London, where I lived for almost three years."

"But you like it here?"

"The neighbours have adopted me," she said, and I thought of the boy who had greeted me outside the front door. "I like it here, yes."

"What were you doing in London?"

"I did all kinds of things. Personal trainer, softball coach, I collaborated with a private detective agency and wrote for a few magazines. But you know what the most interesting job was?"

I shook my head.

"Hotel porter. You learn a lot about people, and your colleagues are often really unusual characters, especially the older ones. The best psychologists I've met in my life have been waiters, police officers and hotel porters."

We continued chatting, eating and drinking. I like women who can have a meal without counting the calories.

"The bottle's empty," she said. "Shall I open another one?"

"Better not, or we'll feel it's our duty to drink it all."

"You're right, especially as I'm going to make you sample a special whisky with the dessert."

She went into the kitchen to get the tart with the ice cream and I spent the time inspecting the bookshelves. There were many volumes on art and architecture, novels by writers from the Far East, comic books, sports books, collections of poetry, lots of DVDs, manuals of psychology, manuals of photography, texts on the training of animals, old school exercise books, photograph albums: a kind of healthy lack of order. While Cat watched me without any hostility from the sofa, I immersed myself in the reading of a poem.

"What are you reading?" Annapaola asked, coming up behind me.

"Sylvia Plath, 'Love Letter'."

"*Not easy to state the change you made. If I'm alive now, then I was dead,*" she recited from memory. "One of my favourites."

After the dessert, she opened a bottle of Scotch whisky of a brand I'd never seen before.

"I'm no expert, but I think it's very good," I said after tasting it.

"I should hope so, too."

"Why?"

"Because that bottle was another gift from a client. When he gave it to me, he told me it was *very* special. Being a *very* unrefined girl, I looked for the price on the Internet."

"And how much does it cost?"

"About seven hundred euros, maybe a little more."

"Excuse me?"

"You heard me the first time."

"Now I won't be able to drink it."

"Are you crazy? I was just waiting for the opportunity to open it. That's what taste is: knowing how much it costs

174

and drinking it all the same. Of course I'd never buy it, but once it's there I think it's completely immoral to keep it. I remember those bottles of spirits in my grandparents' house, preserved intact for decades until they were undrinkable. It made me very sad."

She broke off for a few seconds and, maybe without even realizing it, made a gesture with her hand as if to dismiss an unpleasant thought or memory.

"No, no," she concluded. "Let's drink it without mercy."

Absolutely.

Beyond the window, the lights of the airport and the ones further away flickered like earthly constellations. Annapaola told me she had played softball in the first division for three years, that she had graduated in archaeology and that she still had her press card – which had proved useful in her work as a private detective. She added that she didn't want to this evening, but another time she would tell me why she had stopped writing for newspapers.

"How come you're not smoking?" I asked after a while.

"You know the last cigarette I smoked was the one in your office?"

"Why?"

"I don't know. When I left, it occurred to me that you'd been very kind to let me smoke – you *are* a kind person, which is something I like in a man – and that I'd been rude to take advantage of your kindness. I told myself that I'd been thinking of quitting for ages, and to cut a long story short – I never follow a rational progression in anything – when I left your office I threw away my tobacco, my filters and my papers. It doesn't even bother me very much. I guess the time had come."

We were silent for a while. It was better to stop with the whisky: I wasn't sure I had the situation under control. I sighed, assuming a judicious expression. "I did the right thing not to bring my car," I said. "With what I've drunk, I'd risk a life sentence if the traffic police got hold of me. I'll call a taxi and go, because it's late and—"

"Stay a while longer," she cut in, and before I could reply she stood up and sat down astride my legs, resting her arms on my shoulders. It isn't at all common for a beautiful woman to be even more beautiful from so close up. "I know what you're thinking."

"Oh yes?"

"You're thinking about what I told you in the office a few hours ago. That thing about sex."

"Actually, that too—"

"I've changed my mind."

19

The evening before the pretrial hearing I got a call from Antonio Lopedote, my colleague who was defending Ladisa and his wife. He's a good boy (a sign of the passing years is when you call someone who, like you, is pushing fifty a boy), a dignified lawyer and a genuinely nice person, always polite and well disposed towards his fellow man despite being the size of a bear. At the time, he was mainly defending Mafiosi, and I would occasionally wonder how he reconciled his mild disposition and his courtesy with the type of clients who frequented his office.

"I'm sorry, Guido, I'm calling you about tomorrow's hearing."

"I bet you're not looking forward to it either."

"It's not just that I'm not looking forward to it. I'm not sure I can even be there. Two or three things have come up in the last few hours and I can't get away from Bari tomorrow. You're going, aren't you?"

"I have to."

"In that case, could you deputize for me? I like what you do very much."

I let a few seconds pass. It wasn't a good idea to mix positions. It might create some conflicts of interest in the defence, and above all it might further damage Larocca's image. I thought about how to tell Lopedote, without offending him, that he'd made a bit of a gaffe in asking me that.

"Antonio, maybe it's best not. Your clients' positions might theoretically be in conflict with mine. I don't think he'd appreciate it."

It was his turn to pause for a few seconds. When he spoke, he sounded slightly embarrassed. "You're right. I shouldn't even have asked you. I didn't think it through."

"Don't worry. Look for a colleague in Lecce who can deputize for you officially. I'll see to the rest." I didn't think it was appropriate to go into detail about the evidence I'd be using for the cross-examinations, or how I'd got hold of it.

"All right, I'll make a couple of phone calls. I'm sure I'll find someone."

"Antonio?"

"Yes?"

"Have you ever seen Capodacqua in court?"

"A couple of weeks ago. The Prosecutor's Department brought him out to testify in that trial of the prison guards who were dealing drugs in cahoots with the inmates. I think it was the first time he'd appeared in public as a prosecution witness. I don't know if you remember the trial."

"Yes, I do. And how did he handle himself?"

"He's a tough nut. He has a good memory, he isn't stupid, and as far as I can see he tells the truth. I didn't cross-examine him because what he said didn't concern my client, but I heard how he answered my colleagues. What's your opinion of this case?"

"What do your clients say?"

"I never ask my clients what they've done and haven't done. I sleep easier if I don't know. Ladisa and his wife say Capodacqua is a rat, that he makes things up to get the benefits. The usual thing. The woman told me once that Capodacqua had brought the judge into dishonour, but you know as well as I do that can mean whatever you want it to mean."

"You're right. I find it hard to believe that Larocca is corrupt. He may not be very pleasant, and I'm sure that the Prosecutor's Department and the police hate him, maybe even with good reason, but I'd be surprised if he'd taken a bribe to throw a decision. I find it equally unrealistic, though, to imagine that it's all an invention of Capodacqua's."

"So what do you think?"

"Did you know Salvagno well?"

"We did a few trials together. We weren't exactly friends, but he was a sociable guy. I felt bad when I heard about the accident."

"Did you ever hear him boast about his friendships with judges?"

Lopedote thought this over for a while. "Actually, he boasted of knowing a whole lot of people."

"Did he ever name any names?"

"No." I seemed to see him slowly shaking his big bear head as that unpleasant idea took shape. "Do you think he might have asked his clients for money, saying he had to pay the judges?"

"That would explain everything. Although, of course, it wouldn't be right to pin the blame on someone who's dead and can't defend himself."

"Strange, though, that they haven't petitioned for a custody order."

I was about to reply: oh, but they did. At the last moment, with the words already emerging from my mouth, I realized he didn't know that and I shouldn't have known it either.

"You're right," I said. "I hope I'll get a better idea of their strategy tomorrow."

*

179

I woke up with a headache. A dull pain between temple and eye, the kind I hadn't had for quite a while. The kind that makes it impossible to stay in bed. You have to get up, even though it's early in the morning (this time it really was early in the morning; 5.30 to be precise), eat something, take a couple of pills and wait for it to pass. That usually works, but all day you carry a feeling of menace with you, like a shadow hanging over you.

What's more, even the atmospheric conditions joined in.

When I'd gone to Lecce two weeks earlier, the weather had been wonderful. Now it was May, but looking outside it seemed like late October, maybe even November. It was cold, the sky was grey and dirty, there was a blustery wind and intermittent rain. The air was opaque. The spring was sick, and it looked as if nothing would be as it was before.

Consuelo was supposed to be coming with me, but at 7.30 she phoned to say she had a fever and was aching all over. It happens, in winter, I replied, advising her to take care and thinking all the while that I really didn't feel like driving nearly a hundred miles and handling that hearing all by myself.

I tried to cheer myself up by thinking of the *pasticciotti*, but it wasn't the right morning for that.

Just to have some company, I was on the verge of calling Larocca and telling him that I'd changed my mind, that it'd be better if he was there, too, that I could pick him up from his apartment within fifteen minutes, and so on. But then I dismissed the idea, took from the wardrobe the raincoat that I'd been convinced I'd put away for the summer, now that May was here, and even grabbed an umbrella. By the time I left home, I was in a foul mood.

After half an hour on the road, the wind dropped and the rain came pouring down, heavy and regular. I had to set the windscreen wipers going at maximum speed. It was November, there could be no more doubt about it. I listened to a news bulletin in which the weather expert informed me that it would rain in the morning over the southern Adriatic. I thanked him for the confidential information and switched to a local radio station that was broadcasting a programme of Italian music from the 1970s evocatively entitled *Elephant's Foot*: a wretched potpourri of culture and customs.

The presenter's name was Cosimo. He spoke an elementary, hypnotic language characterized by a radical and ruthless avoidance of the rules of grammar. There were dedications, including one I'll never forget: "This song is dedicated to little Lady Diana, who was born yesterday, and to her lovely parents Vito and Maddalena. We have her dad Vito on the phone. What's the child's real name, Vito?" A stunned pause, as if the man was thinking his questioner must be a bit dumb and that was why he asked stupid questions, then: "Lady Diana. That's her name. Lady Diana Recchimurzo, because I'm Vito Recchimurzo."

Vito Recchimurzo, I want to be like you when I grow up, I said out loud. One of the symptoms of my unbalanced state of mind is my habit of talking to presenters and participants in radio programmes that I listen to when I'm alone in my car. Well, sometimes also when I'm not alone, as some of my girlfriends could tell you, and even my ex-wife.

Listening to that wonderful programme distracted me from the bad weather, external and internal, partly because I started thinking hard about the lyrics of the songs.

One song had been haunting me more than any other since my teenage years: "I untie the plaits of the horses, they run." This is hard to figure out. Firstly, do horses have plaits, which can then be untied? Secondly, do these particular horses in the song run *after* their plaits have been untied, or do the songwriter or the singer, both experienced riders, untie the horses' plaits *while* the animals are running? In another song, the story of a love affair that went wrong, the lyrics ended with a desperate plea from the abandoned male to the abandoned female (who, it was clear, wasn't the subtlest of women, having among other things "the body of someone who's said yes too often"): "My darling, in your room the bed is just as you left it." Does that mean, I used to wonder, that the sheets have never been changed? Which would give a dark, decadent – and somewhat dirty – feel to the whole thing. Or is the singer just referring to the position of the bed, in which case, what's so romantic about that?

Then in a peerless crescendo, DJ Cosimo put on the string intro before the first lines of *Ti amo* by Umberto Tozzi. *The Da Vinci Code* is an easy crossword puzzle in comparison with the incomprehensible lines of that song. For the umpteenth time, I wondered about the meaning of "The love we make is like a butterfly beating its wings as it dies", and for the umpteenth time I was troubled by an image that seems to refer to an ancient Egyptian curse: "Open the door to a tissue-paper warrior". By the time I changed stations, in search of news and better grammar, my headache had passed and my mood, despite the rain that kept stubbornly falling, had improved quite a bit.

So I started to think about the work awaiting me. Cross-examining ex-Mafiosi who've turned state's evidence is something I rarely do, because I rarely appear for the defence in trials dealing with organized crime. This is no reflection on my colleagues who do it regularly – some are very good and perfectly respectable – but the type of defendants you get in those trials are the kind of people I prefer not to have in my office.

In any case, cross-examining one of these people isn't easy: it requires balance and detachment. Usually they're telling the truth, by and large, and going straight on the attack, as many defence lawyers do, is almost always pointless: it gets a harsh reaction from prosecutors and conveys the unpleasant impression that the defender is very close to his clients' mindset and the criminal culture to which they belong. You have to be surgical. You have to isolate the parts that are questionable, so that in the end the judge can say that *those* specific statements are unreliable, without being forced to state that the witness is unreliable *in toto*.

Just before Brindisi, the rain eased off, and after about ten minutes stopped altogether. The sky was still grey and hostile, but at least I no longer had the feeling I was a prisoner in my car. Being slightly ahead of schedule, I decided to stop at a service station cafeteria for a cappuccino.

It had recently been renovated, and yet it looked scruffy and neglected. Counter, shelves, chairs and tables seemed to have just come out of their wrapping after being sent to the wrong place. The barman was a man a few years older than me, sad-looking, badly shaved, with a purple uniform and a cap of the same colour, worn askew. The place was half-empty. There was a labourer having coffee at the counter and a couple in their thirties who seemed as out of place as the furniture. The two of them were sitting at a table, dressed in inappropriately light clothes given the atmospheric conditions, as if they had been surprised by the winter on the way to their holiday destination. The woman was doing most of the talking, in a noticeable Roman accent and – how shall I put it? – not exactly under her breath.

"I told you, darling, that it was stupid to come here in May. The weather in spring is changeable, that's only natural, and you can't be sure of getting any sun. But it's always the same, we always have to do what your mother says, and frankly I'm fed up with it, because it seems to me you're big enough now not to ask her what we should do and where we should go if we want to take a week's break, because—"

"I'm sorry, darling, but—"

"Don't interrupt me, darling, you always do that, just like your mother, always talking and never letting other people talk, it's a question of respect, which I think that if a couple are going to work that's what they need, respect, and their own space without mothers interfering, it's just politeness, but I don't think your mother is—"

"Darling—"

"Dammit, darling, I told you not to interrupt me, dammit, it's just a question of politeness, I almost feel like giving her a video call, your mother, and letting her see the weather we have here in Puglia, she says go to Puglia where it's always lovely, you eat well, and don't spend so much, and then—"

"Darling, please don't raise your voice, people can hear."

"I'M NOT RAISING MY VOICE and if you don't shut up I'll headbutt you because you're pissing me off, too, making me talk like this, I'm not used to using this kind of language."

I exchanged a glance with the labourer as he walked out. I would have liked to go up to the poor husband and pat him on the back, but then it struck me that wasn't such a good idea, because then the woman might give me the headbutt she'd just mentioned, and that it was best to finish my cappuccino, pay and continue on my way.

It was about 9.15 when I walked into the small courtroom, which smelt of paper and dust. The hearing was due to start at 9.30.

For some time now I'd been getting to places early. There must have been some complex psychological explanation, but I wasn't capable of grasping it.

The only people there were two stenographers, who were setting up their equipment and who stared at me for a few moments, slightly puzzled. The atmosphere of criminal courts is like a village club. When a newcomer arrives he sticks out like a sore thumb.

I looked around. The decor was bare: the judge's bench, the bench for the prosecution and the bench for the defence, a few seats, a TV monitor for the long-distance examination of Capodacqua.

I sat down, emptied my bag and wondered what the local custom was – that is, if the time indicated on all the notices, 9.30, was a friendly suggestion, a hypothesis or a strict obligation. Before long, the local lawyer who was deputizing for Lopedote arrived. He asked me to confirm that I would handle everything, then started reading the newspaper and didn't say another word.

Another couple of minutes passed and Capodacqua's lawyer appeared, rather breathless. He was a young guy from Rome who had somehow ended up representing a presumed former Mafioso from Bari. He seemed a little disorientated: the lawyer who'd been handling the brief so far had been unable to get away at the last moment, and he was deputizing for him. He asked me how long the hearing would last, because he was hoping he'd have time to catch some plane or other. I told him I didn't know, but that maybe the judge would have an answer to his question. He didn't catch the irony.

Then the prosecutor arrived.

She belonged to a very different category from that of the young Roman lawyer. She was a woman a few years younger than me, not beautiful but with intelligent, ironic blue-grey eyes that occasionally gleamed in rather a threatening way. The petition for the custody order had been signed by two men, the assistant prosecutor and a deputy, the same men who had taken the statements of Capodacqua and Marelli. So who was she? Was she there only for the hearing, or had the brief changed hands? That would explain some rather obscure aspects of the prosecution strategy. I would try to inquire cautiously about this point.

I introduced myself – her name was Patrizia Greco – and we shook hands.

"Are there many cases being heard today, Dottoressa?"

"Only this one: it's a specially called hearing." She had a slight Lecce accent, which is a bit like Sicilian and very different from the accent of Bari.

At exactly 9.30, the clerk of the court entered, followed by the judge, also a woman: Giuliana Costa, the same one who had rejected the custody petition. She was short, slight and blonde, with glasses and a face like a ferret. She sat down, said good morning without looking at anybody in particular, opened the case file, and we started.

20

The introductory formalities – actually just a check that the notifications had been sent out correctly – took no more than a few minutes. Then the hearing proper began with a surprise.

The prosecutor informed the court that Marelli, whose illness had been the reason for this hearing being requested in the first place, had died the previous Sunday.

I know it was a stupid thought, or rather, a vulgar and even rather horrible one, but I couldn't help it: Salvagno's practice, where Marelli had worked up until a few months earlier, must have been jinxed. I felt a little ashamed and forced myself to follow what was happening in the courtroom. The judge was speaking.

"We take note of this. In that case, I think we should proceed with the examination of the witness Capodacqua, who I believe is present in a safe location—"

The prosecutor broke in before she could finish the sentence. "Your honour, before proceeding with the examination of Capodacqua, I have a request to make."

The judge made a slight, almost imperceptible gesture of irritation. "Go on."

"As I have just informed the court, Signor Marelli died two days ago. The death occurred after this pretrial hearing had already been granted, having been requested in a timely manner by my office. Given that the examination of Marelli's testimony will no longer be possible, I ask that the statements made to my office by the said Marelli during the preliminary investigations be declared usable for the purposes of this hearing and admitted in evidence."

"Are there any observations by the defence?" the judge said, addressing me and Lopedote's deputy, whose name I hadn't caught. She spoke with her head bent over the sheets of paper she had in front of her. The other lawyer said no, thank you, he had no observations. I said yes, thank you, I had a few observations.

"First of all, let me say, in a few words, what I'm *not* going to talk about. I'm not going to talk about the timeliness or otherwise of the petition for a pretrial hearing, because I don't have sufficient elements at the moment to do so. Only some of the papers have been filed along with the petition, and in any case I don't consider that this is the right time and place. I'm sure that in the trial phase, we will be able to evaluate if Marelli's serious medical condition had already been known about for some time and if therefore the prosecutor had *for some time* been able to foresee that the testimony would be unrepeatable and had delayed formulating a request for a pretrial hearing. Because if that should emerge, it would be necessary to exclude the applicability of article 512 of the code of procedure, in other words, the possibility of reading the transcripts of statements made by Marelli. But I repeat: that's a subject that will have to be confronted in any possible future trial. The purpose of today's hearing, a typical pretrial procedure, is simply to bring forward if possible the examination of the witnesses, not to bring forward the *trial* and all the questions of admissibility that will characterize it. I will take the liberty of reminding you that article 512 concerns the *reading* of the statement whose repetition has become impossible, not the admission of the corresponding transcripts as evidence. The decision on this point rests solely with the trial judge. I ask therefore that the prosecutor's request be denied. Or rather, to be more precise – this not being the place to tackle the point – I ask that said request be met with a declaration that there is no need to give a decision."

"Does the prosecutor wish to add anything?"

Greco leaped impatiently to her feet. From the expression of those not very reassuring eyes, even before she said anything, it was clear that she hadn't liked my argument.

"Your Honour, the matter is very simple, despite the attempt by the defence to make it pointlessly complicated. This hearing is an anticipation of the trial. It was expected that the aforesaid Marelli would be examined today. This examination is no longer possible because the individual concerned has died. Therefore it is necessary to admit Marelli's statements into the case file of this hearing, which will then become part of the case file of the trial, in accordance with article 512 of the code of procedure. I repeat my request."

The judge looked at her and then me for a few seconds, still in the same way, with her eyes raised but her head bent over her papers. Finally, she straightened up and dictated her ruling.

"The judge, having heard both parties on the question of the admission, according to article 512 of the code of criminal procedure, of the transcripts of statements made by Nicola Marelli, and having noted that this is not the place for presenting such a request, being a judicial matter that strictly belongs to the trial judge to resolve, for these reasons declares that there is no decision to be made and asks that we proceed. Let us move on to the examination of the witness, if we can make the connection."

The monitor – not exactly a state-of-the-art piece of equipment – emitted a crackle, and the washed-out image of a room all in shades of grey appeared. It looked like a black-and-white

Bulgarian TV programme from the Sixties. Not that I've ever watched Bulgarian TV, either in the Sixties or more recently, that's just to give an idea.

The scene was being captured from a high angle, the camera having been placed about two metres from the floor. A man with not very much hair was sitting at a desk with his back to the camera, slightly stooped. On the right, another man, in profile. The one with his back to the camera was Capodacqua, the one in profile the clerk of the court.

"Can you hear us?" the judge asked, speaking into the microphone.

"Affirmative, Your Honour. We can hear you and see you in our monitor."

"Can you tell us who you are?"

"I am Clerk of the Court Baldi."

"Can you attest the particulars of the person who is with you?"

The clerk of the court read Capodacqua's particulars and confirmed that it was indeed him. The scene, as I'd felt before in similar cases, struck me as taking place in a parallel, unreal dimension.

"Can you confirm that all precautions have been taken to ensure the correct functioning of the remote examination?"

"Yes, I can."

"Signor Capodacqua, can you hear me?"

"Yes, Your Honour. Good morning."

"Do you have a lawyer, Signor Capodacqua?"

"Avvocato Carrozza…"

"Who isn't present today, and has been replaced by Avvocato… I'm sorry, Avvocato, can you repeat your name?"

"Florio, Your Honour."

"Avvocato Florio is here, deputizing for Avvocato Carrozza. Do you have any objections?"

"No, no. It's fine, Avvocato Carrozza already told me."

"Then we may begin."

I stood up before she could give the floor to the prosecutor. She looked at me with a questioning and slightly frosty expression. She had already conceded one point to me, that look said, but that didn't mean I should abuse her patience.

"I beg your pardon, Your Honour, I'd like to make a suggestion to simplify the hearing."

"Go on, Avvocato."

"I declare my willingness to admit in evidence all the transcripts of statements made by Signor Capodacqua during the preliminary investigations. I still have to proceed with the cross-examination, but I think that in this way, if the prosecutor agrees, the hearing could be speeded up."

"What do the prosecutor and Ladisa's counsel have to say?"

Lopedote's substitute, after exchanging a glance with me, said he had no objection. Greco appeared taken by surprise: she hadn't been expecting such a request – just as she hadn't expected my previous objection. She leafed through the case file she had in front of her, just to gain a few seconds, though less excitably than before.

"No, Your Honour, I have no objections to the admission proposed by counsel for the defence. But I still wish to examine Signor Capodacqua, because there are some points I need to clarify with him."

"Then let's admit those transcripts and the prosecutor may proceed."

In actual fact, there weren't many points to clarify, and most of those were of little importance. Everything Capodacqua had to say, from the point of view of the prosecution, he had already said during the preliminary investigations. Once it was over, the judge gave me the floor.

"Go ahead, Avvocato…"

"Guerrieri, Your Honour."

"Yes, I'm sorry. Avvocato Guerrieri, proceed with your cross-examination."

"Good morning, Signor Capodacqua, I'm Avvocato Guerrieri, representing Judge Larocca."

"Good morning, Avvocato."

"I'm going to ask you a few questions. If they aren't clear, don't hesitate to tell me, and I'll rephrase them."

"All right."

"So, Signor Capodacqua, you have stated that your friend Ladisa told you he had in his pocket—"

"At his disposal. He said at his disposal."

"Right, I'm sorry. You said that Ladisa told you that he had members of the state police, carabinieri and even judges at his disposal. Did he also mention the customs police?"

He hesitated for a few moments. "Maybe, yes. I don't remember if he said anything about the customs police."

"Do you remember his exact words?"

"The thing is, he didn't just say it once. He was always boasting that he had cops – excuse the term – and judges at his disposal."

"Do you remember the first time he said this, that he expressed this concept?"

"No, Avvocato, how could I?"

"You don't remember the first time he said this. You told the prosecutor about a dinner at which Ladisa told you—"

"Yes, a dinner at Il Pescatore."

"I'd be grateful to you, if only to make the work of the stenographers a little easier, if you gave me the chance to finish my questions."

"I'm sorry."

"As I was saying, you told the prosecutor about a dinner at a restaurant called Il Pescatore, in the course of which

Ladisa told you about a presumed episode of corruption involving Judge Larocca. Before that dinner, though, he had already told you about these police officers and judges *at his disposal*. Is that correct?"

"I think so, yes."

"Can you remember any specific occasion on which, before that dinner, Ladisa told you this? In other words, the fact that he had judges *at his disposal*?"

"He talked about it… he talked about it lots of times—"

"I repeat, can you remember a *specific* occasion on which, before that dinner, Ladisa told you that particular thing?"

"It must have been at another dinner. Like I said, we often went to dinner together."

"You're an intelligent man, Signor Capodacqua. So you understand perfectly well that saying 'it must have been' isn't a factual reply. It's a hypothesis. Correct me if I haven't understood: you are unable to indicate a specific occasion, previous to that dinner, on which Ladisa spoke of his relations with members of the various law enforcement agencies and the bench?"

Greco rose to her feet. "Objection, Your Honour. Counsel for the defence is arguing with the witness, but not asking any question."

I was about to reply but the judge stopped me with a gesture of her hand.

"Counsel for the defence wants to know from the witness whether or not he is able to indicate a specific conversation on the subject of *judges at his disposal* prior to the dinner in that restaurant. That is certainly a question. Please reply, Signor Capodacqua."

He shook his head, or at least so it seemed from the blurred image on the screen. "No, I don't really remember a particular time."

"Before that evening, had Ladisa ever talked to you about Judge Larocca?"

"No, I don't think so."

"After that evening did he talk to you again about Judge Larocca?"

"He dropped a few hints. He'd say things like: *my friend, our friend*."

"Can you tell us more precisely when – after the conversation at Il Pescatore – Ladisa spoke to you again, even if only in hints, about Judge Larocca?"

Capodacqua had his back to the camera, but the gesture of impatience that preceded the answer was perceptible all the same. "Avvocato, if I'd known then that I was going to cooperate, I'd have kept a diary and written down all the things I was supposed to say. Oh, yes, I'd have kept a diary if I'd known that I was meant to cooperate."

"Please don't become impatient, Signor Capodacqua." Actually, I wanted him to get impatient and lower his guard a little. A good way to induce someone to do something is to tell him not to do it. "So you aren't able to tell us on what occasions Ladisa again spoke about Larocca, if only in hints that you had to interpret. Is that correct?"

"Yes."

"Did Ladisa ever talk to you about other specific instances of corruption of public officials?"

"Yes."

"Can you tell us about them?"

"Objection, Your Honour," Greco said, with a hint of nervousness in her voice. "The question is irrelevant to the facts we are discussing and may damage the confidentiality of other proceedings."

"Sustained. Go on to another question, Avvocato."

I pretended to be upset and disappointed. "The question

was formulated in order to evaluate the credibility of the witness according to article 194, paragraph 2 of the code of procedure, credibility we have reason to doubt. But of course I have no intention of questioning your decision, Your Honour. I'll move on to another subject. Signor Capodacqua, is it correct to say that in the criminal circles in which you have moved, people often have nicknames?"

"Yes."

"Did you have a nickname, for example?"

"Yes."

"What was it?"

"Molletta."

"Can you tell us what that means?"

"A *molletta* is a knife… The kind where you press a button…"

"You mean a flick knife?"

"Yes, that's it, a flick knife."

"Why did they call you Molletta?"

"They didn't exactly call me Molletta. I mean, they didn't say, 'Hey, Molletta'. I mean, they did when I was a boy, but not after that. Let's say that when I wasn't there—"

"You mean they didn't use the nickname Molletta to address you, but they used it to talk about you in your absence."

"Yes, I think so."

"Now that that's clear, can you tell us where the nickname comes from?"

"It was because when I was a boy I already carried a knife – a flick knife – and once I stabbed an older boy, because he gave me a slap. I took out the flick knife and stabbed him, and after that they called me Molletta."

"I see, that's very clear. Thank you. Can you tell us some of the nicknames of people in your circles?"

"There are so many…"

"Tell us a few, just to give us an idea."

"For instance, there was someone they called Cedrata because whenever he went to a bar he always ordered a *cedrata*, a citron juice. Then there was another guy who was called The Tramp…"

"Why did they call him The Tramp?"

"They called him that because… no offence meant, but he was stingy. He never stood a round, he was always careful with his money, even though he had plenty."

"And tell me, Signor Capodacqua, does Ladisa have a nickname?"

"Yes, but it's a nickname nobody ever uses to his face."

"Let's take things one at a time. First tell us, what is the nickname, then explain it to us."

"They call him Il Flippato."

"Can you explain to Her Honour, who isn't from Bari, what Il Flippato means?"

"It means someone… how can I explain this?… someone who's a little bit off his head. Someone who you don't know how he's going to react…"

"You mean: a bit unpredictable?"

"That's it, yes."

"Can you tell us the reason for this nickname?"

"For that very reason, because he was… because he says one thing and does another… It's hard to explain the dialect."

"Of course, I understand. Let's say he showed a certain inconsistency. I've found a vocabulary of expressions from Bari dialect, complete with definitions. To help you, I'd like to read you the one corresponding to *flippato*."

I took the printout I'd made of that vocabulary page and looked at it for a few moments. I remembered the definition by heart, but in these cases reading has a different effect. It makes it sound more official, even if what you're reading comes from a silly website about life in Bari. And anyway, the definition I had found was philologically impeccable.

"So, 'Flippato: scatterbrained by nature or through the consumption of drugs, unreliable, weak in the head.' Do you agree with this definition?"

At this point the prosecutor objected. I couldn't blame her.

"Objection, Your Honour. We've allowed the defence to continue for a while along this line of dubious relevance – nicknames and etymologies, so to speak – but now he's overstepped the mark. The question aims to elicit a personal opinion from the witness and is therefore inadmissible."

The judge turned to me after looking for a few fractions of a second more than necessary at the prosecutor.

"Your Honour, I have no intention of arguing with the prosecutor, but I have to say that the objection strikes me as quite unfounded. As for the admissibility: the aim of the question is to establish if that definition of the word corresponds to the meaning attributed to such an expression in the social and political context to which Capodacqua belongs. It's obvious therefore that in this particular case the witness is not being asked for a personal opinion – which is forbidden by the final paragraph of article 194 of the code of procedure – but a semantic fact, if you'll allow me the expression. The same article 194, as it happens, specifies that the prohibition of personal opinions is reduced when it is impossible to distinguish them from statements of fact. The fact is: Ladisa was nicknamed Il Flippato, a word of which you can't possibly know the meaning. It belongs to the dialect of Bari, which for these purposes should be considered a foreign language. In order to convey this expression into the material usable in the trial, it is necessary to – how shall I put this? – *translate* it, and in particular to translate it into its generally accepted meaning in the context from which the witness comes. The most obvious way to do this is to ask the witness, and, for greater clarity, to consult a text that enunciates with perhaps superior precision – begging Signor Capodacqua's pardon – that meaning in its diverse facets. As for the relevance—"

"All right, Avvocato, I'll allow the question. You may answer, Signor Capodacqua."

"What was the question?"

"I read you a definition of the word *flippato*. I asked you if you agreed with that definition."

"Can you read it to me again?"

"Of course. "*Flippato*: scatterbrained by nature or through the consumption of drugs, unreliable, *weak in the head*." Do you agree with this definition?"

I had emphasized the words *weak in the head* to distract his attention, because the definition that interested me most was *unreliable* and I wanted it entered in the record – and therefore in the trial – without any objections.

"He isn't really *weak in the head*. He's a bit crazy, I don't mean he's stupid, just a bit crazy. I don't think *weak in the head* is right."

"That's a useful clarification, for which I'm grateful. So you don't think *weak in the head* corresponds to the meaning of the word *flippato*. Do the other definitions strike you as correct?"

"Yes."

It had gone well. It wasn't a decisive result, but the record now contained a statement by the principal prosecution witness, Capodacqua, that his former friend, and the source of his information, was nicknamed *unreliable*.

"Thank you. Then I can go on. Just a few more questions and we've finished."

"No problem."

"At the time you started cooperating with the law, you had various proceedings pending, is that correct?"

"Of course."

"On which charges?"

"A bit of everything. Extortion, drugs, arms, robbery, attempted murder."

"Everything but the kitchen sink. Your proceedings are mostly in Bari, aren't they? But I imagine in other jurisdictions, too."

"Yes, in other places. For example, a robbery in Treviso, another in... what's it called?... some other place in the Veneto."

"Have you ever accused anyone falsely of a crime?"

"Objection, not only is the question detrimental to the sincerity and validity of the answer, counsel for the defence is asking the witness to incriminate himself. That's inadmissible."

It was the only moment when young Avvocato Florio seemed to wake from his lethargy. He stood up and said that he agreed with the prosecutor's objection. He wasn't lacking in the gift of brevity.

Costa reflected for a few moments. It was understandable. The prosecutor's objection was correct – I had asked the question in the knowledge that it would be declared inadmissible – but of course, a judge would like to know if the witness whose testimony she is hearing has been suspected of slander in the past. In the end, after a slight sigh, she sustained the objection.

"Ask another question, Avvocato."

"Signor Capodacqua, you're familiar with the offence of slander, aren't you? That is, you know what the word *slander* means?"

"Objection, Your Honour," Prosecutor Greco said, aggressively. "What kind of question is that? Questions should be about facts. Is counsel setting the witness an exam on criminal law? Is he trying to intimidate him?"

"Sustained. Questions about facts, Avvocato."

"Have you ever been tried for slander, Signor Capodacqua?"

"No."

"Allow me to draw your attention to the fact that you are obliged to tell the truth. Maybe you shouldn't be so hasty. I'll rephrase it: are you aware of having ever been *charged* with the offence of slander?"

There was a long hesitation. I was looking out of the corner of my eye at the prosecutor on my left. She seemed on the verge of intervening and at the same time unsure of what to do. Finally Capodacqua replied:

"I've never had any trials for slander. But if there's a case file somewhere and I don't know about it—"

"Well, that strikes me as a more prudent response. You don't know if the carabinieri in San Severo, in the province of Foggia, ever charged you with—"

He interrupted me with an eye-catching movement of the hand, raising it above his head. Up until that moment, he had kept his hands still. "I know what you're talking about. I know."

"I'm pleased. Can you tell us?"

"They did charge me. It was a few years ago."

"Why?"

"It's a complicated story."

"We'll do our best to understand it."

"I'd reported the theft of a car which hadn't actually been stolen—"

"Sorry to interrupt you. As a matter of fact, you're right: the details of that case don't interest us much. Is it wrong to say that you had reported a theft that hadn't actually happened?"

"No, it isn't wrong, but—"

"Do you know if the carabinieri charged you with slander?"

"I know they prepared a charge, but I never saw it. I'd completely forgotten about it."

"Did you report the existence of this charge of slander when you began cooperating with the law?"

"I told you, I'd forgotten all about it."

"I have no other questions, Your Honour. Thank you."

The prosecutor asked if she could re-examine the witness. She was anxious to try to understand the matter, which she herself had learnt about a few moments earlier, because up until that moment I'd been the only one who knew about it, thanks to Annapaola's inquiries. Capodacqua told the story, clarifying it as best he could. In itself the episode was of little importance, and probably it had been merely a minor simulation of an offence rather than a slander. Capodacqua was surely telling the truth when he asserted that he had forgotten all about it and had never mentioned it for that reason.

The fact remained that the hearing hadn't gone well for the prosecution. By the time the examination and the hearing were brought to a close, the unpleasant odour of the word *slander* hung over the proceedings. We all knew it would somehow stay there, and we all knew that the Prosecutor's Department would have to find something very solid if it didn't want this case to end up on the scrapheap of dismissal or exoneration.

21

It was quite late when Annapaola called me.

The whole time I'd been driving back from Lecce I'd thought about calling her to tell her how it had gone. Maybe she'd have replied that she wanted to hear my account in person, and then we'd have seen each other and maybe had dinner together somewhere in the city, or at my place, or maybe again at her place, and I would have told her – soberly of course, avoiding too much self-congratulation, but making it clear that I'd been good. Then later, maybe, we'd have made love again, because I hadn't liked making love so much in quite some time, even though I knew it was dangerous stuff, to be handled with great care.

I hadn't called her. I mustn't harbour unrealistic expectations – I actually said that ridiculous sentence to myself. It had been a great evening, we'd both liked it, but there couldn't be any follow-up. That was very clear from what she'd told me that same evening in her apartment. It had been a pleasant diversion, nothing more.

Don't go having stupid illusions about it, Guerrieri.

Her telephone call arrived after ten, when I'd just finished with my friend Mr Punchbag and was thinking of taking a shower.

"Hi, Avvocato, is it too late to call?"

"No, of course not."

"Am I interrupting anything romantic?"

"Actually, yes. I'm here at home with two girlfriends, Cuban lap dancers. We're having a party."

"Classy stuff, I imagine. Let's talk another time, then."

"Don't worry, they're happy to wait."

There was a brief pause. She was looking for an appropriate line to finish the exchange, but couldn't find one.

"I was letting off steam with the punchbag," I said.

"You're still in the gym at this hour?"

"I'm at home. I have a punchbag in the living room."

"A punchbag in the living room? You really aren't well, are you?"

"I haven't been well for about thirty years, maybe more."

"Well, there you are. So how did it go in Lecce today?"

"Pretty good. We only examined Capodacqua because Marelli died."

"When?"

"Two days ago, after you gave me the dossiers. There weren't any dramatic upsets, but the nickname thing and the slander thing both worked."

"You don't have the record yet, do you?"

"I'll have it in three days."

"Then you can let me read it when I get back."

"Are you going away?" What a clever question, Guerrieri. Your powers of deduction are truly amazing.

"I'll be away for about ten days."

"Where are you going?" I couldn't stop myself from asking the question.

"Oh, different places. I have things to do for work. Then I'll stay for a while with friends in Rome."

There was a note of deliberate vagueness in her answer that produced an absurd pang of jealousy in me. I'll be away *for about ten days*? Do people just go away like that? What the hell!

She was going to Rome, to stay with friends, and God knows who she was supposed to be meeting. A boyfriend, or more likely a girlfriend. Are you *jealous*, Guerrieri? What gives you the right? Haven't you always told yourself that if your woman went with another woman you wouldn't have any problem with that? *Your* woman? But Annapaola isn't your woman.

"Guido, are you there?"

"Yes, I'm sorry, I thought I'd lost you for a few seconds. There are a few spots in this apartment where there's no signal." It was a lie.

Maybe we could meet tonight, that is, now. I'll just have a quick shower and come and pick you up, or if you like you can pick me up, we'll have a bite to eat somewhere and then we'll make love. Sounds like a good plan, don't you think?

I didn't say that, of course. Partly because she spoke before I could add anything. She'd call me when she got back, so good night, kisses, see you soon, bye.

Bye.

I stood there for a few moments with the phone in my hand, looking at it as if it were an object I'd never seen before. Then I turned back to my friend Mr Punchbag. He's my confidant. If I didn't talk to him about certain subjects I don't know who I'd talk to. Some would say he's a comfort object, rather like a teddy bear or Linus's blanket.

"Do you think I have a crush on this girl, Mr Punchbag?"

He was still swaying from the last blows he'd taken before the phone rang. It's his way of nodding.

"Yes, I think so, too. I don't remember how this whole thing works, it's been ages since the last time. The last real time, I mean. But all these palpitations – a bit ridiculous, I agree – when she called me, this jealousy when she told me she was going away God knows where to see God knows who, this wondering how I should behave, what tactics to adopt and so on... well, it isn't good."

"..."

"I was sure you'd agree with me. As usual, I've been running this nice private film in my head, while the reality is quite different. She has someone and she's going to see him – or *her*. She's a very attractive girl, fascinating, freewheeling. We had fun together one evening, it was great – *really* great, actually – but that's where it ends. Better to be aware of that and avoid getting hurt. Right?"

"..."

"Right. Best to go and have a shower instead of standing here talking crap. Although maybe..."

"..."

"I'm going."

As soon as my counterpart in Lecce had sent me the file with the record of the pretrial hearing, I'd forwarded it to Larocca, who'd been waiting impatiently for it. A few hours later, he'd called and said he wanted to come and see me in my office right away.

"Congratulations. That cross-examination is a real showpiece. Both for the strategy and the tactics, and the brilliant way you resolved the legal questions."

I tilted my head slightly and shrugged. A gesture of modesty, almost of indifference. I was just doing my job, you don't have to thank me – strictly speaking, he hadn't thanked me – or words to that effect.

"I'm only sorry I let myself be persuaded not to come. I'd like to have been there, I'd like to have seen the prosecutor's face. The things you said about the admission of Marelli's statements are... *brilliant*."

He was a river in full spate.

"Even the matter of Ladisa's nickname and the charge of slander. Excellent, excellent. That private detective you use is really on the ball. You can't always count on getting hold of information like that. The Prosecutor's Department got what it deserves. But who was this Greco woman? The petition was signed by the other two, so why was she there?"

"I don't know, we'll have to figure it out. I wanted to ask before the hearing began. Then the judge arrived and we started. *After* the hearing, she didn't seem very sociable."

He burst out laughing. The idea of Prosecutor Greco having become not very sociable because of the outcome of the hearing must have really amused him. He was euphoric: it was as if he'd been taking drugs, or drinking. He looked around, wild-eyed, as if he hadn't been in my office twice before.

"I like your office. Very elegant, very original. When this business is over I want to take you out to dinner in my favourite restaurant. It'll be a pleasure for me to spend an evening with you without this whole thing monopolizing our conversation. You know, something good can come from something unpleasant: the beginning – the new beginning – of a beautiful friendship. We'll have a couple of bottles and talk, about ourselves and everything else."

Yes, I said, of course, I'd like that. He was almost too eager. I felt embarrassed.

"All right, Guido. Things are going well. Now what do we do, what's our next move?"

"We wait. It could be several months before there are any new developments. They've just been granted an extension of the investigation. In any case, now the pretrial hearing is over, Signorina Doria" – it had a strange effect on me, calling Annapaola by her surname – "has to find us something on

Salvagno's financial situation so that we can start to explore the hypothesis of influence peddling."

"What about the appeal of the custody ruling?"

"In my opinion, they've given up on that, for the reasons we've already been through many times."

"Couldn't we try to find out, one way or another?"

The question irritated me. I was irritated above all by that expression – *one way or another* – which seemed to allude to the possibility that something unlawful would have to be done in order to obtain a result. Unlawful things had already been done to get the information we'd started with. But I didn't like the way he took it for granted, the way he didn't even consider the ethical dimension of certain actions, or so it seemed.

"Let's not overdo it with requests that are… how shall I put it?… irregular. We have a case that's heading for dismissal, as long as nothing major happens. Better not to interfere with that process, we only risk causing damage."

Larocca didn't seem satisfied with my answer. In his agitated state he required some – any – prospect of action, of movement, he couldn't just keep still and wait.

"Let's do as you say. But when the case is dismissed, we'll come down on them like a ton of bricks. At the very least, we can accuse them of violating confidentiality by leaking the news to the press."

It would have been a pointless accusation. I've never seen a single case in which the person responsible for a leak was identified with any certainty, often because he belongs to the very office charged with carrying out the investigations. I had no desire to remind Larocca of this elementary truth. So I said that once we knew where the proceedings were going and had the whole picture at our disposal, we could decide what to do. Even – I conceded, lying – lodge a possible complaint for violation of confidentiality.

22

The air turned mild, almost summery. Annapaola hadn't phoned me once since her departure. For a couple of days I had hoped she would, while pretending that I didn't care. Then I'd told myself it was better this way.

One of the falsest, most suspect expressions I know is: *It's better this way.*

One evening, after going to the gym, I returned home and made myself something to eat, using the ultra-organic, ultra-healthy and ultra-bland products from a hamper given to me recently by Maria Teresa after she had turned vegan.

Swallowing that stuff – it had everything you could want from food, as long as you're not bothered about taste – was a bit of a challenge, even with the help of half a bottle of good Negroamaro. In other words, the dinner didn't put me in a good mood. I tried to read a few pages of a novel by Jay McInerney, only to get annoyed and come to the final conclusion that I didn't want to read any more novels by Jay McInerney, even though in the past I'd liked them a lot. I thought of switching on the TV – something that was happening increasingly rarely – and looking for a film or a boxing match. I didn't do so, and realized that this was shaping up to be a night when I'd be unable to get to sleep. So I weighed up the various possibilities. The first was to knock back a dozen drops of Minias or some other benzodiazepine. If I have something to do the next morning and have to get up early, that's the best solution. The only one, I'd say. But tonight was Friday and I didn't have any commitments the following morning, so I could avoid psychotropic drugs, which I basically feel uncomfortable with anyway.

The second alternative was to get on my bike and go for a ride around the outskirts of town, trying to out-pedal my anxiety. I dismissed this idea, too, and decided to go to the Osteria del Caffellatte, the night bookshop run by my friend Ottavio. He's a former schoolteacher who suffers from insomnia. He hated his work as a teacher and abandoned it without hesitation or regrets when, thanks to an inheritance from an old aunt, he had the idea of starting a bookshop-café that opens at ten in the evening and closes when the sun comes up. It's my favourite place in Bari.

As soon as I saw the splash of warm yellow light from the Osteria, I already felt reinvigorated. The tables were out on the pavement, and only one was occupied, by two customers who were regulars there, winter and summer. We greeted each other vaguely. From having seen each other there so frequently, we were almost friends, although we'd never actually introduced ourselves.

As always, Ottavio was in his place. I greeted him and he replied with his usual short, cordial wave of the hand. Surrounded by all those books, in that friendly glow in the heart of the night, my anxiety had already passed.

Natalie Merchant's voice spread through the shop at moderate volume, singing a song whose title I couldn't remember.

There was only one customer. A woman of about sixty-five, with perfectly groomed white hair, a plain jacket, and a leather bag over one shoulder.

She was holding two books, which she'd already chosen to buy. Unlike the two sitting at the table, I had never seen her before. I started to wander down the rows of shelves, thinking about how I'd like to find something I really liked, one of those books you can't put down. After taking down several and putting them back again, I came across a title that aroused my curiosity: *How to Talk about Books You Haven't Read*. The cover was like a blank page that had been crumpled then smoothed out again. I had just picked it up and was leafing through it when I heard behind me a voice with a slight, indeterminate Northern accent. An elegant voice. It was the lady with the shoulder bag.

"It's very good. One of the best things that's been written about reading in the last few years."

"About reading?"

"The title's misleading. The book is a reflection on the idea of reading, on the fact that between reading and not reading there are various intermediate gradations, and that the distinction isn't as obvious as it first seems."

"I'm not sure I understand."

"You know Montaigne never remembered anything of what he read? He knew he had read a book and had an idea of its contents only because he'd written notes in the margins. In a case like that – a book we've read and then forgotten – are we entitled to talk about the book or not? I don't know if I'm making much sense."

"Very interesting. I should point out that in moments of grace I am capable of formulating expressions less banal than *very interesting*."

The lady smiled, causing delightful old dimples to appear on her cheeks. She smelt good: a perfume she must have put on several hours earlier. She reminded me of someone, but I couldn't think who.

"The author's a psychoanalyst and a professor of literature."

"Oh, two categories I try to avoid."

"Then you're out of luck tonight."

"Now you're going to tell me you're a psychoanalyst or a professor of literature. Or both. Please tell me I'm wrong."

"Actually, I teach comparative literature. In Paris. What do you do?"

"Put my foot in it. Big time."

Again that smile.

"I'm a lawyer."

We introduced ourselves.

"What's a lawyer doing in a bookshop at two o'clock in the morning?"

"The same as someone who teaches comparative literature. More or less."

"Right. It was a stupid question. Why don't you like psychoanalysts and professors of literature?"

"It was meant partly as a joke, but sometimes both of them strike me as inclined to make statements that are too categorical. Which, since neither psychoanalysis nor literature are exact sciences, does annoy me a little."

The lovely lady didn't reply immediately. She seemed to be weighing up what I had said. "I'm afraid you're right. After a couple of days at a conference with my colleagues, I tend to think the same way."

"Are you here in Bari for a conference?"

"It finished today. I'm leaving tomorrow."

"How did you end up here, at this hour?"

"I'd read about this bookshop and was curious. It's one of the reasons I accepted the invitation without any hesitation. It's really a… remarkable place."

"My salvation on sleepless nights, like this one. Would you like a drink?"

"Yes, I'd love one."

We went to the counter to pay. I felt it my duty to introduce her to Ottavio, because I was actually rather proud of him. This lady lived in Paris and had heard about the Osteria del Caffellatte, a place I felt was mine, as if I were a partner. She had practically come to Bari specially to see it.

"This is Ottavio, the owner."

She held out her hand. "Elena," she said.

"What have you chosen, Elena?" Ottavio asked.

She showed him the two books, the covers of which I hadn't seen. One was called *Italian Beat Poets* and the other was *Of Cats and Men* by Patricia Highsmith.

"I was sure I'd never sell this," Ottavio said, indicating the volume of poetry. Then he touched the Highsmith book with his finger. "I assume you like cats. Only cat lovers buy this one."

"Yes, I do like cats."

So does Annapaola, I thought.

"And you chose the Bayard," Ottavio said to me. "A good book, it clarified a lot of ideas for me. What are you drinking?"

"Can I get a stinger?" Elena asked.

"Of course. What about you, Guido?"

"I'll have the same. I don't know how many years, many lifetimes it is since I last drank a stinger."

While Ottavio fiddled with the shaker, the cognac and the crème de menthe, Natalie Merchant started singing "King of May".

"This is dedicated to Allen Ginsberg," I said. "Talking about beat poets."

"The song?" Elena asked.

"Yes, Natalie Merchant also wrote one in honour of Jack Kerouac, but this one is much better."

She half closed her eyes, as if to concentrate on the words.

"I like to understand what songs are really about, especially to discover the quotations they contain," I added, without knowing why, after a few seconds.

"For example?"

"Well, for example, there's that song by Fossati – 'C'è tempo' – which is from Ecclesiastes."

"I'd never noticed. It's true. Tell me another."

I felt an odd but pleasant sensation. I was like a little boy who has to take an exam but is happy because he's done his revision and can demonstrate how good he is to a grown-up he likes. "There's a song by De Gregori that's really beautiful: 'Un guanto'."

"I remember it. A rather impenetrable song."

"It's inspired by a set of drawings by Max Klinger. It's much easier to understand if you listen to it while you're looking at them. *Paraphrase on Finding a Glove*, I think that's what the cycle is called."

Ottavio placed the two cocktails on the counter. "Would you like to sit outside?"

We went to one of the three tables.

"Max Klinger isn't an artist everybody knows. Are you sure you're a lawyer?"

"No."

"There you are. If you'd asked me to guess what job you do, I'd never have come close."

"Have you got a bias against lawyers?"

"A few years ago I had to deal with lawyers and judges over an inheritance matter. It wasn't a pleasant experience. Yes, I'd say I have a valid bias against the whole lot of them."

I sipped the stinger. I used to drink them when I was married to Sara. Thinking of that time and the fact that it was over gave me a sudden sense of freedom, which left me breathless for a few moments.

"Tell me some more. I mean: quotations in songs."

"The latest I've discovered is 'Alexandra Leaving' by Leonard Cohen. It's a heartbreaking song about a love affair that's ended. I was listening to it and I seemed to recognize something but I couldn't figure out what. Then I realized – it's 'The God forsakes Anthony', by Cavafy."

"I met Leonard Cohen once."

It was an extraordinary piece of information, but on a night like that it struck me as normal. There are nights when normal things seem extraordinary and exceptional things go to make up the whole as naturally as the silent everyday objects in the paintings of Vermeer. That's why I didn't ask what Leonard Cohen was like or how she had come to meet him.

We continued chatting while customers arrived with calm, nocturnal regularity, entered the bookshop, and all came out with a purchase contained in one of Ottavio's famous bags. On one side, there's a drawing of a blue cup without handles, filled with steaming coffee, along with the name of the bookshop. On the other side, a page from a novel, a poem, a quotation from an essay. Things Ottavio likes and that he wants to share with his customers.

We were on first-name terms, but still rather formal with each other. It had a subtle, slightly out-of-focus effect on me. Whenever she said, *Listen, Guido* – the same way you'd speak to the butler or the chauffeur, with warmth but detachment – I felt a rush of intimacy that would have been impossible if we'd become more familiar. We had another stinger, enjoying the unreality of the situation and knowing that at any moment it would fade.

It was after three when we agreed it was time for bed. I asked her where she was staying, and she named a residential development in the centre, just a few blocks away from the Osteria.

"Would you like me to walk you there?"

"Are you making a pass at me, Guido?"

The words hung in the air for a moment. I didn't know what to say – in a situation like that, making a joke can be very risky – and for a few seconds she kept her serious expression. Then she gave a brief laugh, like a chord, with one cheerful note and one sad one in perfect harmony.

"No, thanks. I like walking alone at night. It makes me feel free, although I do get a bit scared sometimes. But you want to know something?"

"Yes."

"Twenty years ago, or even ten, I'd have accepted your offer. And not because I was scared of walking back alone at night in those days."

Then, before I could reply, assuming I'd even found an appropriate response, she came closer and gave me a kiss on the cheek.

"Goodnight."

23

Switching on the phone after recharging it overnight, I saw that Tancredi had tried to reach me three times the previous evening. I had a shower, dressed and decided to have breakfast in a café. I called him when I was out in the street.

"Sodom and Gomorrah yesterday, eh?"

"I'm sorry?"

"Why else would you switch off your phone at ten in the evening?"

"Yes, of course. I switched off the phone so as not to be disturbed in the middle of an orgy. Nothing to do with the fact that the battery only lasts three hours now. Next time, I'll invite you. Why were you trying to get in touch?"

"How about you buy me a coffee?"

"Where are you?"

"Headquarters. And you?"

"I just left home. The corner of Via Sparano and Corso Vittorio Emanuele in fifteen minutes?"

"I'll be there."

"Carmelo?"

"Yes?"

"Is anything wrong?"

"See you in fifteen minutes."

Click. Of course, mobile phones don't go *click*, although I still think it's the clearest way to say that a call has finished, that one person has hung up while the other person is still waiting for an answer.

I arrived a few minutes early. Just as the fifteen minutes were up, Tancredi appeared. He was walking fast, but limping, and there was something dejected in his expression.

"What happened to you?"

"Someone who didn't want to be arrested. It took four of us to stop him."

The only thing I could think of to say was a dumb line about the appropriateness of participating in arrests once you're over fifty.

We went into a café, had breakfast without sitting down, and when we came out Carmelo lit his usual cigar and we walked in the direction of the Teatro Margherita.

"Are you sure you want to walk, with that leg?"

"I wasn't shot, just kicked. Rather hard, but it was just a kick."

"Who was the guy?"

"A crook who'd just punched a local policeman as a mark of his disgust at getting a fine. I was with three of my men, we were coming back from the Prosecutor's Department and happened to pass by just as the radio message came in."

"When was this?"

"Yesterday afternoon. Luckily he didn't break anything, but my shin looks like a plum."

We walked another block without saying anything.

"Is there a connection between this story and the reason you called me?" I asked.

"No."

"So what is this all about?"

"It's sunny; let's go to the sea wall. Maybe I'll get a little colour back in my cheeks, I look like Nosferatu's cousin. I have to put my dinghy back out to sea again. We'll go for a ride one of these days. It's not right for me to be so pale. Do you know what they called me when I was a boy? Carmelo the Turk, because of how dark I got after a few days at the seaside."

He was talking too much. A sign that something was wrong.

We sat down on a bench. At that hour there was nobody about, and the breeze was cool. I was getting restless.

"I've been asking myself for a couple of days if I should tell you what I'm about to tell you, Guido, or else if it was better not to. There seemed to be excellent reasons to choose either of those options. In the end I decided to go ahead."

"Should I be worried?"

"I haven't had any medical tests, if that's what you're thinking. I'm not ill."

That was in fact what I'd been thinking.

"Well, then?"

"You never told me – that'd be all I needed, you telling me everything you do in your work – but I found out you're representing Larocca in that corruption case in Lecce."

He paused briefly, to check that I had nothing to say in reply. I remained silent, merely turning towards him a little more and placing my arm on the back of the bench.

"Actually, it isn't exactly classified information. People are talking about it."

Another pause.

"What do you mean, 'People are talking'? Which people?"

"Different people. The people you mix with and the people I mix with."

"And who do you mean by the people you mix with? The police or the others?"

"The police *and* the others."

"And what are the people you mix with saying?"

"That you're doing a good job for Larocca, and that he's grateful." He hesitated, and took a deep breath as if to steel himself. "They say that before, in order to get… friendly treatment in the appeal court, you had to go to Salvagno, and that now they'll have to see you."

"Friendly treatment? What does *friendly treatment* mean?"

I felt a mixture of contradictory things. Part of me was getting very anxious about what he was saying, which wasn't exactly clear but didn't sound promising; the other part was upset about Tancredi's embarrassment – I had never seen him looking so ill at ease.

"Don't get me wrong. I'm talking to you because when I heard that I felt very uncomfortable, and I'm telling you because I think it's best that you know."

"I'm not getting you wrong, but that's partly because I don't understand a damned thing you're saying."

Tancredi tormented his cigar, crumpling it between thumb, index finger and middle finger, pursed his lips so hard they vanished beneath his moustache, and scratched the back of his neck. "Well, I know perfectly well that you're a defence lawyer, that obviously many of your clients are guilty, and that obviously that's nothing to do with you. Defending them is your profession. End of. It's normal, and I feel stupid just repeating something so banal."

"But?"

"But there are clients and clients. If you defend a corrupt judge it's inevitable that—"

"Hold on. Who says he's a *corrupt judge*? You mean, a judge *accused* of corruption."

He looked at me for a few seconds. His expression said that what he had imagined was indeed happening. He grunted in frustration. I wasn't making things any easier for him.

219

"If you ask me if I have proof that your client is corrupt, the answer is no. Nobody's saying it on the record, apart from Capodacqua. The only proceedings against him are those in which you're defending him, and from what I hear he's going to be exonerated, unless something unexpected happens. So he's a wonderful example of propriety, honesty and competence."

"Go on."

"But if you ask me if anyone in the murky world I have to mix with for my work says that your client is a crook, the answer is: yes, they do, and how."

I felt my head spinning. Not just figuratively: I really did feel dizzy. Maybe this was all rubbish, but I had the feeling that if I stood up, I'd find it difficult to keep my balance. The reason wasn't difficult to pin down. Ever since this whole thing had started, ever since that evening when Larocca came to my office and drained almost a whole bottle of white wine, it hadn't occurred to me even for a moment that he might be guilty. Not even for a moment had I speculated on the possibility that he might have done what he was accused of. From the first moment, I had tried to put together what seemed to me a balanced interpretation of the facts. The crux of this interpretation was: Larocca didn't take money for that ruling, because it's inconceivable and therefore impossible. To use a legal formula: the fact is without foundation. That made it necessary to figure out the reason why Capodacqua had said those things to the prosecutors, because it was highly unlikely he'd made them up: making a deliberately false accusation is a stupid and self-defeating thing for someone who's turned state's evidence to do. Maybe Salvagno was a boaster, maybe Ladisa was a fantasist. The only possibility I hadn't considered even for a second – and it was only now that I realized this – was that Judge Pierluigi Larocca, a judge with what I thought was a blameless reputation, really was corrupt.

And here was my friend Carmelo Tancredi, one of the few people I'd trust in any situation – I'd have believed him even if he announced that extraterrestrials were due to land on the seafront in Bari tomorrow – telling me that this one hypothesis was indeed the truth: Larocca was corrupt.

Corrupt. The word bounced around my head like a blunt object, and with each bump it produced a hollow, painful sound.

"Let me get this clear. Did someone tell you that the story of money changing hands to get Ladisa released is true?"

"No, nobody's talked to me about that particular case. What an informant of mine told me is that Larocca is a crook, and a greedy one at that. Apparently he's been in the habit of taking money – lots of money – ever since he was an examining magistrate."

Maybe the wind turned at that moment, or maybe it was my shock at what Carmelo was saying that sharpened my senses. What is certain is that my nostrils were struck by an intense, nostalgic smell of the sea. All my sadness came crashing down on my shoulders, as if these revelations had all at once drained my life and my work of meaning and made me feel suddenly old.

"Is this man reliable?"

Tancredi nodded like a doctor informing a patient of the seriousness of his illness, a task he's obliged to carry out but which he'd gladly forego. "He's never talked bullshit in the twenty years we've known each other. If he isn't sure of something, he tells me he isn't sure."

"And this time?"

"He's sure. He'd already heard gossip – including from some of your colleagues – about Larocca. But that's all it was: gossip. I didn't even think of telling you. Now it's different."

"When did you find out?"

"A few days ago."

"Why did he tell you only in these last few days if, from what you tell me, it must have been well known?"

"Because the press came out with the story. We met, he commented on the news, and that's when he told me that thing about how you used to have to go to Salvagno and now... Well, you get the idea. Of course he doesn't know we're friends."

We sat in silence for quite a long time. He smoked, while I looked straight ahead. I was confused and didn't know why. A criminal lawyer mostly defends guilty people, that's obvious. Even if the informant was right, what was the problem? What the hell was the problem? I couldn't find an answer, as if my brain were stuck in neutral, unable to change gear, turning on empty without moving an inch.

"Why does it bother me so much?" I asked finally. It wasn't a question for Tancredi, I was just letting it out, trying to get things into focus.

"For the same reason it bothered me. For the same reason I came and told you instead of keeping it to myself."

"Which is?"

Tancredi grimaced, as if a nasty thought had occurred to him and he'd had to suppress it. "If a client of yours is charged with theft, receiving stolen goods, or even something more serious, do you have to know he's innocent to defend him?"

"No."

"Precisely. You do your best, you make sure the rules are followed, you try to get him acquitted if possible or to ensure he gets a light sentence. Everyone's in his place and everyone's happy, more or less. Right?"

"Go on."

"Not being a crook like some of your colleagues, you live by those rules. Your work makes sense if they exist. I'd even say that your world – and mine, too – stands up if these rules are there and if they're generally respected."

He was about to continue when an old gentleman – he must have been in his eighties – passed our bench on a squeaky bicycle. He seemed to have just come out of a time machine. He was dressed to the nines – suit, tie, shiny black shoes, grey Borsalino – and spread around him, to a distance of a few yards, an unmistakable smell of vintage aftershave, identical to the one my grandfather Guido had used. A dog that was sitting in front of a door, and which I hadn't noticed before, stood up as if for a rather trouble-some but unavoidable duty and trotted after the old cyclist. I watched them, and so did Tancredi – they were almost a living allegory – until they disappeared round a bend, against the horizon of the sea.

"That was like a scene from a neorealist film," Tancredi said.

"Right," I said, with a bitter taste in my mouth. "A scene from a film. I guess we also look like a scene from a film."

"Where was I? Oh, yes. The rules make sense if there are judges who make sure they are followed. If that's true, and I believe it is, the idea of defending a judge who takes bribes isn't only upsetting, it also challenges your whole notion of the world, your sense of the things that comprise it. That's why, when Larocca turned to you, you accepted the assign-ment in the belief that he was innocent. You needed to be convinced of his innocence, even if he got on your nerves. Which I think he did, by the way."

The sea continued to diffuse its pungent smell. After the old man on the bicycle, nobody else had passed along the ancient walls. Except for a few details, the place must have been very similar to the way it had been five hundred years ago.

"Am I talking crap?"

"I'm afraid not."

"You may not want to defend a guilty robber and get him acquitted, but that doesn't interfere with your perception of the world. Defending a corrupt judge is another matter. To put it another way: if he took bribes in the past, he'll do it again in the future. It's something you can't accept, and above all you can't accept the idea of being somehow… jointly responsible. So you're forced into an interpretation of the facts that's compatible with you and your vision of the world. It's a moral and psychological survival strategy."

"You're right."

"I wanted to tell you so that you'd know what to do. You'll keep representing him, but maybe you could put a distance between you. You could find a way to make it clear you're not the one who's going to take Salvagno's place, if you know what I mean."

"Please don't ask me if you're talking crap or if I know what you mean."

"It's just that this conversation is making me a bit nervous."

"You were telling me about the friend who told you these things."

"He isn't a friend, he's an informant. Very reliable, but an informant, nothing more."

"All right, I'm sorry. Your informant told you there was a special relationship between Salvagno and Larocca?"

"Yes."

"And that there have been other cases where Larocca was paid to give favourable rulings?"

"Yes. In some cases Salvagno appeared for the defence, in others he acted as intermediary. In other words, some selected lawyers turned to Salvagno and he, in return for a kind of commission, handled the contact with Larocca without being named and without appearing in the proceedings. Oh, and it appears that Larocca also acted as their adviser."

"What do you mean?"

"He suggested to them what to write in their appeals in order to have a greater likelihood of success. And if he wasn't able to guarantee the ruling of the court, for example because there was a risk he might be in a minority, he gave instructions on how to write the appeal to the Supreme Court. In these cases, it seems that he entrusted the writing of the ruling to the most incompetent judge so as to make it flimsier and easier to overturn."

"How did they pay him?"

"I don't know."

"Where the hell does he put this money?"

"Nothing came out from the financial investigations, I suppose?"

"No."

"He must use figureheads or foreign accounts. They can't just search blindly. Without a lead they'll never find it."

He didn't add anything else. He had said what he had to.

Again, the smell of the sea, even stronger. A lady dressed in black, a clear outline between the white of the stone and the amazing blue of the sky. An outburst of yelling: boys playing football in the little field at the foot of the wall, about ten metres below us. The rough surface of the bench beneath my fingers. The noise of a powerful motorbike accelerating along the seafront. A couple of young men passing with rucksacks on their backs, singing a song I didn't know.

Someone once said that the world is a roaring, buzzing mess, made tolerable only by our ability to ignore almost everything that surrounds us.

"What should I do?" I said.

"I don't know." Then: "Was I wrong to tell you these things?"

"No. I don't think so."

24

I was in my office, sitting at the desk, with no desire to work – even less than usual. One of those times when I hope that something will happen, that someone will come and disturb me: a dissatisfied client, the manager of the building, a troublesome colleague.

Nothing.

It took more than an hour of unaccustomed silence for the telephone to ring.

"Hi, I'm outside."

It was Annapaola. I searched for a witty response and couldn't find one. "Outside my office?"

"Outside your office. If you're not too busy, I'll come up and say hello, and maybe you'll let me read the record of that hearing."

"Of course, come on up."

I went to open up for her. Before coming in, she gave me a kiss on the corner of my mouth and I had to make an effort not to turn and check if Pasquale had noticed from his command post. Actually, even if he had noticed, he wouldn't have reacted.

She was very pleased to see me, she said. She must have caught the sun, because she was ruddy, almost tanned, and when she smiled, her very white teeth were even more noticeable; she conveyed a sense of adolescence that was both touching and dangerous.

I was very pleased to see her, too, I said. More than was wise, I thought. To hell with wisdom, I also thought.

I was waiting for a client, but when I'd finished – it wouldn't take long – we could have a chat, maybe go outside for a coffee or a fruit juice. In the meantime, she could read the record of the pretrial hearing.

I told Pasquale to show Signorina Doria into the conference room while I received Signor Oronzo Scardicchio.

This Scardicchio was a builder who specialized in public–private partnerships and financial fraud. His method was simple, not too original but effective – until it had been discovered. He drew up contracts of sale indicating a different and lower price than the one that had been agreed. The buyers paid the regular part by bank transfer or by cheque. The substantial difference – around 40 per cent of the total – they paid in cash, off the books. The money ended up in accounts abroad, transported by Scardicchio and his sons in suitcases, bags and rucksacks. The customs police and the Prosecutor's Department had taken an interest in him and had discovered a total fraud of about twenty million euros. That morning, everything of his that could be seized had been seized – apartments, villas, luxury cars – which was still much less than the amount of tax he had evaded, which in turn was less than he had defrauded over the years.

He felt persecuted by an unjust system, tended to see it in political terms – the judges were communists and things like that: a somewhat overused script, to tell the truth – and demanded justice. I was about to tell him that too pressing a request for justice might turn out to be counterproductive because justice might indeed be done, in the form of a heavy sentence and more seizures. Then I decided that he was in no state to appreciate my subtle sense of humour.

After allowing him to let off steam for a quarter of an hour, I assured him that we would do everything possible, that we would contest the seizure – at that moment, for just a few seconds, the unpleasant thought occurred to me that it might be Larocca's court that would deal with this case – but now I had to say goodbye, he could go to my secretary's office and talk about the advance, and no, thanks, no cash, no, unfortunately I couldn't do a discount without issuing an invoice, yes, I knew that other colleagues of mine didn't kick up all this fuss, but unfortunately, as he had been able to observe, the tax authorities were sharp-eyed and dangerous, in any case I wouldn't be offended if he went to one or other of my aforesaid colleagues who weren't too fussy and weren't averse to cash payments without the pointless formality of invoices, good evening, Signor Scardicchio, see you soon, maybe.

I looked into the conference room where Annapaola was engrossed in her reading. She looked up and smiled at me. Again, those white teeth and those tanned cheekbones and confused images of that night at her house. Oh, I wanted to ask you something: would you mind if we went somewhere now and made love? I mean right now. Wherever you like, maybe not your place, it's a bit far, but my apartment is ten minutes from here. Afterwards, if you like, we can talk. Afterwards.

I didn't say that. I returned the smile and sat down a couple of chairs away from her. The strategy of insecurity.

"You did a good job with Capodacqua," she said, tapping her fingertips on the sheets of paper she had in front of her. "That prosecutor woman can't have been well pleased."

I shrugged. I longed to tell her what Tancredi had told me, and was wondering if now was the right time.

"If nothing new happens they'll have to ask for a dismissal."

I replied with a monosyllable and another shrug of the shoulders.

229

"If you like, I can also use sign language. What's the matter?"

It took me a few more seconds, but I had decided. Actually, I had decided immediately after finishing talking to Tancredi, but I hadn't known it at the time.

"I saw Carmelo Tancredi two days ago."

I told her everything. By the end, I felt at least a little bit relieved. The good old therapy of words, in the sense of telling someone what's eating away at you, always works. Letting everything out. A kind of flushing of the emotions. Opening the floodgates, something like that.

When she was sure that I'd finished, she gave a kind of whistle.

"Well, if it's true, it's a bit annoying."

"A bit annoying strikes me as quite an understatement."

"Tancredi was right to tell you. He acted as a friend."

I nodded. "I feel like a shit."

"That strikes me as rather excessive. Why a shit?"

"Maybe that's not quite right. I can't think of the specific word, but I feel as if I've been made to look a fool."

"To whom?"

"To myself. Probably to him, too. I've displayed all the most hackneyed prejudices."

"I don't follow you."

"You know there are certain kinds of client I don't take on. I don't take people accused of being paedophiles, I don't take Mafiosi, and when it comes to people accused of corruption, embezzlement and similar offences I'm a bit choosy, I decide on a case-by-case basis. I know some might tell me – some colleagues do – that by doing that, I'm refusing to defend the people who might need me most, that is, people unjustly accused of the crimes I find most horrible. It's true, and in fact there have been occasions, rare ones, when I've agreed to defend people on those kinds of charges. It happens when I'm sure – and maybe sometimes I'm wrong – that they're innocent. Do you follow me?"

"I follow you."

"So, if someone comes to me and asks: do you want to defend a corrupt judge, someone who take bribes in order to have people released or for other favourable rulings, my answer is no. In your opinion, why do I do that?"

"For various reasons. I'll tell you one, if you're not offended."

"If I'm offended, I won't show it."

"Vanity."

"What do you mean?"

"You don't take on certain clients out of vanity. That's not the only reason, but it's part of it." She smiled again. One of those smiles – a mixture of provocation, joy, seductiveness, false innocence, real innocence – that some women give at times, and that make you feel irredeemably inferior.

"I am offended. But since the deed is done, tell me more. I assume it's free."

"Each of us, over the years, creates a character for ourselves. One we identify with, which corresponds to a positive idea of ourselves, which encapsulates the qualities we like to think we have. Your character, the one you've created for yourself, the one you identify with, has, among its various characteristics, one that could be described like this: *He's a criminal lawyer, therefore he defends criminals, but not those who've committed heinous and disgusting crimes.* Am I making myself clear?"

"All too clear."

"In this case – apparently – something has happened that's making you doubt the correspondence between reality and the character you like to resemble. That's why you feel this sense of disorientation. Guido Guerrieri isn't someone who defends corrupt judges. It isn't so much his moral sense that won't allow him to do so as his vanity."

A moment after that sentence, before I could even think of a response, someone knocked at the door.

"Come in," I said, at a higher pitch than intended. It was Pasquale: there were papers I had forgotten to sign that had to be given to a courier. I did so, and he slipped away as he had arrived. The unexpected diversion had given me a chance to recover.

"You mustn't get worked up," Annapaola said. "I'm an expert on narcissism because I suffer from it myself. Maybe in a worse form than yours."

"And what form is that?"

"Another time."

"Shall we go for a walk? I feel like getting out."

"All right."

"You don't have your baseball bat, do you?"

"I only carry it in the evening, for after dinner."

The streets of the old city were packed with people. Tourists off the cruise ships, young people sitting at café tables, local oldsters walking along *their* streets like inhabitants of a territory occupied by an enemy power, children zooming dangerously by on bicycles, a young Bengali selling whirligigs and balloons, police officers from the street crimes squad, looking unmistakably like predators, holsters bulging beneath their T-shirts. The sun was low, getting ready to set and spreading orange light over the white walls. It's a moot point whether May is actually the cruellest month, rather than April.

We were walking side by side, at the natural pace of those who have nothing specific to do and who, in the brief space they've given themselves, can ignore time.

"Avvocato Guerrieri!"

He was a man in his sixties, tall, big-boned, a bit ungainly. I was sure I knew him, but couldn't place him.

"What a pleasure to see you," he said as he shook my hand. "How are you? I don't think you remember me."

"I remember your face very well, but if you help me..."

"My name may not mean anything to you either. Seven years ago, you defended my son after he'd got involved in a nasty business..."

"Alessandro. Of course."

"Alessandro, yes."

"Did he resume his studies?"

"He graduated last year. He's been working in Milan for the past few months."

"I'm pleased. When you phone him, say hello to him for me."

"Without you, he wouldn't be there now."

I gave an embarrassed smile. I never know how to respond to compliments. The man and I stood there for a while, looking at each other. I could feel Annapaola's eyes on my right. I didn't know how to take my leave of him without being impolite. He seemed to be searching for the words to say something else.

"I've thought many times over the years about going to your office. I've never summoned up the courage because I felt ridiculous. I wanted to thank you, and not only for what you did for my son. You won't remember this, but while the trial was going on my father died. You expressed your condolences and added a sentence I'll never forget."

"Death is nothing at all, I have only slipped away into the next room." I remembered it a moment before he said it.

"It's incredible how words can ease suffering sometimes. I'm so glad I ran into you."

We said goodbye, and for a while Annapaola and I carried on walking without saying anything or looking at each other.

"It's a beautiful line," she said after a few minutes.

At that moment we again passed the Bengali who was selling the whirligigs. Annapaola bought one and gave it to me. I must have been a sight, in my impeccable grey suit, my blue shirt and my dark blue regimental tie, with my yellow, purple and orange whirligig turning with a slight rustle at every breath of wind.

"I'd like to make something clear."

"I love it when you do that."

"I've said that vanity is *one* of the reasons, but not the *only* reason why I think this case is making you so uncomfortable. I want that to be quite clear, otherwise you make me feel like a pedantic schoolteacher."

"A pedantic, self-important schoolteacher. It seems like an accurate description. But although I hate to admit it, you're right. When Larocca came to me, I immediately took it for granted that he was innocent because I *wanted* to accept the assignment: I was flattered that he had chosen me. To accept it, to satisfy my vanity and remain consistent with my role, as you said, Larocca *had* to be innocent. That's why it never even crossed my mind that he might be guilty."

We sat down at the tables of a little bar much frequented at night by young people because of the low prices of the alcohol. It was called the Blue Papaya and had only recently opened.

"You're getting too worked up about it."

"I'm helping to make sure that a corrupt judge gets away with it. Out of vanity, and for a few other reasons, that upsets me."

"I wouldn't like to dent your self-esteem – I'm sure you did a great job – but even without you and your brilliant cross-examination, they wouldn't have got anywhere on so little evidence."

A waitress emerged from the semi-darkness inside the bar. She was very pretty, with a slightly sleepy expression, several piercings – on her lips, on her ears and on her nose – and enormous breasts. We ordered two spritzes, she said no problem and went back inside.

"Do you like her? She's famous, the boys come here for her. Her name is Maya."

"Maya, gosh. Pretty, maybe a little… overblown. Anyway, I don't suppose she's your type."

"You never know, these girls are unpredictable."

"It's true they would have dropped the case anyway, but that doesn't change the fact that I'm part of the mechanism that will lead to Larocca becoming president of the court, even though he's a crook."

"Maybe you're taking his guilt too much for granted, just as before you took it for granted that he was innocent. What do you actually have on him? What you were told by Tancredi, what he was told by an informant of his who he says is very reliable. With all due respect: Tancredi's good, but he isn't infallible."

Maya reappeared with our spritzes and placed them on the table together with the bill. She passed close by me. She smelt of white musk, and it wasn't hard to imagine what kind of fantasies she aroused in the bar's night-time customers.

"Would you like me to ask around?" Annapaola asked me after sipping at her drink.

"About Larocca?"

She nodded.

I didn't reply immediately. I thought it over for a while. It didn't seem a good idea. Why on earth make those kinds of inquiries, without any reason or objective? The proceedings were going to be dropped, I would continue to practise as a lawyer and he as a judge, and the rest was none of my business.

The guilt or innocence of a defendant is none of your business, Guerrieri. It makes no sense for you to accept her suggestion. Drop it.

"Yes."

"All right."

That was all. For now.

Half an hour later, we were again outside my office, saying goodbye.

"I told a girlfriend of mine that I went out with you, and she asked me if I was interested in you."

"Excuse me?"

"She said that if I'm not interested she'd like me to introduce you."

"And what does she know about me?"

"I don't know. She knows who you are. Should I arrange it?"

"That depends. What's she like?"

"You really are a bastard."

"I get by."

"Why did you never call me over these past few days?"

"You didn't call me either."

"Was it a competition?"

"I've got my hands burnt a bit too often recently. I'm a timid creature. What are you doing this evening?"

"This evening, I have something to do. But you owe me dinner. I'll get in touch in the next few days. My friend is very pretty and I wouldn't even dream of getting the two of you together."

She gave me a kiss on the lips, turned and walked away without adding anything else.

I went back to the office with my yellow, purple and orange whirligig.

25

I had a hearing at the court of appeal. My client was a wholesale shoe merchant who, together with his partner, had been correctly sentenced to five years for fraudulent bankruptcy.

The partner was being defended by an old colleague of mine, Avvocato D'Amore, a man who smelt of mothballs and liked to express radical opinions on every subject under the sun: from the selection of the national football team to the government's foreign and economic policies, and from the state of justice in Italy to the quality – which was in fact questionable – of the coffee in the cafeteria of the appeal court. When he was feeling particularly sociable, he even told jokes – two of them, always the same ones – about people with intestinal problems. I enjoyed the company of D'Amore and his mothball smell about as much as a headbutt to my nasal septum.

The judges were in their chambers, deciding on our hearing. I had asked for my client's acquittal or else a reduction in his sentence, but if I'd been in the judges' place I would have confirmed the sentence without a moment's hesitation.

I was trying to take advantage of the waiting time, searching for a point of law on my tablet for an appeal that I would have to write the following week.

"What are you doing with that, Guerrieri?" D'Amore asked. "Playing video games?"

"I'm looking for a judgment," I said, trying to give my reply a tone of polite disinclination to engage in dialogue. In vain.

"I hate those things. I like paper codes, manuals, law books the size of encyclopaedias."

You also like mothballs, I thought, catching an unusually strong whiff of them.

"The world is getting worse every day, and they call it progress. I hate progress. I wish we were back in the time when lawyers and judges were cultivated people, when school was serious and educated children, when doctors cured their patients. When kids played football in their gardens, not on computers, and for a snack ate bread and tomatoes, or else, if there were no tomatoes, bread with oil and salt. All our problems started with the coming of computers."

The connection between the presumed end of bread and tomatoes and the coming of computers was obscure, but I took care not to ask him to explain it.

Just then, my phone vibrated in my pocket, which gave me permission to escape from the courtroom, beyond the reach of D'Amore, in order to reply. It was Annapaola.

"Hi, boss, I'm in a hurry. I need a piece of information."

"Go on."

"When you told me about the search of Larocca's apartment, you said there was a dressing gown from Claridge's in the bathroom, isn't that right?"

"No, I don't think it was from Claridge's. It was probably from a Mandarin, or the Plaza Athénée. Why?"

"But you did mention something from Claridge's, I'm sure of it."

"Yes, I think so. Why do you ask?"

"Bye for now, boss. I may have something to tell you in a few hours."

She hung up. I stayed outside the courtroom, to avoid being buttonholed again by Mothball Man. A few minutes later, the judges emerged from their chambers and the presiding judge read the decision confirming, correctly, the sentence on the two defendants.

Annapaola called again that afternoon. "I have a couple of things to tell you."

"Shall we meet?"

"I'm going out of town, on business. The usual divorce thing; I can't bear it any more. Maybe I'll become a journalist again, or else I'll look for something else. I could be a softball coach."

"Or else train people to fight with baseball bats."

"Right, that might be an idea. Sometimes I feel so bored. Does that ever happen to you?"

"Oh, yes."

"All right, let's get to the point."

I didn't say anything. There was something strange about her tone.

"Last night I talked about your client with a friend of mine who's a carabiniere. A good man, I trust him. He used to pass me excellent information when I was a journalist. He thinks Larocca *is* on the take, but when I asked him why, he couldn't tell me anything more. Just rumours going around. The same things Tancredi told you, but with less precision and less certainty."

"Okay, let's leave it at that. Basically, it's none of my business, and it's none of yours either."

"Let me finish. I hate dead ends. So I started going over what I knew about this business. After a while, I remembered what you told me about the search of Larocca's apartment."

239

My trainee Federico, the one with a face like a psychotic pigeon, put his head round the door of my office. I raised my finger to tell him to come back later. In four or five years, maybe. It struck me that I ought to find a way to dismiss him, without offending him and without offending my old teacher.

"I told you that when I was in London I worked in a hotel, didn't I?"

"Yes."

"It was a very good hotel. Not famous like the ones your client stays in, but very good. I learnt a whole lot of things and met a whole lot of people there."

I held back from asking her any questions. I couldn't figure out where she was going with this, but I knew she'd tell me when she wanted to. I just had to wait.

"Among the people I got friendly with when I was there was a Pakistani guy. One of the nicest men I've ever met, by the way. Aren't you going to ask me what this has to do with Larocca?"

"I'm trying hard not to, but if you're hoping to arouse my curiosity, you're doing a really good job."

"Good, I like self-control. Hamed – that's my friend's name – works at Claridge's now. I phoned him and asked him if Larocca stayed there often. He told me I shouldn't be asking him for information like that, and he shouldn't be giving it to me. I replied that I knew that. Then he told me that Larocca has stayed there seven times in the last four years."

"I don't in any way want to detract from your inquiries, but the fact that he'd stayed there could be guessed from the objects he had in his home."

"Could you also guess how he paid his bills there?"

"What?"

"Hamed was more reluctant about that. I told him I needed the information for a divorce case, that it was important, and that he owed me one. Which isn't true: he doesn't just owe me one, he owes me lots. In the end he said he'd try to check, but couldn't guarantee anything. He'd call me back."

"What did he tell you when he called you back?"

"The payment always comes by transfer from a bank in Switzerland. Every time it's a large amount, because he charges to the hotel not just the cost of the room and meals – which is a lot in itself – but even his shopping, the rent of a chauffeur-driven car, restaurants, everything."

She didn't add anything else.

I sat there in silence, trying to assimilate the information. It's one thing to imagine something unpleasant in a general, undefined way, it's quite another to hear it described in detail in all its nastiness.

"What made you think of checking this?" I said at last, noticing that my voice had gone down a couple of tones.

"I remembered how the manager of that hotel in London once told me how some guests paid with transfers from coded accounts in Switzerland, Luxembourg or other countries. These accounts are where people put funds from tax evasion, money laundering – and corruption."

"Do you know which bank the payments came from?"

"Yes. I even have the dates of the transfers. No documents, obviously. I took a few notes as I was talking to my friend on the phone. Since I don't trust emails, I'll leave a paper for you in your office letter box. I'll drop by in half an hour, just before I leave."

With this information, I thought, the Prosecutor's Department would be able to issue letters rogatory, and sooner or later it would emerge that a judge being investigated

241

for corruption in Italy had a bank account in Switzerland, and that this account contained sums incompatible with the salary of the said magistrate – or any magistrate – and it might also emerge that fifty thousand euros had been deposited in it in the days following Ladisa's release.

I felt nausea rising inside me. "What do you think I should do?"

"I don't know. The bastard is your client. It's up to you to decide."

"You're right."

Another long pause.

"I'll drop by and leave that paper."

"Thanks."

26

The important events of my life have happened by chance. If there was a design, I never noticed it. I studied law by chance, or as a stopgap, or because I hadn't had the courage to ask myself what I really wanted to do, maybe fearing that *choosing* involved a responsibility I wasn't quite up to. In the same way, I found myself working as a defence attorney: swept along by the current, telling myself that, basically, I liked the work, and that in any case life is a journey partly made up of compromises, and that it's an adult thing to accept this truth. Justifications, most of them, which are like certain rocks just below the surface of the water. You can lean on them, you can grab hold of them, but you can also hit them and hurt yourself very badly.

I had dealt with my unease about my job – a job I had never really chosen – by constructing for myself the character described by Annapaola. She had said things that I knew perfectly well but which I'd been determined never to admit.

I had an image of myself and tried to live up to it. One way or another. Whenever there was a clash with reality, it was reality that had to adapt. But that's a mechanism that can't last forever. Gradually, you lose your sense of balance.

I left my work hanging and walked out of the office. I passed a bakery from which the aroma of freshly baked focaccia emanated. I bought a schoolboy slice – in other words, a big one. I had a cold beer at a bar frequented by habitual drunks who looked at me as what I was: a foreign body.

Then I took my bicycle and started riding with no particular aim, but with the intention of not stopping too soon. I was very, very confused.

Try to simplify, Guerrieri, otherwise you'll never get through this and it'll be another sleepless night. So: a client of yours is accused of judicial corruption. You defend him, convinced of his innocence, then you discover that he's guilty. What to do? Keep defending him or give up the brief? Basically, it's quite a simple question.

Maybe not *so* simple, though. To start with: would you have the same dilemma if you discovered that a client of yours accused of robbery had indeed committed that robbery and maybe had also committed many others? If you actually discovered that he was a professional robber? No, you wouldn't.

Why not?

Because of what Tancredi said.

Because there's a distance between you. He, the robber, isn't part of your world, the world of trials, rules and justice. But a corrupt judge is. A corrupt judge – not his existence, but the fact that he's your client, that his fate depends partly on you – undermines the system, the structure, the whole theatre where you've played your role until now.

Corruption – and in particular judicial corruption – is different from robbery, because it has to do with power. The power of a judge is monstrous, when you think about it. He can decide on a person's freedom, a person's life. I don't want to sound rhetorical, but that's the way it is. Power – any form of power – is acceptable only if it's transparent and clean, if it's exercised in a way that is equal for everybody.

Article 3 of the Constitution: equality and things like that. All right, you're not giving a lecture. But what the hell. With corruption, power gets out of control and becomes unacceptable. Unbearable. Dirty. There, that's the crux of it. If this fellow gets away with it, he'll continue to exercise his dirty power undisturbed.

But there's always been judicial corruption. Pointless to get worked up about it; it's a problem for prosecutors and the police, not you. The imperfection of the world isn't your problem.

Yes, there's always been corruption, but this is different. This is too close. We know a lot of ugly things happen in the world and we can't allow ourselves to get indignant about all of them. We have limited reserves of indignation. But when the events are so close, when they touch you personally, what must you do? It's one thing not being able to do anything – you know something isn't right, but you can't do anything about it – it's quite another when you have in your own hands the possibility of reacting in some way.

Reacting? Reacting how? Maybe you're forgetting that you're a lawyer and he's your client, maybe you're forgetting that there are duties linked to your profession, for as long as you continue to exercise it. You have obligations to that client, and to anyone who trusts you. The client is sacred. If you question that principle, it's over.

And what about justice? Bloody justice? If that man continues to be a judge, how can I continue to be a lawyer?

What has justice got to do with *you*? You said it yourself, you're a *lawyer*. Your duties are simple ones: to defend your client to the best of your ability, not to commit mistakes, not to breach professional ethics. That's it. You want justice? You should have become a magistrate if you wanted justice, if you wanted to change the world. Then the world would have

245

done everything it could to make you change your mind, but that's another matter.

Everything you're saying is just a smokescreen, a way to escape the responsibility of taking a difficult decision. A way of lying to yourself. You say that there are rules of ethics, the protection of the client, the lawyer's obligations, but that's just to avoid the responsibility that comes from knowing certain things. Aren't you hiding behind your presumed professional duties in order to avoid bother, to avoid having to choose? To escape the effort of making distinctions? What was that line from that wonderful film by Renoir – *The Rules of the Game*? "I want to disappear down a hole, so that I no longer have to distinguish between what's good and what's bad." Is that what you want to do? Disappear down a hole in order not to have to distinguish between good and bad? How will you feel about that in ten years' time? What will you wish you'd done, when you look back in ten years' time?

I can't bear these ethical discussions, they're like something from a cheap magazine. Then let's get down to brass tacks, let's drop the abstract chatter. You want to report him? You want to tell the Prosecutor's Department in Lecce everything? Is that what you're thinking? Do you remember article 380 of the criminal code? It's the rule on disloyal advocacy. *The advocate who, becoming disloyal to his professional duties, harms the interests of the party defended by him is punished with imprisonment of three to ten years, if the offence is committed to the detriment of a person suspected of a crime for which the law imposes imprisonment of more than five years.*

A prison sentence of three to ten years, is that clear? Just tell them you instituted an unlawful investigation into a client of yours and now you want to bury him. That's an excellent move. You'll be put on trial *and* have to undergo a disciplinary procedure. You'll be found guilty and, most likely, be struck off. If your idea is to quit being a lawyer, it's the perfect choice.

That kind of argument is a moral anaesthetic. You're exploiting the formal rules to escape your responsibilities and your duty to choose. It's an old trick you've been using for ages. You fill yourself with lies to justify your own cowardice to yourself.

Everybody lies. Anyone who says they doesn't is either an idiot or a bigger liar than anyone else. Mental health consists in finding a point of balance between truth and lies. To think you have to always tell the truth – and that you *can* – is the hallucination of a madman.

You're partly right. Lying to your fellow man is often ethical, and healthy, and excessive honesty frequently conceals – or exhibits? – the worst intentions. Lying to yourself, though, is quite another matter. It may happen – sometimes it's necessary in order to survive – but if it becomes a rule it's just a way to divorce yourself from reality, to protect yourself from the world, to avoid being reached. Yet, sooner or later, the world and reality catch up with you.

You see, there's no question that Larocca is a bastard. The only question is what you can do. You can't bear to keep defending him? Fair enough, that's legitimate. Give up the brief, and leave it at that. Forget this business. The rest isn't up to you. Don't do anything stupid. Behave like a well-balanced adult.

A well-balanced adult.

I didn't know if I was a well-balanced adult, I didn't know if I'd ever been one. Did I even understand the meaning of the words? I asked myself as I got off my bicycle and tied it to a lamp post near my building. I had ridden beyond the San Francesco pinewoods, got all the way to the end of the San Girolamo seafront, then come back across the city as far as Punta Perotti Park and returned to the centre. No more than about twenty kilometres, but I was as exhausted as if I had done a hundred.

As I got into bed, I decided I would call Larocca the next morning, or maybe I would go and see him at the courthouse. And maybe I would also do something else, something that seemed to me as crazy as it was reassuring. Crazy, I repeated, sinking into a sudden sleep.

27

I checked that the hearings at the appeal court that morning were being presided over by the head of the court. When I called the clerk of the court's office, I was told that it wasn't a very heavy schedule and would be over by about two o'clock.

It was raining. I prepared two envelopes with almost maniacal care. I wrote the addresses using an old stencil I had been keeping in a drawer of my desk for God knows how long. When I'd finished, I broke it and threw it in the bin. I stamped the envelopes, then put them in my bag together with a stick of glue. Passing Pasquale's command post on my way out, I told him I wouldn't be back in the office that afternoon. I had just one appointment, with a client who was coming to pay and wouldn't be too upset about our meeting being postponed.

I must have sounded like someone justifying himself, and even though I didn't look Pasquale in the face I'm sure he noticed that something wasn't right.

Ten minutes later, I went into a phone and Internet centre used by young Indians, Bengalis and Mauritians. For the price of two euros I typed out what I had to, printed three copies, then deleted the file and left. On the street, I turned the first corner, took the envelopes from the bag, put one of the sheets I had printed into each one and sealed it with the glue, rather than licking it. It may have been paranoia on my part, or play-acting, or maybe both. The third copy I folded and put in my pocket.

I dropped by the garage, got out my car and drove to the courthouse. The security guard at the entrance, accustomed to seeing me arriving on foot or by bicycle, was surprised and full of admiration.

"Is this your car, Avvocato?"

"No, I just stole it. I'm hiding it here, if you don't mind. Nobody will know."

He laughed. "A pity you never bring it, it's beautiful. Petrol or diesel?"

"Petrol."

"It must drink like a whore," he concluded, laughing like someone who knows what he's talking about. Cars and whores who drink a lot. He let me through, pointing to a rather large free space near the sentry box. When I got out, I noticed that he was looking at me with an expression of respect I'd never seen before.

I dealt with all the chores at the clerk of the court's office that I usually entrust to Maria Teresa, Consuelo or Pasquale. I felt a sense of calm as I withdrew copies of papers, lodged petitions, consulted case files – and even as I queued, which is something I hate. As I went from one office to another, I passed the courtroom where the appeals were being heard and checked how far the hearing had got. At about 1.30, they told me there was only one case left and that they would finish within about fifteen or twenty minutes.

So I got in my car, drove out of the courtyard and parked about fifty yards from the gate of the courthouse, in a position that allowed me to keep an eye on the glass doors. Half an hour later, Larocca came out and immediately went straight down into the underground car park, reserved for magistrates and court staff.

When he reappeared on board his red Giulietta, I started the engine and set off after him, leaving a couple of cars between us in order not to be noticed. I didn't know why I was taking all these precautions, but at that moment it all seemed perfectly natural, almost necessary. Just as it seemed sensible, in the heightened state I was in, to pay obsessive attention to the road.

We got to Corso Vittorio Veneto and drove along it slowly, because of the traffic. When we reached the Castello Svevo, Larocca turned right. I thought I would choose a different route, going past the harbour. A longer way round, but less congested. The Isabella d'Aragona Gardens looked sad and desolate in the rain. I looked at the outside temperature indicator: sixteen degrees, not very high for 2.30 on a May afternoon. Why hadn't I simply phoned him and told him that we needed to talk? Maybe it was a way to gain time, to put off something I had no desire to do. On Corso Vittorio Emanuele, the traffic flowed a little more smoothly. Ahead of me, some hundred yards away, the Teatro Margherita looked like a film set. Come to think of it, I told myself, everything looked fake, as if I were taking part in some kind of *Truman Show* of which I was only just starting to become aware.

Larocca was driving calmly, in a very disciplined manner. He signalled changing lanes with the indicator, stopped at yellow lights, gave way when he had to.

I kept following him along the Di Crollalanza seafront, driving past the big, almost metaphysical buildings built during the Fascist period. The clouds were low and oppressive. We turned onto Via Egnatia, then onto Via Dalmazia. The Giulietta drove into a garage about fifty yards from the front door of his house, opposite RAI. Soon afterwards, Larocca came out on foot. He didn't have an umbrella and was hurrying so as not to get wet.

"Pierluigi!"

He turned with an almost frightened expression, as if he were not used to being called by name anywhere near his house and breaking that rule was a dangerous and destabilizing infraction.

"Guido. What are you doing here?"

28

Near the front door of the building there was a broken gutter, with water gushing angrily from the gap. It seemed as if the rusty metal might burst at any moment. As if that violent, threatening water were a symptom or an omen, as if that leak presaged something else, something worse.

"I need to talk to you," I said.

"Has something happened?"

"In a way."

"Do you want to come up? We're getting wet."

"Maybe it's better not. Maybe we could go for a ride and talk in the car."

From the way he looked at me, I realized he thought I was taking precautions because his apartment might be bugged. "All right, I'll go up, leave my bag, and come and join you."

Five minutes later, we were on the move, first in the direction of the sea, then southward.

"What's happened?"

The rain was beating regularly on the bonnet, on the asphalt and on the sea to our right. The windscreen wipers were dancing, and the liquid being moved to the sides of the windscreen looked more like molten metal than water.

"There's a new development," I said, sensing something ridiculous and at the same time disturbing in what I was doing.

"What?"

"The information I have is a bit vague, but I've been told about some inquiries into a Swiss bank account you're apparently able to draw on."

Strictly speaking, I hadn't told a lie: someone – Annapaola – had told me about inquiries – made by her – into an account in Switzerland. I was watching the road, but out of the corner of my right eye, on the extreme edge of my field of vision, I could just about make out, or intuit, that Larocca's face had turned pale and frozen.

"What the fuck have they done?" he said at last. "What the fuck have those sons of bitches done?"

He was breathing in a forced way, conveying a mixture of anger and fear, and rubbing his hands hard together, as if trying to cleanse them of something, to get rid of something so that nobody could find it.

"Can't we go to your office? Talking like this, in a car, in this rain…"

It was only then that I realized why I hadn't called him to tell him I needed to talk to him. I didn't want him in my office. I never wanted him to come there again.

"The office is almost unusable today," I lied. "There are workers in, doing maintenance."

Without realizing it, I drove onto SS16, the road that goes south to Lecce. People who like to read symbols and metaphors into everything would have said that I actually wanted to take him to Lecce. I don't know, but when I realized the direction I'd taken I felt bad, and at the first turn-off I turned round and started back towards Bari.

"Let's at least go and sit somewhere," he said. "We can't talk this way about something so delicate."

I got back to the city, drove all along the seafront in the opposite direction, past the old town then the Castello again, the harbour, and finally parked outside a café not far from the Fiera del Levante.

The place was deserted. We sat down at a table from where we could see both the sea and the street. The rain was still falling, silent and stubborn. Some lines of poetry came into my head – *It rains without sound on the lawn of the sea/ No one passes on the glistening roads* – but I couldn't remember who they were by.

The barman asked us what we wanted and before I could reply Larocca ordered a bottle of chilled white wine.

"Guido, listen to me. I'm sorry if you think I didn't put my full trust in you. I did, and I still do. The problem is that some things aren't all that easy to explain. I didn't know if you would understand. I was afraid that your defence would be less effective knowing... how shall I put this?... the background."

"Background, that's good."

He didn't catch the sarcasm. "But tell me, how the hell did they find out about the Swiss account? It's incredible, because it's coded, I've never done any transactions between Switzerland and my accounts in Italy. Nobody knows about it except for a lawyer in Milan and my adviser in Zurich, who are the most discreet people in the world. I really can't imagine how they did it." He poured himself some wine, drained the glass and refilled it. "How did you find out?"

"I'm sorry, but I don't think that's the point."

"You're right. You're right, there's a risk you may mis-understand, and I want to explain. I was wrong not to tell you the truth. I've treated you with a lack of respect, and I apologize. I've done a few... thoughtless things, but I want to stress that there's never been any major harm done."

"What do you mean there's not been any major harm done?"

"On a certain number of occasions, over the past few years, I've accepted some… gifts, so to speak."

"Before you go any further: did you accept a gift, so to speak, in the Ladisa case? Was Capodacqua telling the truth?"

"Not really, because—"

"I'm sorry, but I'm not in the mood for subtle distinctions today. Did you take fifty thousand euros to get Ladisa released? It's quite a simple question. Maybe later we can go into it in more detail."

"I received a gift, yes. But it's precisely the Ladisa case that allows me to clarify what I mean when I say there's never been any major harm. You've read the ruling in which we – and I emphasize: we, because my colleagues were in agreement, there was no dissenting opinion – released that fellow, haven't you?"

"I've read it. Of course."

"Did it strike you as correct?"

"It was a plausible interpretation," I conceded.

"So you understand what I mean when I talk about the lack of major harm. In the case of Ladisa, and in all the others where I accepted gifts from some grateful lawyer—"

"Through Salvagno."

"Through poor Salvagno, yes. In every case where I've accepted gifts, I've never forced a decision. They were proceedings in which the investigations had been conducted badly, in which there were invalid arguments, legal irregularities, insufficient evidence, unlawful phone taps, and we had to grant release. And sure enough, these rulings have almost always been confirmed by the Supreme Court. There has never been *any* abuse. Only decisions that were right and proper."

He had assumed a didactic tone that sent shivers down my spine.

"What are you saying? If a judge takes money for a ruling, however well founded, however *right and proper*, that's still judicial corruption."

He looked at me with a good-natured, almost affectionate expression.

He was mad.

He took another big gulp of his wine. If he carried on like that, he'd be drunk within half an hour.

"You don't understand, Guido. It's my fault, I haven't explained myself well. We agree on the fact that the punishment should fit the crime, don't we?"

"I don't follow you."

"Let me give you an example to make it clearer. Let's say someone is called to give evidence about a robbery to which he was an eyewitness. During his testimony, in which he relates what he saw on the occasion of the robbery, he also says something that isn't true. For example, let's imagine he does a job he's ashamed of, so he lies about it. Do you follow me now?"

I nodded reluctantly.

"He told the truth about the robbery and a lie about his work. He told the truth about what's relevant to the case and a lie about something completely irrelevant. Technically, his conduct counts as perjury. Article 372 says something like: 'Anyone testifying as a witness before the legal authorities, who affirms a falsehood or denies the truth, is punished with imprisonment of two to six years.' If that man were tried for perjury and you were the judge, would you feel up to sentencing him to two years' imprisonment?"

"Look, Pierluigi—"

"You'd acquit him if you were the judge. Or you'd get him acquitted if you were his lawyer. And the defence argument would be quite straightforward. Even though from a technical point of view he's committed an offence, there is no offence against the legal good, as protected by article 372, because that lie has no possible bearing on the verdict in the robbery trial. It's in no way able to influence that verdict. It's a technical violation of the letter of the law. There's no major harm done. There's no perjury."

"So what?"

"Let's talk about what interests us more closely. Think of a custodial sentence that ought to be overturned because there was insufficient evidence, no need for custody, absence of motive, legal irregularities. Whatever you like. If this sentence is *correctly* overturned, it's of no importance that the judge – who's only done what it was right for him to do – accepts a little gift from the defence lawyer, because that lawyer is pleased about a ruling which in all probability will be upheld in the Supreme Court. And sure enough, as you already know, very few of my rulings are overturned by the Supreme Court. Very few."

"I admire your clever use of euphemism. Not everyone would call fifty thousand euros a little gift."

He shook his head, shrugged his shoulders, and assumed a self-satisfied expression. The expression of someone who's heard a banal observation and doesn't even want to waste his breath refuting it. He has a more important argument to follow through.

"What interest is protected by the rule on judicial corruption?"

He paused briefly, a pause that served merely to give rhythm to his speech. He wasn't interested in my reply, and I wasn't interested in giving it to him. The impulse to tell him to stop talking bullshit was becoming ever more irresistible.

"The interest protected by the rule is the smooth func-tioning of the judicial office. The rule aims at preventing the judicial office from being distorted in favour of personal interests. The payment of money, the remittance of other utilities, should not interfere with the correct forming of decisions. That's all.

"Let's apply this to my work in the appeal court. If, in exchange for money, I overturn a custodial sentence which has no irregularities, then clearly I'm committing the offence of judicial corruption. But think of a suspect who's been unjustly arrested, for lack of evidence or procedural irregularities. In this case, the verdict ought to be overturned: that's the duty of the appeal court judge. What happens afterwards – gratitude, gifts, things like that – is irrelevant."

It struck me that when you find yourself caught up in certain arguments, arguments that have their own erroneous and deadly inner logic, the cold wind of madness touches you, too.

"If they ought to be released," I said, "they will be released and that's that. It's what you have your salary for."

"An unjustly arrested suspect who receives justice pays a lot to the lawyer who defends him. If part of that money goes to the person who's the real architect of his freedom, I don't believe there's anything wrong in it."

That isn't true, as any student of criminal law could have said: article 319c considers *any* collection of money or other utilities on the part of a judge an offence, regardless of whether the decision for which he has been paid is correct or not. The idea is that when there's money involved, the entire mechanism is altered and it becomes impossible to distinguish correct decisions from incorrect decisions. They're all incorrect, because they're influenced by the personal interest of the judge who's prostituting his office.

Larocca the highly experienced jurist knew that perfectly well. Larocca the man, who had lost his sense of balance and was living in a world of his own lies and justifications, didn't. What was that sentence from *The Brothers Karamazov*? "The man who lies to himself and listens to his own lie comes to such a pass that he can no longer distinguish the truth, within him or around him." My grandfather often quoted it, and said that the rule of moral balance is the opposite of the behaviour described in that sentence. It means not lying to ourselves about the significance of, and the reasons for, what we do and what we don't do. It means not looking for justifications, not manipulating the account we make of ourselves to anyone, including ourselves.

I didn't say these things to Larocca. I was feeling terribly weary. "Why did you do it?" I asked, almost without meaning to.

He sighed. He was about to pick up his glass again, then changed his mind. "Did you know I suffered from gastritis for a long time? Terrible burning sensations, I could eat almost nothing, just horrible thin soups, I couldn't drink wine, I was pumped full of gastric inhibitors. An impossible life. I decided to drop my gastroenterologist and go to see a psychotherapist, because people kept telling me that gastritis is the most psychosomatic of illnesses. To cure it, you really have to identify the cause. The man was good and he explained to me, in a very simple, clear way, that gastritis is caused by anger. By the sense of injustice we feel regarding something, or someone, or life in general. He told me that in order to get at the root of the problem I had to identify who or what was at the basis of my repressed anger. That's when I started to understand."

"Then help me to understand."

"Do you remember which of us had the highest marks at university?"

"There was no contest. You never got anything less than top marks, if I'm not mistaken."

"You're not mistaken. Do you remember what I said I wanted to be?"

"Either a notary or a university professor and lawyer."

"And then what happened?"

"You took the bench exams immediately after graduation, you passed with flying colours, and you became a magistrate before you were even twenty-four. You must have a quarter of a century's length of service by now."

"Excellent summary. I like your ability to always get straight to the point, never wasting words. Your arguments are always the best. You're the best lawyer I know. I liked being a magistrate when I wasn't even twenty-four. Not many people have managed that. I admit my weakness: I'm competitive, I like coming first. I thought I'd be able to be a magistrate for a few years, while continuing to study. I thought I'd write articles and essays and then decide whether to be a notary or a university professor."

"So what happened?"

"Life happened. The work took up more of my time than I'd thought. I married very young – maybe you remember, although you and I didn't see very much of each other at that time – then we separated and it wasn't an amicable separation. To cut a long story short, ten years later I was still a magistrate. I'd lost contact with the university and had stopped studying to be a notary. I was trapped in this profession which I'd considered just a temporary occupation."

It was only now that I managed to take a sip of wine, whereas he, carried away by what he was telling me, seemed to have forgotten his drink. It was as if it was what he had been waiting for: the opportunity to tell his story. As if he had never told it before. Maybe he *had* never told it before.

The waiter asked us if we wanted anything to eat. He could bring us, if we wanted, focaccia, mozzarella bites, olives, pistachios, crisps, celery, carrots, fennel. I nodded, without even thinking. The waiter looked at me, puzzled.

"A bit of everything, a mixture," I said in an impatient, dismissive tone. He looked at me for a few seconds, then must have decided that I was a strange character, the type of customer you have to humour if you don't want any trouble. He gave a half-bow and walked away. I turned again to Larocca, who was just waiting for a sign from me to resume.

"And so I kept on being a magistrate. It was a stopgap, but on the outside I made it seem like a choice. To tell the truth, I managed to convince myself for a while, but soon I realized that I had committed an injustice towards myself. People much less capable and gifted than me – or you," he added after a few seconds, "had become notaries and were making lots of money, or were filling university seats, becoming professors and therefore rich lawyers. Real idiots, people who floundered at university and have never understood anything about the law."

About this he was right. Some people who in our university days had struck us as common imbeciles – because they *were* – now occupied major seats. Boys we had laughed at had become full professors, revered and respected as great jurists.

"They put themselves in the right place, licked the right arses. They were patient, they wrote unreadable monographs full of things they'd cribbed and ended up with university posts. You remember Di Maio?"

I did remember Di Maio. A young man of incomparable mediocrity and ignorance, now a full professor and a rich lawyer. His biography could have been entitled: *The Triumph of the Idiot.*

"Villas, boats, holidays, luxury hotels. With just one of the judgments he gets one of his slaves to write for him on behalf of a bank or a business company, he earns what I get as a salary in six months. Do you think it's possible, do you think it's right, that some of the two-bit bunglers who appear for the defence in my court earn ten times what I do?"

"If you don't think it's right, resign and start practising as a defence lawyer."

He ignored my words. He didn't even hear them. He wasn't interested in my comments. The light of madness shone in his eyes.

"I was telling you about the gastritis. Since I started accepting… gifts, I've got better. I didn't realize immediately, but after a few months I didn't have any more symptoms. None at all. It wasn't hard to link the two things, even though, as you can imagine, I couldn't tell that to my therapist."

"What did you tell him?"

"That I'd followed his advice. Abandoned trying to control everything, let go, stopped judging myself. Actually it was all true; there was just that one thing missing."

He gave a knowing little smile. At that moment the waiter arrived with the focaccia, the mozzarella bites, the olives, the pistachios, the crisps, the celery, the carrots, the fennel, just as we'd ordered. I don't know why, but I was struck by the odour of the celery: it set off one of those roller coasters of memory that only smell can. Within a few moments, I was in my grandmother's kitchen. She was cooking, cutting something I couldn't see on the old streaked marble table and holding it out to me. It was the stem of a plant, and she told me to taste it. I bit into it a little suspiciously, it was crunchy beneath my teeth, I liked it. Then someone else came into the kitchen, but at this point the memory faded.

"I want you to understand, Guido. Have I ordered the release of any of your clients in the past few years?"

"Yes."

"Have you ever wondered about it?"

"No."

"Doesn't that tell you anything?"

"What should it tell me?"

"Your clients were well defended. You're a good lawyer and a decent person. Sure enough, when I needed a lawyer, I turned to you. I take gifts only from rogues and rascals, for clients who should be released anyway and whom they – their lawyers, I mean – may not be capable of defending adequately. Just imagine, I've sometimes had to suggest myself the things they ought to write in the appeals."

"But how much—"

"A lot. Since I started accepting gifts, I've made more money than I would have earned in thirty years of work."

"What do you do with all that money?"

He looked at me with a strange expression. There was surprise in it, but it wasn't just that. It was as if this question placed us on a level he hadn't thought about. He took several seconds to reply.

"Almost nothing. It's there, put aside. I'll use it when I retire and have a very comfortable old age."

"Tell me about that account in Switzerland."

"I opened it in 2001, just before my fortieth birthday. At that time, some kinds of operation were still quite common. Today, everything's much more complicated. Just imagine, back then some banks even provided smugglers."

"You mean people to carry the money over the border?"

"Yes, they'd come here and collect the bags with the money. Because cash is a nuisance, you know. Whenever possible, it's much better to transfer money from one foreign bank to another, using confidential accounts. Accounts created for that purpose, where the money usually comes from over-invoicing or invoicing for non-existing operations. In such cases, it doesn't matter if the transfer is made to an account in Switzerland, or Luxembourg, or the Isle of Man. Someone presses a button somewhere and the money is transferred to the other side of the world. It's much better when I receive gifts like that. It happens when the people involved are big companies which have had their assets seized."

Big companies. I recalled some controversial cases in the last few years where Larocca's court had ruled the release from seizure of considerable assets: land, manufacturing plants. In each of these cases, tens of millions of euros were involved. I felt rather nauseous, the kind of nausea you feel on a winding mountain road when you aren't in the driver's seat.

"But when it's a matter of cash, as I was saying, things are a little more troublesome, less sterile."

"Less sterile?"

"Cash needs to be taken to a safe bank abroad, and the physical distance is quite important. That's why Switzerland is better than other places. And that's why using the services of smugglers was very... *convenient*. Expensive but convenient."

"How does it work?"

Larocca smiled, and drank some wine. He seemed pleased to be able to explain it to me. "Imagine you've opened an account in a bank in Zurich and you have to deposit some cash in it, but you don't want to take unnecessary risks crossing the border with so much money on you. You call your bank, your trusted official, and you arrange for it to be carried by smugglers. In some cases, for large sums, they even flew down on private planes."

"And today?"

"Things have become more complicated. In Switzerland now they're no longer so... *tolerant*. No more smugglers. Every time I can do a transfer from one foreign bank to another, I do it... or rather, I have it done. Otherwise you need to sort out the cash."

He carried on for a while, eating and drinking as he spoke. With a hint of smugness, he also told me about the luxury hotels, and I found it hard to restrain myself from telling him that he could spare me the details, because I already knew.

I realized I was getting bored. Weary and bored to death. He was talking about money, about that bank in Switzerland, about how he would reward my valuable work, and I was thinking I'd rather be somewhere else. I half closed my eyes, sure that he wouldn't notice, and in fact he didn't. I could hear the sound of his voice more clearly, not what he was saying, which no longer interested me. That's how I became aware of something that had escaped me. A kind of obscene, unhealthy self-importance. It was as if that tone – much more than the words, the concepts, the arguments – sucked away all meaning, all distinctions, all possibility of separating right from wrong. I don't know how much time passed before I started actually listening to him again.

"Now that I've told you everything, I think we should put our heads together and decide on a strategy. First, we need to have a better idea of what exactly they've found out about the account. It may be necessary to get in touch with a lawyer in Zurich. What do you suggest?"

I let his words hang in the air between us for a long time. It wasn't calculated, I was simply looking for a way to say what I had to say.

"I'm sorry, Pierluigi," I said finally, "but I'm going to have to give up the brief."

"What do you mean?"

266

"I'm giving up the brief. You'll have to find another lawyer."

"Have you gone mad?"

"Unless…"

"Unless?"

"Unless you resign from the bench."

He looked at me as if I'd suddenly spoken in a completely unfamiliar language. My hand went to my jacket pocket, where I had put the two envelopes. I ran my fingers over the short side of the rectangle and pushed the tips of my thumb and middle finger into the sharp edges. Unconsciously, I must have been looking for a sense of strength and security, but it actually made me feel weak, lost and alone. At that moment, I realized I wouldn't be capable of sending those two envelopes.

"What are you saying?"

"I don't feel I can continue to represent you. I don't think I'd be able to guarantee an effective and unconditional defence after hearing the things you've told me. I can't conceive how you can continue to do your work, in the way you do it, thanks partly to me. It'd be quite different if you handed in your resignation, but I know you won't do that."

There. I'd said it. It wouldn't make any difference, but at least I'd managed to say it.

"You're mad."

"It's possible."

His face was transformed. He opened his eyes wide, and his mouth twisted in a grimace that was meant to express anger and indignation but was as grotesque as a living caricature. "You want to judge me. You *are* judging me. You want to turn into a prosecutor, a judge, and even an executioner."

"I don't think you're in any position to formulate these opinions."

"People like you disgust me. You think you're superior and judge other people only because you're afraid of the wickedness you have inside you."

"You're raving. It's best if I drive you home."

"You moralists don't understand something that Aristotle understood and talked about over two thousand years ago: all men commit wicked and immoral acts, if they have the opportunity. All of them."

"It's a very convenient argument. All men are wicked, therefore *I* haven't done anything wrong. Very convenient."

"Did you never cheat on your wife when you were married? Have you always declared everything you earn to the tax people? Have you never bought a property and put in the contract a figure lower than the one you paid, then paid the difference in cash to save on the registration tax? Have you never driven through a red light, after checking there was nobody at the crossing? Have you never exceeded the speed limit on a clear, deserted road?"

"What are you talking about?"

"You know perfectly well what I'm talking about. We all break the rules, you at least as much as the others. The difference isn't between breaking them and not breaking them. The difference is in the consequences. We need to claim the right to evaluate and decide, using our intelligence and common sense, when breaking the rules doesn't cause any major harm, as I said before. If it doesn't, then there should be no obstacle to the legitimate human desire for freedom of action."

"It seems to me you were saying rather different things in your lecture to the postgraduates. But maybe I'm not intelligent enough to grasp certain nuances."

Once again he ignored my words and my futile sarcasm. "Have you ever smoked grass and offered it to your friends?

That's an offence, you know. Have you ever driven after drinking? That's also an offence. Have you ever been in a fight? Another offence. Who do you think you are to judge? Who the fuck do you think you are?"

"I'll drive you home."

"Go fuck yourself. You're not driving anyone. Let me give you a piece of advice, you arsehole: in future, try not to take on any defence in my court."

He stood up and left. I sat there, not moving.

29

By the time I left, maybe half an hour later, it had stopped raining. Everything was wet and shiny and precarious. They must have been doing roadworks in the area, because there was a strong smell of water and asphalt. The air was grey, with a few gaps of blue in a sky like thick cotton wool. I got in my car, set off, and called Annapaola. The phone rang for a long time, but she didn't pick up. I tried again, but she still didn't pick up. I was thinking of phoning Tancredi – the only other person I could talk to about this business – and wondering if it was a good idea when Annapaola called me back. I stopped the car near the gate of the San Francesco pinewoods and answered.

"I'm sorry, I didn't hear the phone. How's it going?"

"I can vaguely remember better times."

"Are you all right?"

"No, I don't think I am."

"Actually, your voice—"

"I met Larocca. I spoke to him."

The silence hovered between our two phones. In the end she gave an audible sigh.

"Shall we meet and you can tell me about it? How does that grab you?"

"Weren't you supposed to be away on business?"

"I just got back. Well, how about it?"

"Yes."

"All right, I'll take a shower and join you in your office."

Pasquale seemed to be on the verge of contravening his rigid personal protocol and asking me if something was wrong. He managed to restrain himself, but he looked worried. First Consuelo, then Maria Teresa came into my office to say hello. Both asked me if something had happened. To both I replied, no, thank you, nothing had happened. I was sitting there with my feet on the desk. I never do that. Your posture can set alarm bells ringing.

Consuelo said, "If you want to talk, boss, I'm here," and went out.

Maria Teresa said, "Don't get me all worried now, Guido. Please," and also went out.

Annapaola arrived.

I gave her a complete account, starting with those two absurd letters I'd written, which I still had in my pocket.

"I didn't know what to do, so I did something stupid. I wrote a letter, using a fictitious signature, and made two copies, one for the Prosecutor's Department and one for the customs police, basically saying what you told me about the Swiss account and giving them some useful tips for their investigation. I thought... It was idiotic. I thought of telling him to hand in his resignation. If he accepted, I'd destroy the letter, otherwise I'd send it. That was what I thought."

"And did you do it?"

"No. It was a stupid thing, something I *thought* of doing. I realized it was nonsense, as well as an offence – making a personal threat. So I told him I'd learnt from my sources that inquiries about a Swiss account were in progress, but that the information so far was vague, and I asked him to explain."

"And he told you the whole nasty business."

"He told me the whole nasty business, yes. And then, as if nothing had happened, he asked me how we should formulate a defence strategy in the light of this information."

"Because you'd made him think that the account had come up in the course of the investigations; in other words, that the investigators were aware of it."

"Precisely."

"So: he asked you how you should formulate a defence strategy. What did you say?"

"I told him I didn't feel up to representing him any more and that I was giving up the brief. Unless he resigned from the bench."

"And he said you were crazy and could go to hell, something like that."

"More or less."

"And the letters?"

"They're here," I said, touching my jacket where the inside pocket was.

"You didn't send them."

"It was stupid even to *think* of writing them. Apart from anything else, it was your confidential information and I had no right to use it in that way. But that isn't even the main reason. In theory, I could have asked you for your permission."

"What is the main reason?"

"I'm a lawyer. I can't harm a client of mine. If I did, I'd face charges, I'd be struck off, maybe even sent to prison. That didn't only just occur to me, it's why the letter is signed with a fictitious name. It's an anonymous letter, and I can't send an anonymous letter. I wouldn't be any different from him if I did something like that."

"An original theory."

"What do you mean?"

"That it's an absurd idea putting the two things on the same level. We judge people's actions – those they've done or those they're thinking of doing – according to their motives. His motive is pure, unadulterated greed. Yours is disgust at that greed, your dismay at seeing the work of a judge being prostituted. Forget about legal subtleties: one motive is nasty and immoral, the other is moral and – forgive the rhetoric, I know you don't like it – inspired by a need for justice."

I didn't reply. That wasn't exactly it. It was a bit too simplistic as an argument. Things are more complicated, I told myself. But I had no desire to explain it to her. Maybe I was afraid I wouldn't be capable, or maybe I was afraid she was right, that things were actually quite simple, and that I would have to confront that unbearable dilemma again.

"Could you show me the letters?"

I took out the envelopes and handed them to her. "They're sealed with glue. But I have a third copy."

I gave it to her. She took it and read it.

"I think you should send them," she said when she had finished.

I barely moved my head. "I'm not capable. I can't."

"Then I'll keep them. If you don't mind. It's a pity to waste stamps."

I looked at her face. She had the neutral but threatening expression of a boxer just before a match.

"No," I said. "You can't."

"I'm not a lawyer; disloyal advocacy is an offence that doesn't apply to me—"

"Annapaola—"

At that moment it struck me how much I liked her name when I said it.

"Anyway, I was the one who found that information, and I can do what I like with it. I can give you back these letters if you like, but be aware that as soon as I leave here I'm going to rewrite them. And you can't do a damn thing about it."

She took a paper handkerchief and started to carefully clean the surface of the envelopes. Then she put them in her bag.

"See you," she said.

See you, I replied, when she had already left.

30

I left too, almost immediately after Annapaola, thinking that however this thing ended, being a lawyer would never be the same again. Maybe now was the time to quit, as I had said a few weeks earlier to Tancredi. A lifetime seemed to have gone by since that morning when we had stood talking in the sun, leaning on the wall of the courthouse. And maybe it had, because the true measurement of time isn't days, weeks, months, years. The true measurement of time is the unexpected events, the kind that change everything and make you realize how many other things happened before that you weren't aware of and should have been, and how many things you took for granted will never happen again.

Once again, I asked myself how I would remember the events of these days in a few years' time, or even when I was old. I couldn't find an answer.

And naturally I thought about what would happen after Annapaola had dropped the two envelopes into a postbox.

They would reach their destination in a couple of days and in all probability, in spite of precautions, nobody would think of looking for fingerprints. Instead, the prosecutors and the customs police would immediately ask themselves how to use this statement. In theory, anonymous letters should not be used; the law forbids it. In theory they should be thrown away immediately.

In theory.

In practice, all prosecutors' departments find a way to make use of them, employing the most diverse arguments to interpret the law.

I hadn't the slightest doubt that would happen in this case, too. Within a few weeks they would send letters rogatory to Switzerland, and within a few months the reply would arrive. Then Larocca really would be in trouble, and there was little chance he'd be able to squirm out of it. An account in Switzerland filled with millions from cash transactions or bank transfers doesn't exactly look good for a judge accused of corruption.

I thought these things and many others all of Friday evening and the whole of Saturday. An interminable Saturday, spent in solitude. Annapaola hadn't called me back. She had taken it upon herself to do what I should have done. This probably hadn't increased her respect for me, and I assumed she had no desire to speak to me, let alone see me. I didn't feel up to disagreeing with her: at this point I wouldn't have enjoyed Guido Guerrieri's company either.

It certainly wasn't anything new – a solitary weekend, I mean – but with all these things to mull over, it was very hard, at times unbearable. I considered the people I would have liked to speak to. I thought of calling Tancredi, Nadia, Consuelo. I even thought of calling my old friend Alessandra Mantovani, now a prosecutor in Palermo, who I hadn't seen for years and hadn't spoken to for months. I didn't call anybody. I've always been reluctant to ask for help.

The day passed, as certain days pass, after certain other days.

Those *after* days. They drag slowly, and in the end you feel as if only a few minutes have passed since you got up, rolling out of bed with every muscle and joint aching. Aches you didn't have the day before.

About nine, after wandering through the city; after going shopping for such indispensable products as nacho rolls, cassava chips, a jar of fruit mustard, a yogurt cake mix and a box of soluble cocoa – purchases a psychiatrist might have found intriguing; after going out again and again wandering through the city; after buying a few books and a few CDs; after eating a vegetarian sandwich and drinking a small bottle of grape juice at an organic fast food place, I returned home. I put on a CD of golden oldies, took off my jacket, my shoes, my trousers and my shirt, took the rope that was as always on a shelf, next to the works of Bertrand Russell, and did a couple of rounds of skipping. The short, dull, rhythmical sound of my feet hitting the floor started to relax me. Just for me, David Gray was singing "Please Forgive Me".

I took the bandages and the punching gloves, which I kept on the shelf, near some old books from when I was a child. The very few I had kept. Among them, my favourite, *Tell Me Why*: five hundred questions and five hundred answers on the most varied aspects of science and modern life. It was a present to me when I was eight years old. Some of the happiest moments of my existence have been spent leafing through that thick volume.

I carefully bandaged myself, watching the bandage turning around my wrist, the back of my hand, between my fingers, over the knuckles and again around the wrist, the back of my hand, between the fingers, over the knuckles, around the wrist.

I put on the gloves. I opened and closed my fists three or four times.

Neither I nor Mr Punchbag had any desire to talk. It was one of those evenings. So I gave him a push, starting him swaying and, to the tune of "Against the Wind" – which had started at that exact moment as if by chance, assuming the concept of chance had any meaning – I started boxing and forgetting myself.

31

At first, I thought it was the alarm on my phone. Why the hell had I set the alarm on a Sunday morning? Apart from anything else, for once I hadn't opened my eyes wide at the first light of dawn and was sleeping as peacefully as I used to, many years ago.

Recovering a modicum of contact with the world, I realized it couldn't be the alarm. It was a very different sound, an antiquated, petulant buzzing. A sound I'm not very used to hearing at home. The entryphone.

"Who is it?"

"Annapaola."

Annapaola. It's a nice name. I like the sound of it, both when I say it, and when she does. Annapaola.

"Hi, has anything happened?"

"No, I don't think so."

"I haven't looked at my watch. What time is it?"

"7.35."

"Oh, 7.35. Do you want to come up?"

"Can you come down for a minute?"

"All right. I'll put my trousers on."

"That's a good idea."

Three minutes later I was downstairs, in faded jeans and a white T-shirt with the words *Call me Ishmael.*

"I tried to call you last night, but your phone was off."

"It had run out of battery. I should change it."

"You're not bad in the morning. You're much better scruffy than in a jacket and tie."

"Are you going away again?"

"For a couple of days."

The street was deserted, the shadows were long and friendly, the air fresh. It was like a morning when I was a boy. Annapaola looked away for a moment.

"Are you coming with me?" she said.

"Where?"

"Let's just get out of the city, then we'll decide."

"That's a bit random, as a plan."

"I'm happy with random."

Me too, I thought. "I have to take a shower," I said.

"I agree. Throw something in a rucksack. We'll have breakfast on the way."

"Will you also teach me to ride?" I said, pointing to the motorbike.

"If we find an empty enough road."

"I need about twenty minutes. Want to come up?"

"No, I'll wait for you here. I like this breeze."

"Then I'll be right back."

"Hey."

"Yes?"

"It's been quite a while since I liked a man."

"That hasn't happened to me for some time either."

She stifled a laugh. "Why do I laugh at these stupid jokes?"

"I really don't know."

"I have an awful feeling I do."

NOTE

The lines on pp. 181–2 are taken from the songs "Balla", sung by Umberto Balsamo, "Anima mia", sung by I Cugini di Campagna, and "Ti amo", sung by Umberto Tozzi.

TEMPORARY PERFECTIONS

Gianrico Carofiglio

It all began with an unusual assignment, a job better suited for Marlowe than for defence counsel Guido Guerrieri. Could he find new evidence to force the police to reopen their investigation of the disappearance of Manuela, the daughter of a rich couple living in Bari? The stories of Manuela's druggy university friends don't quite add up. Her best friend, Caterina, too beautiful and certainly too young for Guerrieri, is a temptation he doesn't need. He fights his loneliness by talking to the punchbag hanging in his living room and by walking the streets of Bari late at night, activities that somehow lead to solving the riddle of Manuela's vanishing.

PRAISE FOR *TEMPORARY PERFECTIONS*

www.bitterlemonpress.com

A WALK IN THE DARK

Gianrico Carofiglio

When Martina accuses her ex-boyfriend – the son of a powerful local
judge – of assault and battery, no witnesses can be persuaded to testify on
her behalf, and one lawyer after another refuses to represent her. Guido
Guerrieri knows the case could bring his legal career to a
premature and messy end, but he cannot resist the appeal of a
hopeless cause. Nor deny an attraction to Sister Claudia, the young
woman in charge of the shelter where Martina is living, who shares his
love of martial arts and his virulent hatred of injustice.

A Walk in the Dark, Carofiglio's second novel featuring defence
counsel Guerrieri, follows on from the critical and
commercial success of *Involuntary Witness*.

PRAISE FOR *A WALK IN THE DARK*

"Carofiglio is a prosecutor well known for his courageous
anti-mafia stance, which has attracted death threats. *A Walk
in the Dark* features an engagingly complex, emotional and
moody defence lawyer, Guido Guerrieri, who takes on
cases shunned by his colleagues. In passing, Carofiglio
provides a fascinating insight into the workings
of the Italian criminal justice system." *Observer*

"Part legal thriller, part insight into a man fighting his own
demons. Every character in Carofiglio's fiction has a story to
tell and they are always worth hearing. As the author himself
is an anti-mafia prosecutor, this powerfully affecting novel
benefits from veracity as well as tight writing." *The Daily Mail*

"At one level an exciting courtroom thriller, but what places
it in a superior league is the portrayal of a slice of Italian
society not normally encountered in crime fiction and an
immensely appealing flawed hero." *The Times*

www.bitterlemonpress.com

REASONABLE DOUBTS

Gianrico Carofiglio

Counsel for the defence Guido Guerrieri is asked to handle the appeal of Fabio Paolicelli, who has been sentenced to sixteen years for drug smuggling. The odds are stacked against the accused: not only the fact that he initially confessed to the crime, but also his past as a neo-Fascist thug. It is only the intervention of Paolicelli's beautiful half-Japanese wife that finally overcomes Guerrieri's reluctance.

Reasonable Doubts, Carofiglio's third novel featuring Guerrieri, follows on from the critical and commercial success of *Involuntary Witness* and *A Walk in the Dark*.

PRAISE FOR *REASONABLE DOUBTS*

"The role of lawyer Guido Guerrieri is to take on impossible cases that have little chance of success. The lawyer accepts this case only because he's fallen in lust with the prisoner's wife; his efforts to prove his client's innocence bring him into dangerous conflict with Mafia interests. Everything a legal thriller should be." *The Times*

"This novel is hard-boiled and sun-dried in equal parts. Guerrieri stumbles into a case involving old enmities, a femme fatale and a murky conspiracy. But where Philip Marlowe would be knocking back bourbon and listening to the snap of fist on jaw, Guerrieri prefers Sicilian wine and Leonard Cohen… The local colour is complemented by snappy legal procedural writing which sends the reader tumbling through the clockwork of a tightly wound plot." *The Financial Times*

"Carofiglio, until recently an anti-Mafia prosecutor in southern Italy, is particularly well placed to write legal thrillers, and he does so with considerable brio, humour and skill." *The Daily Mail*

www.bitterlemonpress.com

INVOLUNTARY WITNESS

Gianrico Carofiglio

A nine-year-old boy is found murdered at the bottom of a well near a popular beach resort in southern Italy. In what looks like a hopeless case for Guido Guerrieri, counsel for the defence, a Senegalese peddler is accused of the crime. Faced with small-town racism fuelled by the recent immigration from Africa, Guido attempts to exploit the esoteric workings of the Italian courts.

More than a perfectly paced legal thriller, this relentless suspense novel transcends the genre. A powerful attack on racism, and a fascinating insight into the Italian judicial process, it is also an affectionate portrait of a deeply humane hero.

PRAISE FOR *INVOLUNTARY WITNESS*

"A stunner. Guerrieri is a wonderfully convincing character; morose, but seeing the absurdity of his gloomy life, his vulnerability and cynicism laced with self-deprecating humour. It is the veracity of the setting and the humanity of the lawyer that makes the novel a courtroom drama of such rare quality."
The Times

"Involuntary Witness raises the standard for crime fiction. Carofiglio's deft touch has given us a story that is both literary and gritty – and one that speeds along like the best legal thrillers. His insights into human nature – good and bad – are breathtaking." *Jeffery Deaver*

"A powerful redemptive novel beautifully translated."
Daily Mail

www.bitterlemonpress.com